CHAOS AT CARNEGIE HALL

A FIONA FIGG & KITTY LANE MYSTERY

KELLY OLIVER

Boldwood

First published in Great Britain in 2022 by Boldwood Books Ltd.

Copyright © Kelly Oliver, 2022

Cover Design by bnpdesignstudio

Cover Photography: bnpdesignstudio

The moral right of Kelly Oliver to be identified as the author of this work has been asserted in accordance with the Copyright, Designs and Patents Act 1988.

A CIP catalogue record for this book is available from the British Library.

Paperback ISBN 978-1-80483-162-5

Large Print ISBN 978-1-80483-158-8

Hardback ISBN 978-1-80483-157-1

Ebook ISBN 978-1-80483-155-7

Kindle ISBN 978-1-80483-156-4

Audio CD ISBN 978-1-80483-163-2

MP3 CD ISBN 978-1-80483-160-1

Digital audio download ISBN 978-1-80483-154-0

Boldwood Books Ltd
23 Bowerdean Street
London SW6 3TN
www.boldwoodbooks.com

1

THE ASSIGNMENT

The men huddled around the electric kettle. No. It couldn't be. Were they making their own tea for once? Heads together, whispering, you would have thought they were a gaggle of gossips instead of two of Britain's greatest codebreakers.

Handy for me, the kitchenette was visible from my desk, which sat in a cubby hole at the far end of Room 40, the heart of British Intelligence in the War Office. Although I could see the gossips, I couldn't hear them. I had a photographic memory, not supersonic hearing.

I tiptoed to the threshold of the kitchenette and strained to hear what they were saying.

Blast. The tapping of my leather soles on the wooden floor had given me away. The men clammed up.

Were they talking about me? I crossed the threshold into the narrow kitchen. Like a dark cloud passing in front of the sun, their silence followed me to the sink. I pretended to tidy up.

One glance at the dodgy contents of the sink and I scrubbed in earnest. As usual, a pile of dirty dishes nearly reached the tap, and crusts of toast and other nasty bits and bobs floated atop milky dishwater. The smell of stale cheese and sour milk was making me peaky, so I held my breath and worked the tea towel double-time to finish the job.

I distinctly heard, "Miss Figg." I pricked up my ears at the sound of my name.

"First, the villain invited her to Austria, and now New York."

Even without turning around, I recognized the baritone whisper as belonging to Mr. Dillwyn "Dilly" Knox.

"Either our little Fiona is having an illicit liaison with the bounder..." Mr. Dilly Knox knew all about illicit liaisons. Contrary to his doughy and disheveled appearance, he was not a reserved classics scholar. No. He was infamous around the War Office for bedding women and men alike. And he was a notorious tease.

Mr. Knox chuckled. "Or Fredricks has turned her into a double agent."

What rubbish! The dish I was drying slipped out of my hands. I dived after it and caught it on its way to the floor. Me, a double agent? Was he completely barmy?

The kitchen was a narrow galley and only twenty feet long, so he had to know I could hear him. Cheeky devil.

"What do you mean?" Mr. Grey came to my defense as usual. Nigel Grey, also known as "dormouse", was soft spoken, but open-minded. "Miss Figg would never—"

Was I invisible?

"Oh, I don't know," Mr. Knox interrupted. "Our Fiona will do anything for King and country, don't you know?" He tittered, obviously enjoying knowing that I was within earshot.

I tightened my lips as I rinsed a grimy teacup... probably one of his. I wouldn't give him the satisfaction of turning around.

"Miss Figg?" Mr. Grey whispered. "She'd never turn."

"Well, then." Mr. Knox raised his voice, obviously hoping to get a rise out of me. "She must have done her patriotic duty and seduced that traitor, Fredricks." Fredrick Fredricks was a South African huntsman and spy for the Germans who was posing as a journalist for a New York newspaper. Just thinking about the blackguard made my head spin. I threw the tea towel into the sink and whipped around to face my accuser.

Mr. Knox snickered and jumped back as if I'd flicked the rag at him.

"You know very well that Captain Hall has ordered me to follow Fredrick Fredricks to New York." I'd trailed Fredrick Fredricks from the English countryside, through Paris and Vienna. At first, I'd had to persuade the War Office that Fredricks was a German spy sent to kill double agents. At least now, most of them believed me. Then there were the others, the skeptics, who would never believe a woman was capable of telling the truth, let alone discovering it.

My friend and chaperone, Captain Clifford Douglas, was among the latter group. Well, that wasn't quite fair. He had a high regard for women. Perhaps too high. But it wasn't his attitudes toward women that made him loyal to Fredricks. He considered Fredrick Fredricks a mate because they had hunted together in Africa. Clifford was constantly nattering on about the Great White Hunter. Seems killing things was a stronger bond than the truth.

If I could just catch Fredricks in the act of murder, then everyone would have to believe me. Trouble was, he never left enough evidence at the scene to pin anything on him. He was a sneaky bounder; I'd give him that.

I wiped my hands on my skirt and then thought better of it. The infuriating man had me flustered, but that was no reason to sully a perfectly good skirt.

"He ordered you to attend an opera?" Mr. Knox winked. "Sounds more like you're courting than spying."

"I don't know which is worse. Accusing me of being a double agent, or of having a romantic liaison with Fredricks." Then again, Fredrick Fredricks did have an impressive history of romantic liaisons. Most women swooned at the sight of his muscular form and swagger stick. *Why? I don't know.* I found the man insufferable.

"Use your feminine wiles." Mr. Knox raised his eyebrows. "That's why women make such good spies, don't you know." He jumped back again to avoid the imaginary tea towel.

Hands on my hips, I glared at him. I'd been working in Room 40 of the War Office for over a year now and the men still didn't trust me. "Women make good spies because they think with their brains instead of their... their..." I stammered, unsure of where to go with this. "It's 1917, for heaven's sake. Not the Dark Ages. Women are just as capable as men."

I may have started out as a filing clerk in Room 40, but I'd recently been promoted to *temporary* special agent, British Intelligence. Although I had yet to catch the infamous Fredrick Fredricks in the act of poisoning one of my fellow agents, I *had* helped catch a murderer who preyed on Parisian war widows, prevented the assassination of an Austrian monarch, and found a dognapper with a fondness for Sachertorte.

"Then why aren't women fighting and dying on the front lines in this Great War of ours?" As if to add insult to injury, Mr. Knox lit a fat cigar.

"Dilly, be reasonable." Mr. Grey's pinched face flushed. "Women on the front lines. That's the most outrageous thing I've ever heard. How could you even—" he sputtered.

"If women ran the world..." I waved my hand in front of my

face to disperse the smoke billowing from the cigar. "We wouldn't be at war."

"I suppose, instead of wars, we'd have baking contests and sewing galas." Mr. Knox shook his head and then took a big puff. "Women would make a right mess if they were in charge of anything more than a nursery or the kitchen." He blew out another cloud of foul smoke.

"Our boys are coming back blown to bits, missing limbs, and blind from mustard gas." My cheeks burned, and I wanted to slap him. "It couldn't get any bloody worse than the mess men have made of it." I wasn't in the habit of swearing, but Mr. Knox had hit a nerve. In my time volunteering at Charing Cross Hospital, I'd seen my share of the misery men inflicted on each other in the name of righteousness and truth. Witnessing the horrors resulting from combat should make any sane person—man or woman—question the legitimacy of war.

"She's got a point." Mr. Grey gave me a melancholy smile.

"Admit it, Fiona." Still puffing, Mr. Knox folded his hands as if in prayer. "The only reason you're playing at espionage is because men are busy doing serious jobs like breaking codes and blowing up bridges."

"You don't need dynamite to catch a fox." I took a deep breath and immediately regretted it. Coughing, I reached for a cleanish glass and turned on the tap.

"Fredricks is a fox, alright." Mr. Knox grinned. "One who preys on pretty young chicks like you."

Cheeky cad. I didn't know whether to be outraged or flattered.

"I can handle Fredricks." I took a sip of water. "My assignment, *as you well know*, is to trail Fredricks and find out how he is undermining American participation in the war."

America had entered the war against Germany and the Central

Powers six months earlier. They'd sent troops to France four months ago. But they had yet to set foot on the front lines. The War Office wanted to know why. Obviously, they suspected foul play.

"I'm sure you can." Mr. Knox tapped cigar ash onto a saucer. "If anyone can smoke him out of his hole, it's you, my dear."

"Well, I won't be smoking cigars. That's for sure." I banged the glass on the counter just a little too hard. The contents splashed onto the sleeve of my blouse. "Blooming hell," I said under my breath, wiping at my sleeve.

Mr. Knox exploded with laughter, and Mr. Grey joined in.

"There you are." Clifford poked his head into the kitchenette. "I say, what's so funny?" Captain Clifford Douglas was a good sort, a sturdy, reliable chap. With his lanky form, receding sandy hair, and aquiline nose, he wasn't bad looking either.

Since Captain Hall insisted on sending Clifford with me as my chaperone, out of necessity, we'd become friends... *just friends*, as I'd had to remind him.

Just for the record: I didn't need a bloody chaperone. Unfortunately, Captain Hall disagreed. For better or worse, ever since Ravenswick Abbey, he'd sent Clifford with me on assignments. Truth be told, Clifford had saved my life once or twice. And occasionally he overheard useful information while chatting up strangers, which was his forte.

Clifford joined me at the sink, removed his hat, and smiled down at me with his kindly blue eyes.

"Yes." I glared at Mr. Knox. "What's so funny?"

The tea kettle whistled. As if taking his cue, Dilly Knox led Mr. Grey out of the kitchenette. When he reached the threshold, Mr. Knox turned back. "Be a good girl, won't you, Fiona, and bring us a nice cuppa?"

Grrrr. My throat emitted a low growling sound that surprised even me. I'd been promoted and gone on three moderately successful field missions. Yet the men still expected me to make their tea and deliver it too.

"If you're making tea, old girl, I'll have a cup." Clifford sat down in a rickety chair someone had left in the middle of the kitchenette.

Obviously, I was the only one in the office who cared about order. As my dear granny used to say, "Everything in its proper place is the definition of style." She was a farmer's wife living with a dirt floor and still her house was spotless.

"Of course you would," I said through clenched teeth. I rinsed the teapot with warm water, dried it with the tea towel, poured in a healthy dose of rough-cut black tea then filled it with boiling water.

"Are you all packed?" The cigar smoke hadn't yet dissipated when Clifford lit a blasted cigarette. "Should I come round and collect your trunks?" He grinned. "I know how you love your disguises."

I used to be able to fool Clifford with my disguises. Now that he was on to me, I'd never hear the end of it. "I can manage." I prepared the tea tray with four cups on saucers.

"I'm just trying to help." He crossed his long legs and balanced his hat on one knee.

"I know," I said to placate him. He was so easily hurt. And he did try to help, after all. "And you're a dear." I forced a smile, hoping to change the subject. Clifford and Captain Hall might make fun of my disguises, but they'd come in bloody handy in the past. After all, it was my manly Dr. Vogel disguise that wooed Lady Mary and got the goods on the spy ring at Ravenswick. And without my maid's costume, I wouldn't have discovered Fredricks's plot to blow up British cargo ships. Not to mention the helpful gen I gathered as Harold, the helpful bellboy.

Clifford's eyes lit up.

I should know better than to encourage him. Poor man had already proposed to me twice. Then again, while "just trying to help," he'd proposed to half the women in London.

At least Clifford was loyal. Unlike my ex-husband, Andrew, who had cheated on me with his secretary... and then died in my arms from German mustard gas.

I suppose if he hadn't left me for Nancy, I'd never have left London. After the divorce, I had to get away. *What's the best way to forget an unfaithful husband? Become a spy for British Intelligence, of course.*

Clifford reached into his jacket pocket.

No, not an engagement ring. He'd never gone quite that far before. I blushed.

He withdrew an envelope and waved it in the air. "Our tickets."

"*Our* tickets?" I spilled the milk. *Curses.* "Don't tell me Captain Hall has ordered you to protect me." I shook my head. Didn't anyone in the blooming War Office have confidence in me?

"You can't very well travel to America by yourself." Clifford returned the envelope to his pocket.

"Why not?" I wiped up the spilled milk from the tray.

"Good Lord, Fiona. A woman alone on a ship?" He glanced around and then pinched out the end of his cigarette. At least he didn't soil a saucer or leave his filthy butts lying around. "I say, it's just not cricket."

"I won't be alone." I poured the strong tea through a strainer into the teacups. "I'm sure there will be other passengers aboard the RMS *Adriatic*."

"Yes, and I will be one of them," he said. "The orders come directly from Captain Hall. He may not outrank me, but he is the head of British Intelligence."

"Certainly, Captain Hall can't expect us to share a cabin." I hoped to heaven I didn't have to pretend to be Clifford's wife on the ship... or while in New York. I'd barely survived my last assignment posing as Mrs. Clifford Douglas. I didn't relish trying it again... even as a cover. I rearranged the milk jug and the sugar bowl on the tea tray. Given how little I had to work with, the tray was neat and clean, if not pretty.

"You're in for a surprise, old girl." Clifford chuckled. "I've just come from Captain Hall's office and—"

A round-faced delivery boy interrupted us. "Miss Fiona Figg?" He looked from Clifford to me as if either one of us might answer to Miss Fiona Figg. "The Guv wants to see you in his office."

"I told you." Clifford winked.

"By Guv, I assume you mean Captain Hall?" I wiped my hands on a towel and picked up the tea tray.

"That's right, Miss." The boy nodded and waved a grubby paw at me. "Better hop it. He wants ya, today and not tomorrow."

"I'll hop it." I squinted at the lad. "Right after I deliver this tea."

"Let me." Clifford took the tray from my hands.

"Well, I'll be..." Wouldn't the men be surprised when Captain Clifford Douglas delivered their tea? I nodded in gratitude, and then "hopped it" upstairs to Captain Hall's office.

No sooner had I arrived than Captain Hall's secretary ushered me into his office. Captain Reginald "Blinker" Hall was seated behind his mahogany desk shuffling papers. He looked up and gestured toward a chair across from his desk, his eyelids blinking as if sending out Morse code, as usual.

I sat down as ordered and waited while he continued with his papers. My gaze wandered to the large window facing Whitehall Street.

The winter sky was gray. Even from the second floor, I could hear the traffic below... bells on horses, motorcars and lorries, vendors in the streets. Despite the war, London was as lively as ever. Only instead of men keeping shops open, those jobs fell to their wives.

I couldn't imagine women wanting to go back to dreary days filled with domestic chores after a taste of freedom afforded by the war.

A birdlike twittering and a high-pitched bark made me twist around in the chair.

The door had blocked my view and I hadn't noticed them when I'd come in—a girl and a dog.

Sitting behind the door, a pretty girl dressed up in lilac frills, wearing lace gloves, a sailor hat, and neat little white boots was cuddling the ball of fur squirming in her lap. She could have been on her way to Easter Sunday service at St. Bartholomew-the-Great—except that it was early November. She had to be at least seventeen or eighteen, but her incessant giggling made her seem younger.

She waved at me, and I swirled back around to face Captain Hall.

He must have sensed the question on my lips. "Miss Figg, may I present my niece." He gestured toward the girl. "Miss Eliza Baker, my, er, sister's daughter."

Avoiding eye contact with the fidgety puff of lace and ribbons, I nodded in her direction. If Captain Hall had company, why in the world had he summoned me to his office?

"Eliza has won a scholarship to the Institute of Musical Arts in New York." Captain Hall blinked with pride.

On another occasion, I might have been delighted to stay and chat with Miss Baker. But given my departure to America in the morning, I had many stops to make this afternoon—including Angel's Fancy Dress Shop—before I could lay my head on my pillow. "Congratulations." I forced a smile.

When she smiled in return, she went from a pretty girl to a beautiful young woman. If only she'd lose the frothy trappings of girlhood, she would be a very attractive young lady. Although I had to admit, that rose petal hat was precious.

"Eliza is sailing to New York tomorrow." Captain Hall's voice became stern. "Her mother wants her on her way as soon as possible."

"Mother wants to get me away from Billy, you mean." The girl stomped the floor with a booted foot. "It won't work. We love each other, and nothing you—"

"Enough, Eliza." Captain Hall stopped blinking to glare at the girl.

Unnerving, to say the least.

Ambushed by talk of love, my thoughts turned to Lieutenant Archie Somersby, the handsome soldier I'd met when he was convalescing at Charing Cross Hospital.

Last time I'd seen Archie, he'd kissed me with such passion, surely my own mother had turned over in her grave. Yet I hardly knew him. What did that kiss mean? No sooner had he planted it on my lips than he disappeared again. Would I ever see his adorable crooked smile again?

Eliza's lower lip trembled. Her little dog growled.

"Miss Figg." Captain Hall turned back to me. "I'm appointing you Eliza's chaperone until she is well settled in New York. She will stay with you until the campus opens in less than two weeks."

Two weeks! My mouth fell open. When I tried to speak, no sound came out.

"I'm trusting you to look out for her." Captain Hall stood up. "As of tomorrow, she's your responsibility. Miss Figg, I'm counting on you."

He's got to be joking. "Yes, sir." I cringed.

"We're going to be such fast friends." Eliza adjusted the bow of her puppy's topknot and then lifted the Pekingese, so it was standing on her lap. "Aren't we, Poppy?" she cooed. She gently placed the dog on the floor. "Go and say hello."

The furry creature ran at me with her tongue lolling. And I swear the little beast was smiling.

Eliza clapped her gloved hands. The girl's countenance was as changeable as a London sky in springtime. "Won't it be a lark?"

I thought of a line from a poem. The larks, still bravely singing, fly, scarce heard amid the guns below...

"Indeed." I bit my tongue.

Good grief. I'd been demoted from spy to babysitter.

2

ABOARD THE ADRIATIC

The RMS *Adriatic*, a huge, majestic ocean liner, was one of the only passenger ships not yet requisitioned by the War Office. Even so, on the return trip from America, the now empty swimming pool would be used as a cargo hold for ammunition and war supplies. One of the dining saloons had been converted into a hospital to transport injured American soldiers back home.

It was surprising how many civilians braved the war to cross the Atlantic. The only cabins open to civilians were the first-class berths, which was fine with me. The 450 first-class berths were all occupied. The second-class cabins went to officers, and regular infantry were quartered in steerage.

Too bad I had to share my cabin with Captain Hall's excessively chatty niece... and her overly talkative Pekingese. The girl was even worse than Clifford, whose nattering was at least melodious, if not profound.

Despite whole areas of the luxury liner being reserved for the military and off limits to passengers, the ship was as nice as any hotel I'd seen, including the finest in Paris and Vienna. Lush satin upholstery, wood paneling, and crystal chandeliers made me feel like I was back at Schönbrunn Palace. And although the cuisine was disadvantaged by war rations, the presentation was lovely. Adorned with sprigs of unidentifiable herbs, I'd never seen meat pies and peas looking so elegant.

Calm seas and mild autumn weather had made the first three days of the voyage pleasant and uneventful. This morning, however, the puffy clouds that had followed us from England turned to steely streaks echoed by the stormy seas below.

Not one to let a little seasickness ruin my appetite, I ventured to the breakfast room. Eliza and Clifford were already there, obviously unaffected by the roiling waves.

This morning's breakfast was the usual toast, tea, and jam. Cut with who-knows-what, the war bread was dark and heavy. The sugarless jam was thin and tart. But, having been declared a *weapon of war* by the Cake and Pastry Order of 1917, the tea was stout and fortifying.

After a few bites of breakfast, I managed to slip away while Clifford lectured poor Eliza on the virtues of a healthy appetite. It was true. Eliza ate like a bird. Still, Clifford's incessant nagging didn't help. He wasn't her father, after all. At least while he was watching her like a hawk, he wasn't bothering me.

I headed to my favorite place on the ship.

After three days on board, one particular easy chair near the fireplace in the reading and writing room had my name on it. I'd spent many hours hiding out there in my special place.

The turquoise and gray décor, offset by a wall of curtained windows, was soothing yet cheerful. And since most of the passengers preferred playing games on deck when the weather allowed, or having cocktails in the saloon when it didn't, the reading room was usually quiet. That was, until Eliza tracked me down—which she always did—and hounded me until I promised to accompany her to the evening's entertainment. It seemed her mother had expressly forbidden her from going anywhere after dark without me. *More's the pity.*

With the latest issue of *Strand Magazine* tucked under my arm, I settled into my chair in the corner of the reading room. I ran my hand across the chair's smooth satin fabric. My finger caught on a gash that ran across the arm. *Ahem.* Best not look too closely at the finery. As so often happened, just beneath the lovely veneer lay a deep wound.

The harsh morning light was transformed by the stained-glass windows into an inviting warm glow, which spread across the pretty room. *Ahhh.* With my stomach settling, I opened the magazine. I quite felt as though I was on holiday instead of crossing the ocean on behalf of King and country.

A new Sherlock Holmes story and the room to myself. What could be better?

"His Last Bow." I devoured the story like a hungry bee feasting on nectar. I should send this to Captain Hall. Maybe then he'd stop ridiculing my disguises. The venerable Sherlock Holmes often used disguises to catch evildoers off-guard. In this story, play acting had allowed Holmes and Watson to catch a German spy who was selling British naval secrets.

I chuckled to myself. I dared not show this story to Clifford or he'd be off playing Sherlock... and I'd be demoted to Watson.

Hiding away in the reading room, I felt like an adolescent sneaking my mother's copies of *Strand Magazine* up to my room to enjoy the latest Holmes story. If it hadn't been for Sherlock's adventures, my childhood would have been very dull indeed.

"I found you, Aunt Fiona."

So much for peace and quiet.

Eliza had taken to calling me "Aunt Fiona." Only seven years her senior, I was hardly old enough to be her aunt. Technically, I suppose I was old enough. Still, "Aunt Fiona" sounded positively hideous—the kind of homely aunt one locked in an attic and only allowed out when the company had gone home—and altogether too informal for my tastes.

Anyway, at twenty-five, I was hardly out of the running yet—no matter what Mrs. Benson, my theater teacher at North Collegiate School for Girls, had said about "the bloom going off the rose" at twenty.

Eliza plopped down in the chair next to mine with an exaggerated sigh. "I'm bored." She dangled her legs over the armrest and kicked her feet. The girl just couldn't sit still. "What can we do?" She laid her head against the back of the chair, languishing in ennui. "Isn't there something we can do for fun?"

"You could read." I held out the magazine.

"Read!" She flung herself against the back of the chair. The way she carried on, you'd think I'd suggested she throw herself overboard. "Can't we at least go to the dance tonight?"

"Do you think Captain Hall—your uncle—would approve of girls dancing while so many men are off at the front risking their lives and dying?"

Her rosebud lips turned down in a practiced pout. "What are they risking their lives for, if not dancing?"

What were they risking their lives for, indeed?

"What's more divine than dancing?" She lifted the folds of her skirt and her torso swayed back and forth to an imaginary waltz. "On Mount Olympus, there's even a god of dance."

The girl had a point. I'd met my late husband, Andrew Cunningham, at a dance. Poor dear cheating Andrew. If only he hadn't gone and got himself killed at the front, I could have strangled him myself for divorcing me to marry Nancy, his husband-stealing secretary. To make matters worse, they'd had a son. Something I'd never managed to do. Poor little mite was fatherless now.

Eliza let her feet fall to the floor. "You don't want me to end up twenty-five and alone, do you?"

Touché. I tightened my lips. *Don't count me out yet.* "Alright. We'll go to the dance." I dropped my magazine onto my lap. "But I'm not letting you out of my sight."

Eliza clapped her little hands together. "Thank you, Aunt Fiona." She jumped up and kissed me on the cheek. "You're simply marvelous."

I couldn't help but smile. *Is this what it's like to have a daughter?* I winced. I'd never know. If only I could have had a baby, Andrew might not have left me. A vice gripped my heart and I inhaled sharply. *Deep breath, Fiona, old thing.*

My father's voice echoed through my head. Water under the bridge. No use crying over spilt milk. Stiff upper lip, and all that.

I suggested we prepare our outfits for tonight. Brushing the felt on an elegant hat always worked wonders for my nerves.

Eliza was only too happy to oblige.

For the rest of the day, Eliza fluttered around our cabin like a hummingbird-moth in a garden of valerian and verbena, flitting from one pretty frock to another. She laid her dozen evening dresses across her bed and mine. Trying on gown after gown, one minute she would settle on a frothy pink chiffon and another she was committed to a canary-yellow gaberdine. For someone so young, she had quite an assortment of eveningwear.

She modeled a magenta crinoline with huge yellow flowers on one shoulder. With each accessory she added, she turned to me for approval. "What do you think?"

The feathered hat was nice. The silk wrist corsage was a bit much. But when she added a gaudy purple beaded necklace with beads the size of lemons, I couldn't take it.

"Let's not gild the lily, dear." I shook my head.

Since I only had one evening gown appropriate for a fancy

ball—the one the War Office had purchased for my last assignment—my struggles were limited to accessories.

Satin gloves or lace? Lavender or beige?

Feathered hat or turban?

And then there was the question of which wig to wear. I'd shorn my own auburn locks in the service of King and country. As a result, I had nearly as many wigs as I had hats. Should I go with the strawberry-blonde bob? Or my towering white Marie Antoinette?

The last time I'd worn my one and only evening gown, I'd been dressed as the unfortunate monarch. With its tight-fitting bodice, intricate embroidered flowers, and half-length sleeves with large satin bows at each elbow, it was already a bit much for a dance aboard a partially commandeered passenger ship. The white beehive hairpiece would most certainly put the outfit over the top.

I held a white lace glove up to my gown and scowled. I went to the wardrobe to fetch a small case. Moving Eliza's emerald-green sheath dress out of the way, I sat the case on the end of my bed and opened it. I pulled out a pair of beige gloves. *Egad.* They were even plainer than the white ones.

I paced the length of the berth. *Come on, Fiona.* It was not like this pair of gloves would decide the future of Britain.

I went back to my bed and lifted the tray from inside my case. Underneath was my collection of mustaches. A rush of adrenaline coursed through my veins. If my days in espionage had proven anything, it was that clothes do indeed make the man.

The mustaches would have to wait. And so would the brilliant new disguise and mustache I'd purchased at Angel's Fancy Dress Shop before I left London. I glanced at the wardrobe where it was hanging. I couldn't wait to try it out. Smiling, I glanced down and stroked my favorite handlebar mustache, then closed the case.

Tap. Tap. Tap.

Bark. Bark. Bark.

A knock at the door, followed by Poppy's barking, interrupted my jubilations.

I opened the door. A portly porter stood holding a giant pink box. "Delivery, Miss."

Did Eliza have a secret admirer aboard already?

The porter handed me the box and then disappeared. *Doeuillett* was embossed in silver on the lid. Even I'd heard of the famous Parisian fashion house.

Good heavens. Attached to a string tied around the box was a small envelope... addressed to me. Did *I* have a secret admirer? Could it be a present from dear Archie? Even though I'd only seen him a few times, each time, I left another piece of my heart with him.

I twittered like a schoolgirl. Get a grip on yourself, Fiona.

I hadn't seen Archie in over a month. And more to the point, I didn't know when I might see him again. Whatever he did for British Intelligence was above my security clearance, evidenced by the way he secreted himself and then dashed off at a moment's notice.

Of course the box could not be from Archie! What an absurd idea. He didn't even know I was on my way to America, let alone aboard this ship.

So, who was sending me a gift? And such a big one too?

I carried the box to the dressing table.

Eliza appeared at my side. "What is it, Aunt Fiona?"

Before I could read the card, Eliza snatched it off the string and held it over her head. I jumped at it, but as she was taller than me, I had no chance of recovering it.

"Open it." Eliza danced around the room, chanting. "Open it."

"Very well." I untied the string, eased off the lid, and gently tore open the tissue paper. My breath caught. "Oh, how lovely!" I pulled the black satin gown from the box and held it up to my torso.

I'd never seen such a beautiful ballgown. The argent roses at the waist added just enough color to signal elegance over funerary. And the sprinkle of silver sequins nestled among the jet on the bodice and the hem gave the embroidery a shadowy, mysterious quality. Whoever sent it had impeccable taste. A pretty pair of mother-of-pearl opera glasses and a matching fan accompanied the dress.

Eliza pulled a tiny card from the envelope. I held my breath as she read it. "To my darling Fiona, with love..." She snickered.

I swear, my entire body was shaking in anticipation. Archie? With love, Archie?

Eliza raised her eyebrows and gazed at me expectantly. "Fredrick."

"Oh, no!" I instinctively dropped the gown as if I'd accidently mistaken a dirty nappy for a dishcloth.

"What's wrong?" Eliza rushed over and rescued the dress.

"Fredrick Fredricks," I huffed. "The rotter, the scoundrel, the cad."

"If you don't want it..." Eliza held it up to her torso. "Can I have it?" She admired herself in the dressing table mirror. "It *is* lovely."

"It's gorgeous." Was it wrong to accept a gift from one's enemy? My assignment was to follow him to New York and learn what nefarious scheme he was hatching. And he *had* invited me to the opera. And I did need to look the part, after all. *Yes. Keeping the gown is my patriotic duty—at least until I catch Fredricks in the act of murder... or worse.*

"Who is Fredrick?" Eliza asked, a coy smile creasing her face.

"A German spy," I blurted out. *So much for my secret mission. I* grabbed the gown from her hands and shook it at her. "He is decidedly *not* an admirer."

"Golly." She dropped like a sack of flour into the chair near the dressing table. "A German spy?"

Tap. Tap. Tap.

Bark. Bark. Bark.

Another knock left us both gaping at the door. At least it had distracted Eliza from my slip about Fredricks being a spy.

More tapping.

More barking.

Good heavens. Not another poisonous gift.

As I headed for the door, Eliza dashed into the lavatory with Poppy hot on her heels. Traitors. Abandoning me to whatever sinister presents awaited me on the other side of the door.

With the gown draped over my arm, tentatively, I answered the door.

"I say." Clifford stepped into the berth. "What's going on in here? A fashion parade?"

Eliza emerged from the lav swaddled in peach gauze. Poppy was sporting a matching ribbon in her topknot. "What do you think of this one, Auntie?" She twirled around. The gown's abundance of ribbons and bows didn't hide its excessively low neckline.

I gaped at her. "Do you think you're Mata Hari performing the dance of the seven veils?" I had seen the infamous beauty removing said veils at a garden party in Paris, and it hadn't ended well for her. Sadly, I'd seen that, too.

"Good Lord." Clifford stared at her. "You'll catch your death in that wisp of a dress." He turned to me. "I say, Fiona. You aren't going to let her go out in that, are you?"

"Stop being such a prude." I shook my head. "All the fashionable young ladies are wearing these now." I had no idea what the fashionable young ladies were wearing. But I wasn't going to let Clifford dictate Eliza's wardrobe, or mine.

After all, no matter how paternalistic his behavior, he wasn't the girl's father. *And I'm not her mother.*

I hung Fredrick's gown in the wardrobe. I couldn't wait to try it on.

"Yes, well," he stuttered. "I came to fetch you ladies for tea." He stuffed his hands in his trouser pockets. "You both look as though you haven't had a decent meal in weeks."

"With this bloody war, none of us has had a decent meal in years." As if on cue, my stomach gurgled. "If I see another fish pie or suet pudding, I'll scream."

I closed the wardrobe and whispered to myself, "See you soon, my lovely."

"At least you haven't had to eat cold Maconochie's stew or break your teeth on what passes for a biscuit." Clifford pulled a pipe from his jacket pocket. "War rations are one thing. Trench rations quite another."

"Poor dear." I patted his arm. I did feel sorry for those poor boys fighting on empty stomachs, blistered feet, and precious little sleep. At Charing Cross Hospital, I'd seen the pitiful consequences of war.

Clifford put his hand on mine and smiled down at me as he clamped the bit of his pipe between his teeth. He removed what looked like a brass bullet from his pocket, flipped it open, flicked the flint, and proceeded to light his pipe.

I squinted at him and clucked my tongue.

He stopped puffing and put the blasted thing back in his pocket. If it burned a hole in his jacket, it would serve him right. Foul thing.

I turned to Eliza. "Go and change, dear. *Uncle* Clifford is taking us to tea."

"Yes, Auntie." She flitted back into the lav. When she emerged a few minutes later wearing a plaid skirt, white blouse, and flat Mary Janes, she looked like a schoolgirl again. *Thank goodness.*

* * *

As the November weather was too brisk to serve tea outside in the café, it was served in the smoking room. The smell of stale cigar smoke put me off my appetite. The sight of fresh toast, jam, and biscuits quite restored it.

With its low ceiling, thick drapes covering one windowless wall, and substantial wooden furniture, the smoking room had an oppressively masculine feel. In the center of the room, a large round table was adorned with flowers and laid with tea trays, which offset the dark mood considerably.

As I filled a small plate with biscuits and an orange—my word, I hadn't seen an orange in two years—I felt a stab of guilt. Such luxuries seemed extravagant given the situation of our poor Tommies fighting in France. One bite of a sweet biscuit and my tastebuds overpowered my conscience in the fight for my attention.

Clifford led us to a table with a direct view of another table, around which sat the smartest set of Americans aboard the ship. I'd seen them in their finery, dining at the captain's table.

Out of the corner of my eye, I spied a man slip out of the room. Something about his gait made me think of Archie. I swung around just in time to see the white-haired man disappear down the hall. Definitely not Archie.

"See the couple with their heads together," Clifford whispered. His voice was full of excitement. "Newlyweds. Dorothy Rothschild and Edwin Pond Parker II, a stockbroker. Dottie is one of New York's bright young things."

"Dottie?" I raised an eyebrow. With her pixie haircut, petite frame, and foot-long golden cigarette holder, Mrs. Parker looked like a mischievous wood nymph. Her husband looked like he'd just crawled out from under a rock.

Eliza's eyes lit up. "Are they old or new money?"

"Money is money, old or new." I scowled at her. "Anyway, doesn't it just depend on when you start counting?"

"And the woman to her right." Clifford pointed with a biscuit. "That's Margaret Sanger. Surely you've heard of her?"

I shook my head.

"The rabble-rousing American advocate of..." His voice trailed off.

"Advocate," I repeated encouragingly.

"I can't say in mixed company." Clifford blushed.

"Birth control," Eliza blurted out. "That's what she calls it."

"Oh, my word." I gawked at the woman. Margaret Sanger's demure pose and high collar, along with her girl-next-door freshly washed freckled face, didn't betray whatever depths of spirit lay beneath. I turned to Clifford. "How do you know these people?"

"Why shouldn't I know them?" His teacup clinked as he crashed it into the saucer. "I'm a sociable sort of chap."

Busybody, more like.

"Don't you read the newspapers, Aunt Fiona?"

"What newspapers?"

"The American papers." Eliza smiled. "They're splashed all over the social pages."

"Why would I read—"

"Weren't you just telling me I should read?" Eliza interrupted. She gave me a coy look. "Now who is the dullard?"

"I've heard that Mr. and Mrs. Parker have wild parties," Clifford whispered. "And Mrs. Sanger has been arrested." His blue eyes danced. "That gorgeous woman in red is a famous opera singer." He was positively potty with excitement. "And the man next to her invented aspirin." He waved a biscuit in the general direction of the celebrities.

Busybody and gossip. Judging by the pained look on his face, the glum man next to the famous singer needed to imbibe some of his own invention. The man glared at me, and I averted my gaze. My cheeks burned like I'd been caught in a lie.

The man stood up. *Good heavens.* He was coming straight toward me.

The gorgeous woman in red reached the table first. "Captain Douglas, how good to see you," she gushed.

Blimey. Clifford really did know her.

"Miss Case." When Clifford stood up, his napkin fell off his lap onto the floor.

I bent down to retrieve it.

"I'd like you to meet my... my... my..." Clifford stammered. "Miss Fiona Figg."

At the sound of my name, I jerked up and hit my head on the table. "Pleasure," I said, emerging from under the table and extending my hand. She did not follow suit.

"May I present Anna Case." Clifford bowed his head. "The famous opera singer."

The high-pitched tittering did not become Anna Case. How did I know that name?

"This is my *friend*, Mr. Hugo Schweitzer." Anna Case put her hand on his arm. He patted her hand with his own bejeweled paw. Mr. Schweitzer had a bald pate, round spectacles, and an enormous handlebar mustache.

"Happy to meet you." He sounded anything but happy. And his accent was German. I was sure of it. What was an American soprano doing with a German pill?

"I hear you invented aspirin," I said, not knowing what else to say.

"No. No." He shook his head. "That is not correct. I am a chemist, but—"

"Don't be so modest." Anna Case waved her gloved hand. "Dear Hugo was head chemist at Bayer in New York. Now he owns the Chemical Exchange Association—"

"Anna," he interrupted. "These good people are not interested in my business." It was clear from his tone that Dear Hugo thought his chemical interests were none of our business.

"Are those real pearls?" Eliza asked. "From oysters?"

I wanted to crawl back under the table.

"We're very much looking forward to your performance at Carnegie Hall." Clifford saved the day.

Carnegie Hall. Anna Case. *Aha!* The opera ticket Fredricks had hidden in the pocket of my dress on my last mission before I escaped from Vienna with the German authorities on my heels. It was a ticket to Anna Case's performance at Carnegie Hall. *What does Fredrick Fredricks have to do with this twittering soprano?* I glanced around the smoking room. *Is he here?* A chill ran up my spine.

"You should come backstage after the concert, and we—"

Hugo Schweitzer held up his hand and stopped Anna mid-sentence.

Oh, my sainted aunt. His ring. It had the exact same insignia as the pinky ring worn by Fredrick Fredricks. A panther insignia. What did it mean?

I had the queerest sensation... like someone was watching me, ready to pounce.

3

MAN OVERBOARD

While Eliza was busy with her toilette, preparing for tonight's ball —which wasn't for another two hours—I snuck back to the smoking room and gathered up several American newspapers: *The Sun, New York Herald Daily, The Evening World,* and *The New York Times.*

Good heavens. That was an awful lot of papers for one city.

The whole bunch under one arm, I planned to educate myself before the ball. Eliza and Clifford wouldn't catch me out again.

Blast. I heard Clifford's voice coming from the corridor. Flustered, I bolted to the exit. Could I sneak past him? I didn't want him to have the satisfaction of seeing me brushing up on my knowledge of the social set. I stopped short and listened. Men's laughter receded into the distance. I peeked out of the door. The coast was clear. I dashed down the hallway, up a set of stairs, and out onto the deck.

The sky glowed orange as the sun dropped below the horizon. A brisk breeze made me shiver, and I took cover under the roof of the outdoor lounge. The space was dark except for a sliver of artificial light coming through a window from the outdoor café's interior counterpart.

Since no one in their right mind would sit out here in November, except for one lonely deck chair, the tables and chairs were stacked and chained to the wall. I pulled the chair closer to the light and then plopped down, ready for my crash course in the American social scene.

The pile of papers on my lap, I snapped open *The Evening World*, and held it up to the light. This was no frivolous pursuit. In my line of work, it was essential to know who was who and where to find them.

"Giants and White Sox in Battle" was the big bold headline on the front page. I knew America was our ally, and so too were France and Russia, but who were the Giants and Sox? Rubbish. A battle between sports teams gets top billing when there are far deadlier battles being fought across the Atlantic.

Further down, in smaller print was, "Americans sink U-boat in 22-minute battle." I bet that battle didn't involve bats and balls but deck guns and torpedoes. Huff. I flipped to the back of the paper. Where was the bloody society section?

I scanned paper after paper, memorizing names and faces. Many of the passengers aboard the ship appeared in print. I learned that Mrs. Sanger had been imprisoned several times for distributing birth control, which apparently was illegal in America.

A familiar-looking, and very well-dressed, young man had just been promoted to head of the Justice Department's Alien Enemy Bureau. According to the article, this lad—John Edgar Hoover—was given free rein to arrest anyone suspected of anti-American sentiments. He'd vowed to rid America of vice.

Clifford was right. These newspapers were a *Who's Who* of New York society. I'd cut my stack in half, when a photograph in the midsection of the *New York Herald Daily* caught my eye. I held the paper closer. It couldn't be.

Crickey. It was him, alright. Riding crop in hand, a jodhpur-clad Fredrick Fredricks leaned against a tree, chatting up a beautiful woman. Given that Fredricks often wore that ridiculous South African riding costume, I knew better than to assume he'd been riding. What was he doing in the newspaper?

I squinted at the caption: "Renowned New York journalist interviews soprano about contract with Edison Records." *Renowned. Ha!* Were they having a laugh?

I took a closer look. The beautiful soprano was none other than Anna Case. How could she be on this ship and in Central Park with Fredrick Fredricks at the same time? I scanned the article for a clue. *Aha!* The photograph was taken over a year ago, before I met the scoundrel.

I squinted at the photograph. There was a man standing on the path in the background. His erect but graceful posture reminded me of... No. It couldn't be. Good grief. Now I was seeing Archie Somersby everywhere. What was wrong with me? I had to get Archie out of my mind.

Dear Archie. The last time I'd seen him, he'd kissed me. Then there was that heavenly kiss in Austria, over a month ago, when we were both behind enemy lines.

Concentrate, Fiona.

Fredrick Fredricks. Anna Case. Hugo Schweitzer.

If Fredricks knew Anna Case, did he also know her *special friend*, Mr. Hugo Schweitzer? The two men's rings shared the same insignia. Were they members of the same club? Or something more sinister.

Fredricks was a known German spy. At least, *I* knew he was a spy—he was such a slippery eel that not all the top brass at the War Office were as convinced. Or perhaps they just weren't convinced that I was the woman for the job. Lieutenant Archie Somersby knew Fredricks was a spy. He'd been chasing the blackguard even longer than I had.

If Fredricks and Schweitzer were members of the same club, was Dear Hugo also working for the Germans? His name was German. His accent was German. But was his heart German?

Tonight, at the ball, I had to keep my eyes and ears open. While Clifford and Eliza were dancing, I could slip off and do a quick search of Hugo Schweitzer's cabin. I did have my handy maid's outfit tucked away in my suitcase. Would I have time to change, snoop, and then get back to the ball without anyone noticing? But what excuse could I give Clifford and Eliza for disappearing?

By now, of course, Clifford knew I was assigned to follow Fredricks. Clifford was loyal to King and country, but he was an incorrigible blabbermouth who couldn't keep a secret if his life depended on it. And when it came to Fredrick Fredricks, it just might.

Eliza was clueless and I hoped to keep it that way.

Shadows moving in front of me along the deck stopped my scheming. Two figures struggled to carry something large between them.

I froze, holding the paper still to keep it quiet. My heart skipped a beat. Peering into the darkness, I could only tell that the two men were dressed in such dark colors they faded into the night sky, and the parcel they carried was long, of irregular shape and wrapped in a tarp.

Good heavens. A body?

Fiona, get a grip. Don't be so bloody morbid. Of course it's not a body.

Slowly, I laid the papers on the floor and then slid out of the deck chair. On tiptoes, I skirted the wall of the café, following the shadows. When I reached the end of the café, I ventured to the corner and peeked around.

The two figures were standing next to the railing. One was wearing a long dark trench coat, and the other was wearing dark wool trousers and a pullover jersey. They both had dark knitted hats covering their heads. They lifted the parcel, which, given the way they struggled with it, must be deuced heavy.

Splash.

Bloody hell. They'd thrown it overboard.

I gasped, sucking in cold night air.

The two men turned in my direction, and I ducked back behind the corner. My heart was racing. Who were they? And what had they just thrown overboard?

I clasped my hands over my mouth to keep from screaming. I flattened my body against the wall and held my breath as the two men walked past.

"*Merci aux Français,*" the shorter of the two said in a high voice.

So, they were French. I had to find a way to check the passenger list. I should tell someone. But who? Clifford? The ship's captain? One of the soldiers?

When I was sure the two men were out of sight, I gathered up the newspapers and headed inside. My fingers and toes had turned into icicles.

Back inside the smoking room, I sat the papers on a table, and then rubbed my frozen hands together.

"Good Lord, Fiona." Clifford's voice startled me.

"You scared the living daylights out of me!" My hand flew to my heart.

He'd come out of nowhere, puffing on a cigar, and looking jolly elegant in his evening suit. "What were you doing outside?" He took my hands in his.

The warmth was reassuring.

"They threw a body overboard," I whispered. "Two men. They threw it overboard."

"I say. Are you feeling alright?" Clifford stubbed out his cigar in a nearby ashtray. "Let's get you a brandy." He glanced around the smoking room, which had filled with men, who were smoking, drinking, and shouting.

"Can we go somewhere quieter? And with less foul smoke and fewer loud men?"

"You missed dinner." He took my elbow and led me through the maze of smokers. "Where were you?"

I scanned the smokers as I passed. Could a pair of them be the perpetrators? Was someone murdered aboard ship and then thrown overboard? What a ghastly thought.

As soon as we stepped into the interior hallway, I pulled out of his grasp. "Didn't you hear me? I saw them drop someone overboard."

"Come on, old girl. Let's get you some brandy." Clifford tilted his head and half-smiled.

"Don't you believe me?"

"Of course I do." Clifford put his hand over his heart.

I didn't believe him. I narrowed my eyes. "I saw them dump someone overboard."

"It was dark, and..." Clifford patted my arm. "You do have an overly active imagination—"

"I saw it as sure as you're standing there." I stomped my foot. *Ouch.* Perhaps a bit too hard.

"I say, you're white as a sheet." He removed his evening jacket and draped it over my shoulders. "Let's get you that brandy, and you can tell me what you saw."

I pulled the jacket closed around me and followed Clifford to the lounge.

* * *

The lounge was crowded too. But at least it wasn't as smoky, and, more importantly, there were other women. While I was determined to hold my own among the men, given a choice, I preferred not to do it alone.

I led Clifford to the back corner, hoping to find a quiet table. Like the rest of the first-class accommodations, the lounge was extravagant in its luxury, and yet lurking just below the shimmering surface was something darker, something sinister, like bodies thrown overboard. The wood paneling, low hanging lamps, and red satin upholstery gave the room an air of mystery and romance. And since there were no windows, blackout curfew was not an issue.

I glanced around at the well-heeled men and women. In the middle of an ocean and they were dressed to the nines. *Take away our pearls and silk ties, and we're one step closer to chaos.*

A small table in the back corner of the room was as secluded as we could get in this public space. What from a distance looked elegant, even dazzling, showed signs of age, up close. The heavy wooden table had scratches on its surface, and the slightly uneven legs of my chair tilted to the left. I fiddled with a button on Clifford's jacket, waiting for him to finish charming every table as he passed. How in heavens could he know so many people after only four days?

Under the circumstances, Clifford's amiable demeanor was more annoying than usual. I wanted to shake him. Didn't he realize there was a murderer—murderers—aboard this ship?

As if exhausted from the biathlon of crossing the crowded lounge and greeting every person in it, Clifford dropped into the chair across from me with a self-satisfied sigh.

"Finally." I tightened my lips.

"What's eating you?" Clifford crossed his long legs and leaned back in the chair.

"Murder." I glared at him. "Or have you forgotten about the poor corpse thrown overboard?" I shuddered just thinking about it.

"Really, Fiona." He sat up. "You've been reading too many Sherlock Holmes stories."

"For all we know, they could be in this very room, smiling and sipping brandy as if nothing happened." I stood up, removed his evening coat, and handed it to him, which gave me the opportunity to survey the crowd. Just who was missing?

He glanced around the room.

"Although I doubt they've had time to change into evening kit and get back to the lounge." I shivered, wishing I hadn't surrendered his coat so soon.

"Speaking of changing." Clifford looked me up and down. "Shouldn't you be getting changed for the ball?"

"How can you think of dancing?" I shook my head.

Clifford shrugged.

The waiter appeared from around the corner, and Clifford ordered two brandies.

"We can't just sit here." I hugged myself. "We should do something."

"Like what?"

"Find out if any passengers are missing. Examine the scene of the crime. Look for suspects. I don't know. Something."

"Calm down, old girl." Clifford reached across the table and touched my arm. "Don't get hysterical."

"I'm not hysterical." I huffed. "Surely by now you know me better than that, *old boy*. How many cases have I solved with you in tow?"

The waiter delivered the brandies. I took a sip. The burning sensation in my mouth enlivened me.

Clifford swirled the brandy in his snifter. "If there has been a crime, I'm confident we'll get to the bottom of it."

"What do you mean, *if*?" I wriggled away from his hand. "I tell you. I saw two men throw a body overboard."

"Righto." He removed a packet of cigarettes from his jacket pocket, tapped out a smoke, and lit it with his metal lighter. "Describe these two blokes." At least his countenance was serious now.

"It was dark, and they were wearing dark clothing." I gritted my teeth. "I didn't get a good look. I couldn't see their faces. They were speaking French."

"That's a good start. How many frogs are aboard ship?" He blew out a cloud of smoke and stared up at the ceiling as if calculating the number of frogs present.

"We should ask one of the crew."

"Good plan. Now be a good girl and drink up," Clifford said with a smile. "You'll feel better for it."

A nice hot cup of tea would have been more to my liking. But needs must... I took another sip. At least the brandy radiated heat throughout my body. After I'd finished the snifter, my muscles began to relax. I didn't realize how cold and shaken I was until the spirits took the edge off.

"Now tell me again exactly what you saw." Clifford sipped his brandy.

"Two men dressed in black struggled to carry a body and then dropped it overboard."

"How do you know it was a body?" He puffed his cigarette.

"What else could it be?"

"Rubbish, soiled linens, kitchen refuse... a thousand things besides a body."

He had a point. Maybe I'd jumped to conclusions. Perhaps I had read too many gruesome stories. I shook my head. "I suppose you're right."

"I know I'm right." He ground out his cigarette in an ashtray. "Let's forget all about it and enjoy our last evening aboard." He finished his brandy.

"How can we enjoy ourselves when some poor soul has been tossed overboard?"

"Look, why don't we go to the ball, and I'll discreetly ask around to see what I can find out, while you look out for the men you saw on deck." He tilted his head. "What do you say?"

"Alright." I doubted very much if Clifford was capable of discretion. He might not be able to keep a secret, but he was good at chatting up strangers. Although Captain Hall sent him as my chaperone, his sociability and easy manner came in handy. Not that I needed a chaperone, mind you.

"How about I escort you to your room so you can change? Eliza will be chomping at the bit by now."

Eliza. Good heavens. I'd forgotten all about the girl.

4

THE BUTTON

Where was that girl? Poppy jumped down from the bed and came to my side.

"Eliza?" I rapped on the door of the lav.

Panting, Poppy sat at my feet, looking up at me expectantly.

I rapped again. "Are you in there?"

No answer. She wasn't in our cabin. She wasn't in the lav. Where was she?

"Where are you, girl?" I picked up a pillow off her bed. Ha. As if she might be hiding underneath.

"Stay." I pointed at Poppy. "And don't worry. I'll find her."

I dashed back out into the hallway, just in time to see Clifford round the corner. I ran after him. By the time I caught up to him, I was winded and panting. "She's not there." Breathless, I bent over and put my hands on my knees. Corsets and espionage do not mix.

"Good Lord." Clifford's face fell. "You don't think..." His voice trailed off.

No, I didn't think. And blast him for putting the idea in my head. A chill ran up my spine. If I didn't find Eliza alive and well and still on board, Captain Blinker Hall would have my head on a platter. "Silly girl probably just went to the ballroom on her own." She was instructed to stay put and wait for me. Still, I prayed she'd just gone on to the dance on her own, which was quite bad enough.

"Why don't you get changed?" He patted my hand. "I'll pop down to the ballroom and find her."

I stood blinking at him, unsure of what to do. What if she was hurt? Or worse? Should I really be thinking about dressing for a ball?

"Don't worry, I'll find her." Clifford stuffed his hands in his trouser pockets. "But unless you change your clothes, you can't search the ballroom for her... or the, the, the..." He stammered. "Two men in black."

"So, you do believe me?"

"Yes, old bean." He smiled. "I believe you."

"Right." I sprinted back to my cabin.

"But hurry," Clifford called after me. "I know how women dilly-dally when dressing."

I was sure he knew no such thing. "I never dilly-dally," I called back without turning around. I hadn't time to debate the virtues of expedient toilette on behalf of my sex. I had to rescue poor Eliza from a tainted reputation if nothing else. And I had to discern what—or who—went overboard and why.

Where was that blasted girl? Keeping tabs on a teenage girl was proving more difficult than trailing that bounder, Fredricks.

Back in the cabin, I ripped off my clothes, threw on the nearest gown, and tugged on my fanciest wig, an auburn chignon with wispy curls across the forehead. Poppy sat on the floor, watching me intently.

No time to lose, I glanced in the looking glass just to avoid any glaring mishaps. Oh, my sainted aunt. *Or should I say uncle?* If not for those feminine wisps, I was the spitting image of my uncle Frank, red face, and all. Although my new black and silver gown was stunning, and it matched my silver mesh evening bag perfectly.

I tucked my trick lipstick and nail kit into the handbag. The spy lipstick had a mirror so I could watch my back. And the nail kit was really a lockpicking set. I hadn't yet persuaded Captain Hall to give me a miniature espionage camera. He insisted my photographic memory was just as good and easier to carry around. As a backup, I packed a small notebook and pencil.

He may have had a point. With the addition of Mata Hari's pearl-handled gun, my small mesh evening bag was already bulging. I wound the handbag's dainty chain around my wrist.

The cold wind on deck had burned my skin the color of a ripe tomato—which, by the way, I hadn't seen since the start of the war. I dabbed a powder puff into my small jar of face powder and then patted my cheeks. Blimey. *Forget about peaches and cream.* The layer of powder had turned my complexion into tomatoes and cheese curd.

Clifford might be right. More time for my toilette would have been an advantage. But no amount of time would turn ketchup into a satisfying meal. I wiped excess powder from my chin with a handkerchief and waved it at the mirror in surrender.

When I turned the doorknob to go, Poppy whimpered.

"I'll find her," I said and bent down to pat the little creature. Bending in a corset nearly took my breath away. Poppy licked my hand.

Wait a minute. I had an idea. I fetched the pup's leash. Maybe the little bloodhound could sniff out her mistress.

"Be a good girl." I scratched under her chin as I attached the leash to her collar. "Let's find your mama." I tugged the leash, and I swear Poppy smiled up at me.

Tongue lolling, the little dog trotted after me down the hall and out onto the deck.

I'd forgotten how difficult it was to move quickly wearing a corset and a tight skirt. Only a man could have invented the hobble skirt. What could he have been thinking? *If a hobble keeps my horse from running away, maybe it will work on my wife?*

I wrapped my silk shawl around my person. If I was cold before, I was positively freezing in this evening gown. "Poppy, you'd best make it quick."

In the darkness, alone outside, a full moon shining on the deck, the stars bright in the night sky, I would have felt a sense of peace if I wasn't frantic over Eliza.

Poppy took off running and the leash slipped out of my hand. Curse it! I tried to keep up. I'd already lost the girl. I couldn't lose the dog too. Where you go, I go, little beast... even if it's overboard.

The dog stopped near the railing where I'd seen the two men disposing of their hideous cargo. Perhaps Poppy was a bloodhound after all. Could she sense something? I watched as she sniffed and panted, turning in circles.

Oh. I see. At least she'd done her business.

Poppy gave a few kicks with her back feet. The pup trotted back to the door, and I followed. I opened the door, and the dog stepped inside. *What's that?* Poppy had something in her mouth.

I bent down to remove it, but the little beast growled through her teeth. Sigh. Trying to maneuver in full evening dress was no mean feat. Carefully, I squatted and yanked the thing from her mouth and took up her leash.

What in heaven's name was it? It was round, tan, made of rubber and thick, flexible wire. Poppy had chewed a hole in it. I tucked it into my bulging handbag. Could it be related to the man overboard? If so, it could be crucial evidence.

"Well done." I not so gracefully stood up. "Now let's go and find your mama."

I returned to our room, hoping Eliza might be back by now. No such luck.

"You stay here in case she returns." When I unclipped her leash, Poppy stared up at me with those big eyes. "Yes, I'll find her." I hoped Clifford was right and Eliza had slipped off to the ball without us.

Next stop. The ballroom.

Rushing down the hallway and up the stairs, I nearly fell on my face... more than once. With each misstep, a torrent of adrenaline flooded my brain. By the time I arrived at the ballroom, I was in a lather.

A small orchestra played a waltz and couples swirled around the dance floor. The ball had been underway for over an hour, and judging by the laughter and glowing faces, the combination of dancing and spirits was a much needed, if temporary, antidote to the horrors of war.

I scanned the ballroom for the billowing pink gown Eliza had chosen for tonight. Surely it would stand out in any crowd. While I didn't spot Eliza's candy floss frock, I did spy Clifford's cowlick standing up above the crowd. He was a good deal taller than most. And the sprout on his crown added a good inch.

I snaked my way through the throng, using Clifford's periscope as my guide. When the music stopped, the dancing also stopped abruptly, causing me to miscalculate the distance between my person and that of a brick wall of a man.

"Pardon me," I said, holding my shoulder where it had rammed into his back.

He waved me away like a bothersome insect.

Applause gave way to the rustling of skirts as ladies made their way off the dance floor.

Blast. I'd lost Clifford in the crowd.

Aha! I spotted a pink puff exiting the dance floor on the arm of a soldier in uniform, an American uniform. I'd found Eliza... hanging off the arm of a doughboy and giggling like a schoolgirl. "Eliza, there you are." I strode up to her. "You were instructed to wait in our cabin until—"

"Aunt Fiona, may I present Billy." She grinned from ear to ear. "Billy Buck, meet Fiona Figg."

The forbidden Billy? "*The* Billy?" I asked.

When Eliza nodded, her blonde curls danced.

The handsome young doughboy chuckled and then extended his hand. "Good to meet you, Aunt Fiona."

Oh dear. What would happen when Captain Hall found out about his niece's clandestine liaison and Billy's manifestation on the ship? The girl might as well have been thrown overboard... and me along with her.

Forbidden Billy still had his hand extended. In a state of shock, I took it. His overly enthusiastic handshake yanked my entire arm and nearly shook my evening bag off my wrist and onto the floor.

"What happened to your face?" Eliza asked, the smile disappearing from her face.

I touched my cheek. "Whatever do you mean?"

She laughed. "Why, you've applied so much face powder, you look like a ghost."

I scowled. Where was Clifford when I needed him?

Eliza was wearing a necklace exactly like the one she'd admired on the opera singer.

"Where did you get those pearls?" I pointed to her necklace.

She blushed. "These old things?"

"I say, there you are, Fiona." *Speak of the devil, and he shall appear*. Clifford was all smiles, obviously enjoying himself. "See, old bean. I told you there was nothing to worry about."

Nothing to worry about! Under orders from the girl's mother, Captain Hall had arranged passage for Eliza precisely to separate her from Mr. Billy Buck. And now, here she stood, chaperoned only by my unreliable self and the hopelessly oblivious Clifford Douglas.

I took hold of the arm of his evening coat and pulled Clifford aside. "This Billy is the very boy... young man... Captain Hall warned Eliza to stay away from. What is he doing on board?"

"He's a nice sort of chap." Clifford lifted his knee and tapped it. "Injured at the Somme, don't you know." Clifford walked so well that I'd forgotten he too had been injured in the war. When I first met him a year ago, he'd walked with a cane. Now, no one would know he'd been shot in the leg.

"He doesn't look injured." I glanced over at the lad. He was attractive, I'd give her that.

"Not all injuries are visible," Clifford whispered.

"Yes, quite right." I was dying to know but didn't ask. Maybe Billy Buck suffered from what the doctors were calling shell-shock. But how did Clifford know so much about Mr. Buck? Were he and Eliza in cahoots on the Billy front? "How long have you known about Billy?"

"Why, I just met him." Clifford smiled over at the boy. "Jolly good sort of lad. We got to chatting."

"I bet you did."

Clifford could chat to an ironing board and come away with a new mate. I supposed that was part of his charm. And it came in jolly handy too. The way he put people at ease loosened their lips.

Her face glowing, Eliza hung on Billy's arm and looked up

into his face with obvious admiration. Thank goodness Captain Hall wasn't here to witness the touching scene.

I tugged at Clifford's sleeve. "Keep your eye on them, would you?"

"Why?" Clifford stood blinking at me. "Where are you going?"

"Never mind." I didn't want him interfering. Anyway, someone had to stay and chaperone the girl. "Don't let Eliza out of your sight."

"I say." He cocked his head and looked at me out of the corner of his eye. "What are you up to?"

"Just promise you'll keep an eye on her." If I told him my plan, he would insist on tagging along. The last thing I wanted was Clifford breathing down my neck. He was such a nosy busybody.

He huffed.

"Promise me." I tightened my lips.

He nodded.

"Say it," I demanded.

"Good Lord, Fiona." He huffed again. "Don't you trust me?"

"You have good intentions." I patted his arm. "But there's many a slip between cup and lip."

He pouted.

It wasn't that he wasn't trustworthy. He did mean well. But sometimes, he was completely incompetent. This time, I was banking my career on him. If anything happened to Eliza, Captain Hall would have my head.

* * *

First things first. Before I searched Mr. Schweitzer's cabin, I must find the captain, and tell him what I saw. Perhaps he could determine if someone was missing from the passenger manifest. What a gruesome thought. Now where was the captain?

I zigzagged through the throng of partiers. Whoops and hollers made me wonder what in the world they'd been drinking. Whatever it was, most of the men and some of the women had had quite enough of the stuff.

"Miss Figg." Mrs. Dorothy Parker stopped me on my way past. "Are you enjoying the ball?"

"Yes, very much," I said, looking over her head toward the bar. "Are you enjoying the party?" I really didn't have time for small talk.

"If I enjoy it any more than I already have…" She lifted her glass. "You'll find me under the host."

What did she say? I looked down at her. The mischief in her eyes made me uneasy.

"I'd better not find you under the host, unless I'm the host," Mr. Parker said. "I find this crowd utterly boring. I can't bear fools."

"That's queer," Mrs. Parker said. "Obviously your mother could." She burst into laughter. Her poor husband joined her.

I hoped that wasn't what passed for wit in New York.

"If you'll excuse me," Mr. Parker said. "I need to find the little boys' room."

"He really needs to use the telephone." Mrs. Parker touched my arm. "But he's too embarrassed to say so."

I forced a smile. As my father would say, "She eats vinegar with a fork." I wouldn't want to be on the receiving end of her acid tongue.

I spied Margaret Sanger out of the corner of my eye. "If you'll excuse me," I said. "I see a friend." Of course, Margaret Sanger was no more a friend than Mrs. Parker. The ruse worked, and I managed to escape Mrs. Parker's nail-sharp grip.

"Excuse me, Miss Sanger—"

"Mrs."

"Apologies. Mrs. Sanger." I looked around for Mr. Sanger but didn't see anyone nearby who might fit that bill. "Have you seen the ship's captain?"

"I'm afraid I haven't." She shrugged. "Why do you ask?" I may have overdone it with the face powder, but she'd been overly enthusiastic with her rouge. She looked like a radish.

"Apologies." I scooted past her. "But I really must find the captain."

"I'll accompany you." She trailed me as I made my way through the crowd.

"What did you see exactly?" she asked. "When did it happen?" She followed so closely she trod on my heel at one point. "Where did it happen?" Her incessant interrogation was distracting to say the least. But I wasn't about to confide in her. I hardly knew the woman.

I caught up with Captain Stamest munching on a piece of shrimp toast and entertaining a small group of dignitaries. The captain, a balding man in his forties, stood up so straight he was rigid. The circle of posh patrons parted to give us access to the man in charge.

"May we speak in private, sir?" I asked.

Captain Stamest cocked his head. "And you are?"

"Fiona Figg, sir." I curtsied. Why I don't know. I must have spent too much time around the Austrian royalty on my last assignment. My cheeks burned with embarrassment. "I saw something suspicious on deck."

"Suspicious?" He continued munching.

"Two men threw something—or someone—overboard."

"When was this?" He sat his plate on the table and brushed crumbs off his jacket.

"About an hour ago."

"And why didn't you report it earlier?" he asked, his steely eyes trained on me. "You say a passenger went overboard?"

"I don't know who went over." I fiddled with my bag string. "I saw two men in black throw something that looked like a body overboard."

"Alright." He wiped his mouth with a napkin. "Let's get to the bottom of this."

To his credit, Captain Stamest immediately flew into action. He summoned the ship's bursar and ordered an accounting of all the passengers and crew right away. I had to persuade him not to stop the ball and alert the murderers that their dirty deed was known. If the killers thought they'd got away with it, we would have the element of surprise on our side.

While the crew, with the help of Mrs. Sanger, was busy counting passengers, I led the captain out on deck to the scene of the crime. Luckily, the captain had a torch to illuminate our path. Unfortunately, the temperature had dropped since my last excursion. My gown provided about as much protection against the cold as hopes and prayers protected against artillery shells.

My teeth were chattering, and I hugged myself, bracing against the frigid wind. I couldn't be sure of the exact spot where the two men had thrown the body overboard. But I did know the general vicinity of the misdeed.

The captain and his first mate examined the deck and railing but found nothing out of the ordinary. Then again, it was dark, and the criminals had thrown the most important *evidence* overboard.

As the first mate shone his torch on the railing, a sparkling reflection caught my eye. Arms out to keep my balance as the ship tossed on the waves, I joined him at the edge of the deck. I ran my gloved hand over the railing.

Aha! What's this? I pulled a small metal button out of a seam in the wooden rail. One of the perpetrator's sleeves must have caught on the railing and torn off this silver button when they threw the body overboard. "Evidence," I said triumphantly. "Hard evidence."

I held it in front of the beam from the torch. The button was round and about the size of a grape, with a fleur-de-lis design. Was the culprit French? Or an American soldier who favored French clothing? One of the culprits was speaking French, after all. My next step would be to check the passenger manifest for French nationals.

I opened my mesh bag and was about to drop it in when the captain stopped me.

"I'll take that." Captain Stamest held out his hand.

"Of course." When I turned the button over to examine the back, I noticed a dark hair stuck to the shank. I yanked it off and slipped it into my handbag. After a few more seconds of memorizing every detail, I handed it to the captain.

Next on my agenda: Find a French soldier missing a silver button from his shirt sleeve.

5

LEAVING THE BALL

With the help of Mrs. Sanger, the ship's crew had managed to count passengers without stopping the ball. To my astonishment, not a single passenger was missing. Even the pet dogs and live chickens were accounted for.

"What a relief." Mrs. Sanger wiped the back of her hand across her forehead.

"You put us through a lot of trouble, Miss Figg." The captain's voice was stern. "Don't let your imagination run away with you again."

"Yes, sir."

Once he was gone, I squeezed my eyes tight to keep from crying. I know what I saw. Something or someone went overboard. Perhaps there had been a stowaway aboard. Someone not counted on the official roster. Someone hiding out from their assassins.

"Cheer up, old girl," Clifford said, patting me on the shoulder. "This means no one was murdered."

"You're right." I was miserable because everyone was still

alive. *Good grief.* What was wrong with me? I had to be the most morbid person on earth.

"How about a spin around the dance floor?" Clifford smiled and held out his hand.

"Why not?" Maybe it would distract me from murder and murderers. *One nail takes out the other.* Then again, it would give me a chance to examine the gentlemen's shirtsleeves for missing buttons. I wrapped the chain of my handbag more firmly around my wrist and then took his hand. He led me out onto the floor.

The small orchestra was playing an upbeat waltz. Clifford whisked me along so quickly, I felt like I was flying. My feet seemed to leave the ground entirely. Only when Clifford's large shoe kicked my shin or stomped on my toe did I come back to earth.

The gentlemen's shirts were a blur—forget about their shirtsleeves. If only I were a man, I could go about the room introducing myself and shaking hands to expose missing buttons. Should I enlist Clifford's assistance? He was such a blabbermouth; he'd probably spill the beans to the killers and ensure their escape. No. I'd have to find another way.

"Why is this waltz so fast?" I was breathless.

"It's a polka," Clifford shouted above the music. "It's supposed to be fast."

The music stopped, and so did Clifford. I slammed into him as the other dancers broke into applause.

I turned to leave the dance floor, but Clifford took my arm. "How about another?"

The music—if you could call it that—started up again. The trumpet wailed and the clarinet screamed. The trombone answered with a roar. *What in the world?*

Wriggling like excited puppies, Eliza and Billy bounded onto the dance floor. Their feet were twisting and kicking the air. Eliza twirled, and Billy spun around. *Good heavens.* Billy lifted Eliza clean off the floor. Was this dancing or calisthenics?

Blimey. Eliza returned the favor. How could such a petite thing lift that strapping doughboy? The girl was stronger than she looked.

"What is this?" My eyes were glued to the dance floor. "American music?"

"It's called jazz," Clifford said. "Isn't it marvelous?"

There may not have been a murder on deck, but there was a horn section in this ballroom being strangled. For a five-piece orchestra, they were making a jolly lot of noise.

"My head is killing me." I put my hand to my forehead. "I'm going back to my room."

"Oh dear. Are you quite alright?" Clifford's concerned expression was endearing.

"I'll be right as rain after a good night's sleep." Of course, I had no intention of sleeping.

"I'll escort you to your cabin." Clifford took my elbow.

I wriggled free. It was time to get back to my original mission, search Hugo Schweitzer's room. "You stay here and chaperone Eliza." I nodded toward the dance floor where Eliza and Billy were making quite a spectacle, spinning, twirling, and practically throwing one another in the air. "Make sure the girl gets home— alone—and at a reasonable hour."

* * *

Before exiting the ballroom, I scanned the dance floor one last time, concentrating on extended arms and exposed shirtsleeves. I may have a photographic memory, but from this distance, my eyesight wasn't good enough to discern whether any buttons were missing. I would have to devise another strategy to find the maltreated garment and its dodgy owner.

I did, however, spot Mr. Hugo Schweitzer, a cigar in one hand and a cocktail in the other, gesticulating at Miss Anna Case. *Good.* He was engaged, at least for the time being.

I stepped out into the hallway and took a deep breath. It felt good to leave behind the stuffy room and boisterous crowd. I needed to clear my head and work out the details of my plan. Perhaps a bit of night air would do me good. I headed downstairs and back out onto the deck.

As I rounded the corner, I heard voices and stopped in my tracks. I pricked up my ears. *Men's voices. Speaking German!* Good heavens. Was everyone on this ship brazenly conducting nefarious business openly on deck? What kind of ocean crossing was this?

I crept along the wall until the ember from one of the men's cigarettes came into view. I could make out two men standing under the awning of the café. They both were wearing long trench coats. The one facing me wore a bowler hat and the one with his back to me wore a fedora and had a knapsack over his shoulder.

I took a deep breath, held it, and listened.

My German wasn't great. But I had learned enough to get by for my last assignment in Vienna.

"*Krieg der Chemiker.*" *Chemists' war.* When the man took a drag of his cigarette, the glow illuminated his round spectacles and enormous mustache.

Aha! Mr. Hugo Schweitzer. I knew he was up to no good. But how in the world did he get from the ballroom to the deck so quickly? He must have left right after I did.

The man with his back to me was animated in his response

and spoke German with a strong accent. *British? American? Australian?* I couldn't tell.

From what I could make out, the men were talking about some chemical called carbolic acid, also known as phenol, extracted from coal tar. Either my German was worse than I thought, or this chemical had many uses, including aspirin, explosives, and... vinyl records. I shook my head. *That can't be right. Records for phonographs?* If only I had my German dictionary.

Hugo Schweitzer dropped his cigarette and ground it under the heel of his dress shoe. "I'm going back to the ball before Anna gets suspicious," he said in English.

"I'll just drop my coat off in my cabin and then I'll see you there." Speaking English, the second man's voice sounded familiar. Maybe it was the London accent. One of my countrymen was in cahoots with Hugo Schweitzer.

"Good idea," Mr. Schweitzer said. "I'll do the same."

The Englishman took out a pocket watch. "See you in ten minutes."

When the men were out of sight, I slid around the corner and entered the hallway through the same door they had to have used. Darn. The door squeaked as it closed, and I ducked into a stairwell.

I peeked out into the hall in time to see Hugo Schweitzer turn the corner. Lifting the hem of my gown, I dashed after him. It was not easy to keep tabs on him and stay out of sight. The long corridors and hallways did not offer many hiding places. Still, the telescoped spaces afforded me unobstructed views of his movements.

After following him the full length of the ship, which was considerable, my shoes pinched my toes, and my feet hurt. The French heels on my patent opera pumps were killing me. Fashion be hanged. I didn't care what people said. From now on, evening gown or not, I was wearing my practical Oxfords.

I glanced around. The coast was clear. I lifted my dress to pull up my silk stocking. My garter had slipped, and my blooming stocking lay pooled at my ankle.

A noise made me duck back into the stairwell. The sound of heavy footfalls was getting louder. Horsefeathers. There was nowhere else to go. So what if he saw me? For all he knew, I could be returning to my own cabin after the ball. I cleared my throat and steeled myself for the encounter.

Slowly, I stepped out into the corridor. "Good heavens." I brought my hand to my heart. "You startled me." I did study acting at North Collegiate School for Girls.

"Apologies, Miss." My performance lost on him, Hugo Schweitzer didn't make eye contact as he brushed past me and then disappeared into the stairwell.

I leaned against the wall and exhaled sharply. After a few minutes, I tiptoed down the corridor and stopped in front of Mr. Schweitzer's cabin. Hopefully, Anna's charms would keep him occupied long enough for me to snoop... or I should say, carry out some espionage.

I slipped my handy lockpicking set out of my mesh handbag. Disguised as a nail care kit, the small leather pouch contained a tension wrench, a pick, and a rake, all neatly tucked into individual sleeves. Just opening the pouch, I was chuffed.

I slid the thin metal tension wrench into the lock and applied pressure. Next, I skated the metal pick in under the wrench and felt for the pins. *Voilà.* The lock gave, and I turned the door handle. *As easy as sago pudding.* My stomach gurgled.

Good grief. The room was in disarray. The bed wasn't made, and clothes were strewn everywhere. The dressing table was an unholy clutter of cups, papers, and toiletries. I resisted the urge to tidy the room.

In such chaos, where did I start?

Usually, I would begin with the wardrobe. Clothes did make the man. But, by the looks of it, his entire wardrobe—trousers, shirts, jackets, socks, and underwear—was wadded and tossed about the cabin.

Still, in such a small berth, there weren't many places to hide state secrets other than the wardrobe. With such mess, how did he find anything? And more to the point, how would I?

The room had a sour smell that I couldn't quite place. *Pickles? Milk? Socks?*

Stepping over shoes and discarded magazines, I made my way to the dressing table. Without touching anything, I bent down and examined the papers strewn across the tabletop: a receipt for a box of expensive cigars, a laundry list, filled out but obviously not yet bagged and set out to be cleaned, and a playbill for *The Bing Girls are There*, complete with the lyrics of "Yula Hicki Wicki Yacka Dula".

Nothing suspicious. Unless you counted his taste in musical theater.

I tackled the obstacle course to get to the wardrobe. Inside hung jackets only slightly less wrinkled than the ones lying across the furniture, and trousers that looked fine from a distance but upon closer inspection had tiny stains and tears. A tumble of shoes and boots were piled on the floor. I bent down to take a closer look. *Aha! What's this?*

Carefully, I pulled the briefcase out of the wardrobe. It was heavier than it looked. The black leather was scuffed and worn, and the handle was barely hanging on. I depressed the latches on either side. They didn't budge. The case was locked.

Surely this flimsy little lock was no match for my lockpicking set. But where to do it? I couldn't very well sit on the floor in my evening gown. With the gown wrapped around my legs, I'd never be able to get back up. I glanced around the berth. My best option was an empty chair whose wooden back doubled as a hanger for only one dirty shirt.

I was sorely tempted to bag up his dirty laundry and put it out myself. Instead, I took the briefcase to the chair, and sat down with it on my lap. I let the chain of my mesh evening bag drop off my wrist, removed my lockpick set, and went to work.

Blast. The case was so old, the lock was rusted. Double blast. My rake skid across the metal lock and scratched it. I'd better hurry and get this bloody thing open before the ball ended and Mr. Sourpuss came back.

Holding the case between my knees, with all my strength I pressed the wrench and pick into the lock. *Grrrrr.*

The blooming thing finally popped open. *At last.*

Oh no! The momentum sent the case flying out of my lap and onto the floor.

Brilliant. Just brilliant. Even a barmy slob would notice someone had tampered with the briefcase and its contents.

I fell to my knees and began scraping up the papers and pawing them back into the case. An official-looking letter caught my eye. *Good heavens.* It was from Kaiser Wilhelm.

My German wasn't good enough to actually read the letter. But I did make out the words *Das Aspirin, Phenol,* and *Karbolsäure,* which if I wasn't mistaken meant carbolic acid. How was aspirin involved in a plot against the allies?

I scanned the letter to commit it to memory. I could recreate it later and then have Clifford translate. His German was much better than mine.

I stuffed the papers back into the briefcase as best as I could, giving them a quick look as I did so. Since most of them were in German, I had no idea what might be important. The case was pregnant with file folders and thick stapled reports, and I had to put it back together and get out before Hugo Schweitzer returned.

Maybe I should just take the whole kit and caboodle. After all, unless he was completely daft, he would know someone had been in his room. Then again, I couldn't very well hide the blasted thing under my evening gown. And I didn't dare walk down the hallway carrying it.

I glanced at my watch. How long had I been here? It seemed like an hour already, but I knew it was only minutes. Still, how did I know Mr. Schweitzer would return to the ball instead of to his cabin? The hairs on my arms stood up. The ballroom wasn't that far away, after all.

There was nothing else I could do. I returned the briefcase to the wardrobe, and then quickly left the cabin. As I shut the door, I heard voices. Crikey. Hugo Schweitzer rounded the corner with Anna Case on his arm. The man got around.

My face was on fire. I gritted my teeth and walked straight toward them. I hoped to heaven he didn't see me exit his berth. If he was high enough up the German food chain to receive a letter from the Kaiser, then he must be an important agent... and probably a bloody dangerous one too.

As they approached, I took a deep breath. "Good evening." I forced a smile as they passed.

Hugo Schweitzer glared at me.

If looks could kill, I would be lying dead in the corridor.

6

CAUGHT IN THE ACT

After my near run-in with Mr. Schweitzer, I made a beeline back to my own cabin. I was traveling as fast as my sore feet would allow, which was darn slow considering the toes of my new shoes pinched something awful.

To make matters worse, my cabin was on the opposite side of the ship. And it was a whale of a ship. I could just go back to the ballroom, which was closer. But I needed to jot down what I'd seen so I could report it to Captain Hall.

Anyway, I couldn't wait to take off these shoes, trade my silk gown for a flannel one, and crawl into bed. It had been quite a day. Chaperoning a teenage girl only to find out her forbidden love was aboard. Watching as two figures dressed in black threw another overboard. Overhearing a mysterious Englishman plotting with Hugo Schweitzer. Breaking into his berth and finding evidence of his treachery.

I only just escaped his cabin in time. He'd almost caught me in the act. If he had half a brain, it was only a matter of time before he put two and two together and realized I had just come from his cabin when he passed me in the hallway. Surely he would have noticed that someone had broken into his case and rearranged his papers.

Caught up in my thoughts, I was barely aware of my surroundings. Yet, when I approached the last stairwell leading to my deck, I stopped. A shiver ran up my spine. Again, I had that queer feeling I was being watched.

I whirled around to confront my pursuer. The stairwell was empty. Sigh. Clifford was right. I had an overactive imagination.

I took a deep breath and opened the heavy door to the last corridor between me and my bed. A blast of warm air hit my face, and I stepped inside.

Good gracious. There he was. The other man. The one in the fedora with the knapsack. The one who was plotting with Hugo Schweitzer. Although I still could only see him from behind, I recognized that silhouette. My pulse quickened.

Had he seen me? If he had, he made no sign of it.

With my back up against the wall, I watched as he removed a key from his trench coat, unlocked the door, and then disappeared into his cabin. As it happened, his was only three doors down from mine.

I tiptoed down the corridor—which only made my feet hurt worse. I'd taken two steps when I heard a noise and stopped again. Damnation. The man opened his cabin door and stepped out in the hallway. *Good grief.* It was after midnight. Where was he going now? Was he meeting Hugo Schweitzer again? Or some other good-for-nothing German agent?

My breath caught, and my hand flew to my mouth. Now he would see me for sure. What of it? I was going to my cabin. Nothing suspicious about that. Anyway, there was no way he could have seen me watching him with Hugo Schweitzer. Was there?

He didn't even glance in my direction. *Whew.* What a relief.

Only when I exhaled did I realize I'd been holding my breath.

Still in his trench coat and fedora, the man continued down the corridor. There really was something uncanny about his gait. Thank goodness, he didn't double-back in my direction. As soon as he'd turned the corner and was out of sight, I scurried to my room.

I stood in front of the door to my cabin. Should I, or shouldn't I? *What the heck.* I glanced up and down the corridor. Except for the sounds of the ship's engines, it was quiet. And there was not a soul in sight.

I dashed to his door, opened my bag, and withdrew my lock-picking set. It had been such a breeze picking Hugo Schweitzer's lock. Hopefully, I could get in and out quickly.

If I was lucky, I would find a clue as to what my mysterious compatriot had planned... why he was scheming with Hugo Schweitzer... and what aspirin had to do with it.

* * *

Inside, the cabin was the opposite of Hugo Schweitzer's. Whereas the German's room was disorderly and repulsive, this man's berth was tidy and attractive. In fact, it hardly looked occupied. The bed was made in a neat military style. There wasn't an article of clothing nor a personal item in sight. A faint scent of pine and citrus graced the room. Like a familiar embrace, the uniform order and pleasing smell put me at ease.

Hugo Schweitzer's disgusting mess had allowed clues to remain hidden in plain sight. This man's neatness required clever hiding places. Where would I hide a secret document in this room? Under the mattress? In the wardrobe? Sewn inside an article of clothing?

I crossed the room. Getting to the wardrobe was considerably easier than it had been in Schweitzer's clutter. When I opened the wardrobe, a waft of pine and citrus caressed my nostrils again. I thought of Archie. When would I see him again?

Concentrate, Fiona. Now was not the time to behave like a lovesick schoolgirl.

Two neat suits hung on hangers, spaced apart like sentries guarding a gate. One was a uniform. A British uniform. Could this traitor be in the British army? The other was a black evening suit. Whatever the blackguard was wearing under that trench coat constituted his third and final outfit. There were no more.

Standing to attention at the bottom of the wardrobe were two tall black boots. I bent down to get a closer look. Inside a boot would make a decent hiding place.

"Looking for something?" a man's voice boomed from behind me.

I gasped and squeezed my eyes shut tight.

If only I were wearing my maid's costume—although what maid would be cleaning at this time of night? I should have changed into Harold the helpful bellboy. At least then I'd be dressed as a man. As it was, I was wearing a flimsy evening gown and as vulnerable as a lamb in a ship full of wolves. Did I dare turn around and face my accuser?

"Did you find it?" The voice was closer now... and softer... and familiar.

Good heavens. I whipped around and practically flew into his arms. "Archie."

He chuckled. "I should have known I'd find you breaking into my room." He pulled me into an embrace. "Fiona. Dear Fiona." He kissed the top of my head.

I buried my head in his shoulder. *Ahhh.* The scent of pine and citrus... and those horrible Kenilworth cigarettes. The scent of Lieutenant Archie Somersby.

My heart was racing. From being scared out of my wits, or from being in Archie's embrace, I didn't know. "What are you doing here?"

"I could ask you the same." He held me tighter.

"You, first." I inhaled his familiar presence.

"I will tell you, but only because it's necessary." He pulled out of the embrace and held me out at arm's length. "It's crucial that you don't expose me."

"Expose you?" I had to censor my imagination. His earnest green eyes framed by those dark lashes and that wild lock of chestnut hair falling across his forehead made it deuced difficult.

"I'm on an important mission." He fortified his countenance with a steely gaze. "You mustn't let on that you know me. In fact, you should stay away from me." He pulled a gold pocket watch out of his waistcoat pocket and glanced at it.

I pulled my arm out of his grip. "Does your mission involve Hugo Schweitzer?" My tone was pained, but I couldn't help it. I wished my feelings for him weren't so strong. After all, I hardly knew him. Still, I knew he worked for British Intelligence, despite Fredrick Fredricks's accusations to the contrary. Afterall, who was more trustworthy? A German spy or a British soldier, an especially attractive one too?

Archie tilted his head and gave me a quizzical look. "How did you know?"

"I saw you together earlier on deck." Without a doubt, the trench coat and fedora Archie was wearing, along with his sleek silhouette and graceful gait, were identical to those of my mysterious compatriot and Hugo Schweitzer's clandestine companion.

He laughed. "I should have known that was you watching us." He kissed me on the cheek. "Fiona, you're an ace. I've never met a girl quite like you." His eyes danced mischievously.

The way he was laughing, I didn't know whether to be

insulted or flattered. *Wait a blooming minute.* "Did you forget something?" I'd seen that amused expression before. "Why did you return to your cabin?"

"To catch you in the act, love." Archie grinned.

"So, you saw me in the corridor?"

He raised his eyebrows and nodded. "Afraid so."

I punched his shoulder. "And instead of saying anything, you pulled this trick?"

"I'm sorry." He intercepted my hand and brought it to his lips. "Can you forgive me?"

I pulled out of his grip. "Only if you can tell me about Mr. Schweitzer and the chemists' war."

"You know I can't do that." He sighed. "It's classified."

"What does the war have to do with aspirin, the headache remedy?"

He led me to the bed, sat down, and patted the bedcover, inviting me to sit too.

My cheeks flamed. It was only then that I realized I was alone in a gentleman's room... after midnight, no less. Dilly Knox's words echoed through my head. "Our Fiona will do anything for King and country, don't you know." That only strengthened my resolve. I was on official business and not a romantic getaway.

I took a seat on the bed and tucked my gown tightly around my thighs. "You were going to tell me about aspirin?"

"You're nothing if not persistent." Archie smiled and put his arm around my shoulders.

I scooted to the head of the bed and out of his reach. "Aspirin?"

He shook his head. "You really are quite a girl."

I folded my arms over my chest and glared at him.

"Righto." His smiled faded. "Aspirin is made from a chemical called phenol."

Phenol. I'd heard Hugo Schweitzer mention it. And phenol was in the letter from the Kaiser. The Kaiser's letter. Should I tell Archie about the letter? Or report it to Captain Hall first? "What does phenol have to do with the war?"

"We need phenol to make trinitrotoluene." Archie gave me a knowing look.

I gave him an ignorant stare in return. "What is trinitrotoluene?"

"TNT."

"The explosive?"

He nodded.

"Golly." Still, why did it matter if aspirin and TNT shared one element? How did that affect the war? Could aspirin be turned into an explosive?

"Golly is right." When he smiled, tiny dimples appeared at the corners of his mouth.

I had to stop myself from reaching across the bed to touch that tempting lock of wavy hair... and those dimples. Stop it, Fiona. You're on an espionage mission and not on holiday. A holiday with Archie... how divine. Stop! Just stop.

"I'm sorry we can't work together in the open." He took my hand and kissed it. "But for now, I'm undercover and I have to stop Schweitzer at all costs."

"I have a confession." I sat on my hands to keep from touching him. "I broke into Hugo Schweitzer's cabin."

Archie sat up straighter. "Go on."

"He has a briefcase full of papers and letters... in German."

"Yes," Archie said encouragingly.

"One of the letters was from the Kaiser." I glanced over at him.

"I don't suppose you can recount the letter verbatim?" He raised his eyebrows. He'd seen me do it before.

"I don't suppose you have a pencil and paper?" I released my hands from their bondage.

Archie got up and went to the dressing table. He opened the top drawer and pulled out a sheet of paper and then withdrew a pencil from his breast pocket and held it up.

I joined him and sat down at the table.

He placed the paper on the table in front of me and handed me the pencil. "Work your magic, my love."

My pulse quickened. Did Archie just call me *my love*? My cheeks warmed. With a smile in my heart, I closed my eyes and let the words form before my mind like captions across a black screen. I didn't know what they meant, but I could see them as clearly as if I were holding the letter in my hands. I opened my eyes and began setting to paper what I had seen. My hand was flying across the page. When I finished, I scanned my reproduction and then held it up to Archie. He'd been breathing over my shoulder as I wrote, which was deuced distracting.

As he read, the grim look on his face spoke volumes. "Good God," he gasped. "So that is what they're up to. And the phenol plot goes all the way to the Kaiser himself." He dropped the paper on the dressing table. "Schweitzer is siphoning off phenol from the allies on orders from the Kaiser himself."

Siphoning off phenol. The chemical needed to make explosives. So that was the phenol plot.

The corners of his mouth turned up ever so slightly. "Fiona, you're a genius."

I couldn't help but smile.

His eyes hardened. "I've got to stop him." Archie's hand trembled as he ran it through his hair. "I've got to stop Schweitzer."

I gazed up at him with as much resolve as I could muster.

"You mean *we've* got to stop him."

7

ALONE AT LAST

Archie and I were both leaning against the headboard with our legs stretched out on the bed. He still hadn't taken off his trench coat or hat. I had my evening gown wrapped around my legs all the way down to my ankles. Even wrapped up like a caterpillar in a cocoon, sitting next to Archie made for the most exciting night I'd had in a long time.

It was nearly three in the morning, and I'd managed to extract mere crumbs from Archie about "the great phenol plot." All I'd learned was that Schweitzer was the mastermind of a plan to disrupt the supply of phenol needed for the allies' munitions. I still had so many questions. But every time I asked one, Archie shook his head and said "classified." I was beginning to wonder whether he and I were truly on the same side.

"Does Bayer Aspirin have stockpiles of phenol?" I asked with a yawn and covered my mouth.

"Classified." He stared at his shoes.

I'd slipped mine off. The blasted things pinched my toes to no end. "I bet you say that to all the girls."

Archie's laugh lit up his face. *His beautiful, perfect face...*

"Are they supplying the Germans with the main ingredient in TNT explosives?" Even though there were a good two inches between us, I could feel the comforting heat of Archie's body and the intoxicating smell of his citrus cologne. Alone with a man was bad enough. But sitting on his bed... without shoes, no less. I trusted Archie more than myself. Although at this very moment, I'd like to throttle him. If he wouldn't tell me about Schweitzer and the phenol plot, then I'd just have to find out for myself.

"Classified." He didn't turn his head to look at me, which gave me an excellent opportunity to study a dear little mole next to his right ear.

"How is Schweitzer preventing the allies from getting supplies of phenol?" Maybe Archie would get tired of saying "classified" and finally answer one of my questions. I really was dying to know how aspirin and phenol and Schweitzer all fit together.

"Classified."

Horsefeathers. I was ready to tear my hair out—or at least pull my wig off. When I got back to London, I was going to have to have a serious chat with Captain Hall about my security clearance level. I tightened my lips and stared straight ahead at my own stockinged feet and the torn hem of my beautiful evening gown.

What would Fredricks say if he found out I was wearing his gorgeous gift while lounging on Lieutenant Archie Somersby's bed? I chuckled to myself. He wouldn't hear it from me. So, unless he had hidden cameras in Archie's cabin, he would never find out. I glanced around the room, looking for peep holes in the walls or recording machines in the light fixtures. I wouldn't put anything past Fredrick Fredricks, especially where Archie was concerned. They were longtime enemies, circling each other in a deadly dance.

My beloved Archie. I still couldn't believe he was aboard the

Adriatic. And I was sitting so close to him, I could reach out and touch him. I slipped my hands under my bottom to prevent myself from doing so. *Espionage, not romance. Espionage, not romance. Espionage, not romance.* I repeated the mantra to myself.

A strange thought percolated up into my consciousness. *I wonder...* "You know, I saw something on deck earlier."

Archie tilted his head to face me.

"Two men threw a body overboard."

He jolted upright and then swung his legs over the bed and made to stand up. He must have thought better of it. Instead, he sat on the edge of the bed, staring at me. "Are you sure?"

Oh, bother. He was as bad as Clifford. "Of course I'm sure." The thing the dog had found. Maybe Archie knew what it was. I pulled it from my bag. "And I found this." I held it up.

Archie's eyes went wide.

"What is it?"

"I'm afraid I'm not the right person to ask about that." Was he blushing? "You do know it has a hole in it?"

"From the dog."

He gave me a queer look.

I curled my legs up under my gown and sat up straighter. "Could it be related to the great phenol plot?"

For several seconds, Archie sat silently wringing his hands. He seemed miles away. "I don't know." His voice was so soft, I hardly heard him. He stood up, paced the length of the cabin, and then tapped out a cigarette from his packet of Kenilworths.

"Do you think Schweitzer killed someone aboard this ship and then threw the body into the ocean?" I shuddered at the memory of the shadowy figures and their uncanny load.

Deep in thought, Archie didn't answer. Smoking that disgusting cigarette, he turned, paced back toward the dressing table, turned again, and retraced his steps.

"Once you've killed a man, your life is never your own." He stopped and stared over at me. "You're haunted forever. The questions won't let you sleep. Did he have a wife? Children? What did he love?"

"Have you killed a man?" I shivered. What did I really know about this man? For all I knew, he was working with Schweitzer. What if Fredricks was right and Archie was a double agent? I just couldn't bring myself to believe it. Not my Archie.

He closed his eyes and exhaled.

Now that he was no longer next to me, the empty space left me chilled, and the full weight of sleeplessness pressed against the backs of my eye sockets. I hugged my knees to my chest under my gown. *I really should go back to my own cabin and get some sleep, or else, tomorrow, I'll be wiped out and worthless.* I closed my eyes and inhaled the scent of pine and citrus. *Who knows when I'll see Archie again?* I wanted to savor every moment.

Movement next to me on the bed startled me, and my eyes flew open. Archie was sitting next to me, sans cigarette. In fact, he was sitting on the skirt of my gown. He twisted around and put his hands on my shoulders. His green eyes gazed at me so intently I had to look away.

"Promise me." His fingertips pressed into my flesh.

"Ouch." I tried to pull out of his grasp. But his weight on my gown had me pinned in place. He loosened his grip but didn't let go.

"Hugo Schweitzer is a very dangerous man." His grip tightened again. "Promise me you will stay clear of him."

"What? Because I'm a woman, you don't think I can take care of myself?" I jerked my arm away.

"No. I know you can." He gently moved my chin until I met his gaze. "Promise me," he said, softer this time. "Fiona, darling, please. I couldn't live if something happened to you... if I couldn't protect you."

"Golly." My cheeks burned.

Archie moved even closer. His lovely face was mere inches from mine, and his eyes pleaded with me. I saw something in those sea-green irises I'd never seen there before. Fear... fear and pain. His lips brushed against my cheek. "Darling Fiona," he whispered.

I wrapped my arms around his neck. His lips moved from my cheek to my mouth. He kissed me. Not the sweet little kisses we'd shared before. This kiss was desperate. His passion both frightened and stirred me. I knew I should leave, but I couldn't. I wanted him with every fiber of my being.

He slipped his hand around my back and held me tight against his torso.

"Oh, Archie," I sighed.

Bang. Bang. Bang.

Good heavens. Who could be knocking on Archie's door at this hour? It wasn't even daybreak. Was it? I'd lost track of time. We could have been huddled together for minutes or hours. Distracted by Archie's smell and that devilishly tempting wave of hair across his forehead, I had absolutely no idea how much time had passed since I last checked my watch.

"Hop it into the loo." Archie jumped up and took my wrist. He hustled me into the lav. "And don't come out, no matter what."

I stumbled backwards and nearly fell over the toilet.

Archie put his finger to his lips. "Shhh." He blew me a kiss and then shut the door.

Was he expecting someone? Did he have a sweetheart on board? *Blimey. For all I know, he has a wife.*

The lav was cramped and dark, windowless, and claustrophobic. I felt like I'd been shut into a coffin. I squeezed my eyes shut and concentrated on breathing. With the door closed, the tiny water closet quickly became unbearably stuffy and hot. I fanned myself with my clutch bag, which I'd had the good sense to grab off the foot of the bed.

The walls were closing in on me. *Come on, Fiona. Get a grip on yourself.*

I heard men's voices. *German.* Archie was speaking German with another man. I pricked up my ears. *My sainted aunt.* I recognized the voice of the other man. It was him. *Hugo Schweitzer. What is he doing here at this hour?*

Hugo spat out words rapid-fire like a machine gun. He raised his voice, obviously upset. Archie spoke in hushed tones, apparently trying to appease the livid German.

Muted by the door of the lav, the words landed on my ears in a secret code that I could not for the life of me decipher.

Hugo Schweitzer kept repeating, "*Sie weiß. Sie weiß,*" so often he sounded like a hissing snake. "*Sie war in meinen Zimmer.*" *She was in my room.* That much I understood.

"*Sich beruhigen,*" Archie said. "*Ich werde mich um sie kümmern.*" Maybe it was because I was completely knackered, but Archie's German sounded like a perverse lullaby. Both calming and terrifying.

If I was wrong about Archie, and he was working with Schweitzer, then I'd given him crucial information. Information I had yet to report to Captain Hall. Information known only to me. I shuddered.

"Frau Figg," Hugo Schweitzer said forcefully. "*Ich sah sie vor meinem Zimmer.*"

Bloody hell. My breath caught. Why had Hugo Schweitzer just used my name? *And it's Fraulein, not Frau, you beast.*

"*Ich werde mich um sie kümmern,*" Archie repeated. If I wasn't mistaken, he'd just said, "I will take care of her." What did he mean by that? I thought of Fredricks's warning. *Don't trust anyone, especially not Lieutenant Archie Somersby.*

Fredricks insisted Archie was a double agent. But I knew better. Didn't I? My stomach lurched, and I felt like I'd swallowed a stone. I didn't trust Fredricks as far as I could throw him. If only I could throw him overboard.

Then again, I didn't know who to trust.

I was afloat in the Atlantic Ocean on board a ship with two murderers and at least one German spy... not to mention suffocating in a floating coffin of a lav.

The men's voices were soft now, too soft to tell what they were saying. I could only decipher their urgent tones. Was Archie cajoling or demanding? Was Schweitzer collaborating or threatening? I couldn't tell.

Come on, lads, get it over with so I can get answers from Archie. I was dead tired and wanted more than anything to crawl into my own bed—alone—and sleep for a week. *To sleep the sleep of the dead* ran through my head. I bit my lip until I tasted blood. Shivering in the darkness, I waited for Archie to release me from my lavatory prison so I could find out what in blazes was going on.

As quietly as I could, I slid down to the floor and rested my head against the wall. Yes, I had resorted to sitting on the floor. I hated to imagine what might be sharing the cold tiles with me. My legs were in an awkward position, wedged between the toilet and the wall.

Blast! A ripping sound announced a fresh tear in my beautiful evening gown... what would be, no doubt, the first of many casualties of this already harrowing assignment.

8

THE REUNION

By the time Hugo Schweitzer left Archie's cabin, and I escaped the lav, my head was pounding. I could have used some of that Bayer Aspirin phenol for my exploding head. I was desperate to crawl into bed, pull the covers up over my ears, and forget all about the war, my assignment, bodies overboard, and most especially Hugo Schweitzer's threats against my person.

Even Archie's form as he held me, or the heady scent of his cologne mixed with a deeper masculine smell, wasn't reassuring. Archie had refused to answer any more of my questions and insisted I go get some "shut-eye" and I didn't have the energy to argue.

I half-heartedly kissed Archie goodbye—for how long, I never knew—and dragged my exhausted backside halfway across the bloody ship and back to my cabin.

As I made my way through the corridors, I wished I knew for certain that I could trust Archie. My heart told me I could. And I knew from past assignments that he too worked for Captain Hall. Yet if Archie was a double agent, then he was a mole within British Intelligence and reporting back to the Germans.

No. I didn't believe it. Fredricks had been just trying to mess with my psyche. At least, I hoped to heavens that was it. Otherwise, I'd just exposed myself to two German agents. I would have to be on my toes. Hugo Schweitzer had seen me leaving his room. My mission—and my life—were in danger. But I was determined to get to the bottom of the phenol plot, Schweitzer's part in it, and how this was all related to Fredrick Fredricks.

The panther ring. They both wore the same ring.

Dawn was breaking and through the portal windows, I could see the horizon turning ominous shades of red and orange. *Red sky at night, sailor's delight. Red sky in morn, sailors be warned.* Not even a tempest on the high seas could keep me from my bed.

When I opened the door to my cabin, I was shocked to see Eliza still in her ballgown, sitting on the end of her bed with her head in her hands. Next to her was the young man from the newspaper. *What the devil?*

Face wan and haggard, Clifford was pacing the floor.

The young man seemed to be watching Clifford's every step. And so was Poppy, as she shredded one of my favorite gloves. It may have been plain, but it was well-loved.

When I stepped into the room and shut the door, all four looked at me with their mouths open. Even Poppy dropped the glove and came running to investigate.

Eliza flew across the room and threw her arms around me. "Oh, Aunt Fiona, we thought you'd gone overboard."

The young man stood up. He wasn't nearly as handsome as Billy Buck, but he was fastidiously dressed, dapper even. Something about his slicked-back hair and asymmetrical face set my teeth on edge.

"Clifford, may I have a word?" I broke free of Eliza's embrace.

"I say, where have you been?" Clifford came to my side. "We've been worried. After your stories of bodies overboard and all that rot."

"In private." I narrowed my eyes. Where to go? Of course, I trusted Clifford, but not Mr. Hoover. Anyway, Captain Hall would have my head if Eliza's reputation was ruined. I needed to get rid of Mr. Hoover as soon as possible.

Clifford glanced around the cabin.

There was jolly little privacy to be had... except in the loo. He stepped into the small lavatory and shrugged. Not again.

I followed him in and so did Poppy. There was barely enough room for both of us to stand shoulder to shoulder. "Why is he here?" I hissed.

"Who?"

"Mr. John Edgar Hoover." I recognized him from the newspaper. The ambitious young man campaigning against vice in America.

"Eliza invited him. Do you know him?" Clifford smiled.

"Really, Clifford." I rolled my eyes. "Young men should not be allowed in a young lady's bedroom." I thought of my own indiscretions. Then again, I was a free agent. Eliza was not. And moreover, I was responsible for her.

"And what about a young lady's loo?" Clifford asked with a sly smile.

"Really, Clifford." I sucked my teeth. "Anyway, what happened to Mr. Billy Buck?" Was Eliza such a flirt that she'd already thrown over Mr. Buck for this Mr. Hoover?

"They had a row and Mr. Hoover took Billy aside." I could tell by the excited look on his face that Clifford was about to launch into one of his longwinded stories. "You should have—"

I had to stop him before he got too wound up. "I asked you to keep an eye on her for me." I shook my head. And I thought the one thing Clifford had going for him was reliability.

"I'm here, aren't I?" Clifford asked indignantly. Poppy barked in his defense.

"Yes, well, thank you for that." I sunk my nails into the arm of his wool jacket. "Now please go out there and get rid of him so I can go to bed."

"I say, old girl." Clifford got that hangdog look of his. "No need to get testy."

"Just a minute." I fished the evidence out of my bag and held it up. "Do you know what this is?"

Clifford came closer and stared at it. He took it and examined it. "I haven't a clue."

"I found it on deck where the man was thrown overboard."

"There's a hole in it." He handed it to me.

"That was Poppy." I glanced down at the little beast and then tucked the whatsit back in my bag.

"Maybe a washer from the ship?" Clifford scratched his chin. "Or a piece of some game they play up there?"

"Or a clue to who went overboard and why." I needed to find someone who knew what the bloody thing was. "Well, why are you just standing there?" I shook my head. "Go and tell that young man to leave."

"Yes, ma'am." Clifford gave me a crisp salute.

* * *

Poppy and I waited in the loo while Clifford asked Mr. Hoover to leave. When I heard the door shut, I emerged. I snatched my mangled glove up off the floor and then flopped onto my bed.

"Oh no!" Eliza shrieked. She knelt on the floor next to my bed and lifted the hem of my gown. "Your beautiful evening gown. It's torn."

"Yes, and now it matches my glove." I held up the evidence.

"What have you been up to all night?" Clifford's hand trembled as he lit a cigarette. Did he really need to smoke in *my* cabin?

I pursed my lips and glared up at him.

"Yes... right... sorry." He glanced around the berth, then pinched the end of the foul cigarette between his thumb and forefinger and dropped it into his pocket.

I hoped it burned a hole in his evening coat.

"So, spill the beans, old girl." Clifford stood near the head of my bed and gazed down at me. "Where have you been?" He glanced at the tear in my frock. "Fighting pirates off the starboard bow?"

"Something like that." I wanted to tell him about my misadventure with Schweitzer and my romantic encounter with Archie —*scratch that... espionage, not romance*—but not in front of Eliza. Anyway, Archie had sworn me to secrecy. Even if I saw him in the dining room or on deck, I was to pretend I didn't know him.

"I say, you weren't single-handedly trying to catch those ki—"

I clicked my tongue.

Clifford stopped himself and looked over at Eliza. "Tell me you weren't." His blue eyes filled with concern.

"I can't tell you my shoe size until I get some sleep." Good grief. My poor shoes were worse for wear. The black silk on one French heel had been rubbed raw and the other shoe was missing its bow. My gown. My glove. My shoes. Espionage was jolly hard on the wardrobe.

Clifford glanced at his watch. "If we go to sleep now, we'll miss breakfast." He smiled. "I, for one, could use a strong cup of coffee... and then, old bean, I want to hear what you've been up to all night."

"Later." I gestured toward Eliza. Coffee reminded me of my last assignment in Austria and those delicious, sweet coffees covered in whipped cream. "I doubt you'll get a strong coffee on a British ship bound for America." At least from what I'd heard, the Americans couldn't make a decent cup of coffee *or* tea. I wasn't exactly looking forward to finding out for myself.

Why did I have to think of tea? I could really go for a nice cuppa. "Sap for the soul," my grandmother used to say. There was nothing like a good strong *English* cup of tea. Sigh. I sat up and threw my legs over the side of the bed. "Oh, alright."

"Brilliant." Clifford's tired eyes sparkled. "I'm famished."

My stomach growled. Food or sleep. I definitely needed one or the other—if not both—*tout de suite*. Wait a minute. "We can't go to breakfast dressed like this." I waved my hand over the front of my dress.

"How about I just dash back to my cabin and change and then come back to escort you ladies to breakfast?" Clifford opened the door and stepped into the hallway. He turned back and smiled. "Back in a jiffy."

I had to admit, there was something reassuring about Clifford and his carefree manner—an ease born of a life of comfort, privilege, and abstaining from contemplation.

* * *

The breakfast room hummed with life—a veritable Tower of Babel, filled with languages from nearly every continent. Thankfully, the buffet was not as colorful. Toast and tea with thick-cut marmalade and traditional English baked beans were enough to nourish any traveler with an appetite for adventure or a desire to avoid wretched seasickness.

Clifford insisted I step in front of him in line for breakfast. I gathered a cup of tea and a plate of toast and then headed for the nearest table for fear my balance wouldn't hold out long enough to make it very far without dumping my breakfast down the front of my skirt.

A striking woman with thick eyebrows, hard eyes, and a stern mouth stood up from a table on the far side of the room. She tapped on the side of her cup with a spoon, obviously attempting to get everyone's attention. She was covered from neck to ankles in heavy woolen garments, an elaborate fur cape, and a large-brimmed ostrich-feathered hat. I wished I had the face to carry off such an extravagant hat. The moment she bellowed out her name, the feathers on her hat shook with rage.

Emily Hobhouse proceeded to give a speech imploring the British to free South African children from concentration camps and deplorable tent cities. What she described put me quite off my food. Malnourished infants covered in flies languishing in tents as hot as infernos. *Good heavens.* How could my countrymen abide such horrors? If it was true, then I could understand why Fredricks was so enraged over the British incursion in his homeland. In the name of freedom, we put children in concentration camps? Truly abominable.

Mrs. Sanger and her sister were breaking their fast at a table directly in front of Miss Hobhouse. Mrs. Sanger raised her hand and then stood up. "We need to educate those poor people on how to limit their families using birth control."

My word, the woman was forward. Mentioning birth control in public.

"Those orphaned children are casualties of war and not poverty." Emily Hobhouse's face was red. "Birth control won't bring their parents back."

A young man sitting at a table near me was becoming noticeably agitated. He stood up and his napkin fell to the floor. "You suffragettes and your contraception," he shouted. "You should all be locked up." His broad nostrils flared, and his dark eyes flashed.

Good heavens. It was Eliza's lad. The one I'd encountered when I returned to our cabin. Mr. John Edgar Hoover.

"How exciting," Eliza said. "A lively debate."

"A shouting match, more like." I took a sip of tea to calm my nerves.

"Did you know there are forty-five concentration camps in South Africa?" Emily Hobhouse balled up one fist and pounded it into her other palm. "We call them refugees and offer our protection. Starvation, disease, filth. I ask you, is that what the British mean by protection?" She held her hands in the air. "No. These people are prisoners in wholesale cruelty."

I felt the blood drain from my cheeks. Even the hot tea was not enough to lift my spirits. No wonder Fredrick Fredricks hated the British. He'd told me how the British army had killed his family during the Second Boer War. I didn't know whether to believe him.

Whatever had happened to Fredricks, those poor children described by Emily Hobhouse met an even worse fate. How could our brave Tommies do such things? Warm tears ran down my cheeks. Lack of sleep. Lack of food. And endless bloody war. I really couldn't stand it any longer. I didn't know whether to cheer her on or break down and cry.

My quandary came to an end when two of the ship's constables dragged Emily Hobhouse from the dining room.

"Good Lord," Clifford exclaimed. "What was that all about?" He shook his head as he took a large bite of buttered toast. "That old dear is barmy as a bandicoot."

"What's barmy about ending human suffering?" I glared at him.

Flustered, his face went red as he gulped down his coffee.

"Her hat was nice," Eliza said as she nibbled on the corner of a piece of dry toast.

Didn't the girl have a compassionate bone in her body? And really, Clifford was right. The girl really did need to eat more.

Thinking of those poor starving children in Africa, I forced myself to take another bite of toast. I allowed my gaze to wander from table to table. Soldiers mixed with high society ladies, and file clerks hobnobbed with spies. The room was abuzz after Emily Hobhouse's speech.

My gaze landed on none other than Mr. Hugo Schweitzer. Obviously no worse for wear after what must have been a sleepless night for him too, he was in a heated conversation with his lover, the opera singer, Anna Case. I strained to hear what they were saying, but within moments it took no straining at all to overhear the couple.

Anna Case stood up and threw her napkin onto the table. She made to leave, but Mr. Schweitzer grabbed her wrist and pulled her back.

"Anna, be reasonable." Mr. Schweitzer's mustache twitched. "I can't do what you ask, you know that."

"Why not?" Anna's eyes welled with tears. "Just tell her. It's simple."

"You know it's not that simple... the children and my career—"

"I hate you," Anna Case shouted as she slapped his face. "I hope you fall overboard."

Mr. Schweitzer growled something at her, something I couldn't make out, but it sounded ominous.

"If you weren't so fat, I'd throw you over myself." The singer wrenched her arm away from Schweitzer and stormed out of the dining room.

Blimey. Even at its cheating worst, my marriage to Andrew Cunningham had never devolved into such a public display of animosity. The singer's reference to throwing him overboard made me wonder. Was it just a coincidence that I'd actually seen a man thrown overboard last night? A transatlantic crossing did provide an excellent opportunity to dispose of an unfaithful lover.

Perhaps what I'd seen last night was two lovers disposing of an unwanted spouse. I shuddered. At least Andrew had settled for divorce.

As my gaze followed Anna Case out of the dining room, I saw Archie leaning against the far wall, smoking a cigarette. My cheeks flushed and I touched my face. He was smiling his crooked smile.

"Is something wrong, Aunt Fiona?" Eliza asked. "You look like you've seen a ghost."

A nervous laugh escaped my lips. "No. It's just the opera singer and the..." I wanted to say blackguard and enemy spy. "Bayer Aspirin man."

Was Archie staring at me from across the room? I thought we were pretending not to know each other. It was deuced unsettling. As much as I tried to avert my gaze, I couldn't help but peek at him every chance I got. He cut a striking figure.

Judging from the assortment of feminine hands in front of tittering mouths and the batting of eyelashes in his direction, I wasn't the only woman to notice him.

"Who is that man you keep staring at?" Clifford asked.

"Me, staring?" I cleared my throat.

"Yes, that fellow leaning against the wall." He pointed with a piece of toast. "Just there."

I batted his hand down, and he dropped the toast. The last thing I needed was Clifford announcing to the dining room that I was staring at Lieutenant Archie Somersby.

"I say, why'd you do that?" He picked up a fresh piece of toast from the rather tall stack he'd piled onto his plate.

Don't you recognize him? Clifford had met Archie before. But I didn't dare ask. Maybe it was because Archie wasn't wearing his uniform. That was probably why I didn't recognize him when I first saw him on deck. I'd only ever seen him in uniform.

I smiled. A warm sensation spread through my stomach. Must be the lack of food. I really should eat something. I snatched a piece of toast off Clifford's plate and took a bite.

"Who is he?" Clifford asked. "He looks familiar."

"I've never seen him before," I lied through my toast.

"Well, he seems quite taken with you." Clifford sounded jealous. "He can't keep his eyes off you. I have half a mind to—"

"Now, now, Clifford dear." I patted his arm. He pouted but busied himself with his coffee spoon.

I stole another glance at Archie, just in time to see him leave the dining hall with Mr. Hugo Schweitzer.

If I didn't know better, I'd think those two were thick as thieves.

9

WELCOME TO AMERICA

As we prepared to disembark, Mrs. Parker slipped a card into my hand. "If you need anything." She smiled up at her husband as he escorted her to the gangplank. "Don't hesitate to ask Mr. Parker."

I examined the card. It was an invitation to luncheon, tomorrow. Golly. I hadn't even set foot in America, and already I'd been invited to dine with a New York socialite. I slid the card into my glove.

Tomorrow. That was when I was scheduled to meet Fredricks. I glanced at the card again. Luncheon. Good. I wasn't meeting Fredricks until later. He'd invited me for cocktails at the hotel. Why, I didn't know. No doubt he was up to something.

"Clifford told me you love a good party." Mrs. Parker winked at me.

I glanced over at Clifford, who shrugged.

"It was such a pleasure, Mrs. Parker," Clifford gushed. He really was a social butterfly.

Eager to disembark, a crush of passengers waited impatiently on deck. The crowd was abuzz with the excitement of finally arriving at our destination.

In the distance, just across the water, another throng waited on the pier. Beyond the docks stretched the city of New York with buildings as far as the eye could see.

And I thought London was grand.

Eliza and Clifford were standing behind me and chattering, and Mr. Billy Buck was attached to the girl's side like a hedgehog tick. Obviously, they'd made up after their row. Even if Eliza was sent to America to get away from Billy Buck, I was not a fan of the other lad, Mr. Hoover.

To counterbalance being pushed forward and back by the horde, I focused my efforts on staying upright. At least the thicket of bodies sheltered me from the stiff breeze blowing off the Hudson River.

After an interminable wait that would have tested the patience of a saint, we finally arrived in the customs hall. We were confronted with another crush of people and baggage... so much baggage. Some passengers had dozens of trunks and a small army of stevedores to carry them.

If the wait went on much longer, I'd have to resort to my emergency rations. I was quite pleased I'd thought to bring some sandwiches from the ship. If we didn't get through customs soon, they'd be stale.

The interval in the customs hall stretched even longer than the wait to get off the bloody ship. Eventually, I gave in and sat on top of my trunk. Even the effervescent Eliza was starting to flag. Despite the heat of bodies, her young man never removed his jacket and valiantly carried one of her larger suitcases. I had to admire his persistence... even as I tried to come up with a plan to get rid of him.

Captain Hall had ordered me to chaperone Eliza until she was "settled" in New York. The school wouldn't be open for almost another week. Another week with the silly creature and her destructive dog. Sigh. I leaned my elbows on my knees and put my head in my hands.

My dear mother would turn over in her grave if she saw me slumped over in such an unladylike posture. Out of deference to her, I straightened, slightly.

Now that's interesting. In my peripheral vision, I spotted Mr. Hugo Schweitzer. A full-figured woman in an unflattering lime-green coat shook her finger at him. Was she his wife, perhaps?

Behind him, wide-eyed and mouth twitching, Anna Case watched. The more the other woman raged, the more the opera singer fidgeted. The way her arms were flapping, she looked like she'd soon take flight.

At least the scene between the wife and the mistress kept me distracted while we waited for the customs agents to search our luggage. I wondered what they'd found in Mr. Schweitzer's trunks. Piles of Bayer aspirin? Bags of phenol? TNT explosives? Or just dirty drawers?

Apparently, Schweitzer's bags were clean. He was allowed to leave the hall long before we were.

After the customs officers inspected our luggage, Eliza bid Billy goodbye. The boy clung to her. She shooed him away, insisting they would see each other again before long.

I looked the other way to give them privacy but continued eavesdropping. I was, after all, the girl's chaperone.

I was quite ready to collapse in a heap by the time we finally left the customs house for the Hotel Knickerbocker.

* * *

The Knickerbocker was a boisterous building with vertical limestone piers, red brick and terracotta trim, and alternating iron balcony rails and stone balustrades. The pediments above the windows sported ornately sculpted scrolls. All in all, it was a handsome building, if a bit excessive. The red and white façade reminded me of a barber's pole.

"I'm dying to try a martini," Clifford said as he pushed the button for the lift.

"A what?"

"A martini." Clifford lowered his voice and gave me a conspiratorial smile. "It's a gin cocktail invented in that bar for none other than John D. Rockefeller." He turned and pointed across the lobby.

The last time I'd crossed paths with gin, I'd nearly caused a pistol duel between Archie and Fredricks... not to mention that coincidentally I came down with an awful headache and wished someone would take a pistol to me and put me out of my misery.

"No, thanks. No gin for me, even if it's offered by John D. Rockefeller himself."

"They put olives in it." Clifford smiled wistfully. "Can you imagine?"

"I'd rather not." A drink containing olives. What would the Americans think of next?

The doors to the lift opened. I stood staring with my mouth agape.

Good heavens. It was Archie... and Mr. Schweitzer. Were they coming up from the cellar? Was I still supposed to pretend I didn't know him? I just stood there, blinking like an idiot.

Archie glanced at me but kept speaking to Schweitzer in hushed tones.

"I say, Fiona, are you getting in or not?" Clifford was struggling with his suitcases and the lift doors.

I stepped into the lift. Eliza followed me, holding Poppy's leash. Clifford managed to get in, but not without nearly hitting me with a large case. When I scooted to the back of the lift to avoid being battered, I found myself standing next to Archie. I stared straight ahead and held my breath. When his hand brushed against mine, I felt a jolt of electricity up my arm and stifled a gasp.

I'd never been so glad to exit a lift in my life. I led the way down the hall toward rooms 717 and 719. Eliza and I were sharing a bedroom again, and Clifford had an adjoining bedroom.

As I approached the door to our room and withdrew the heavy key from my oversized bag, I had an uneasy feeling of being watched. I glanced both ways up and down the hallway. When I saw Mr. Hugo Schweitzer standing in front of the lift watching me, I nearly jumped out of my skin. What in heaven's name was he doing? Spying on me? And where was Archie? Had he continued on in the lift?

I dropped the key back in my bag. "Wrong room." I turned and continued down the hallway. If Hugo Schweitzer thought I would lead him to my bedroom, he had another thing coming.

"Good Lord, Fiona," Clifford stammered. "Where are you going?" He stopped in front of room 719, dropped the cases he was carrying, and inserted the key into the lock. "Your room is just there." He tilted his head toward room 717.

Horsefeathers. Now I had no choice but to enter my room while the creepy Hugo Schweitzer watched from down the hall. And why was Archie here? Was he staying at the Knickerbocker, too? He'd given me a number to call in case of emergency, but I'd rather see him in person.

"Please open the door, Aunt Fiona," Eliza said. She was panting from carrying Poppy and one of her carpet bags. "Poppy and I need to change and prepare our toilette."

I glanced down at the dog, who was looking up at me with those big dark eyes. Although I was more partial to cats, I didn't know how anyone could resist those pitiful eyes.

"Aren't you going to open it?" Eliza asked.

Blast it all. I relented and opened the door. While I waited for the porter to roll a cart into the room and unload the luggage, I fiddled with my glove and tried to look innocent. The cheeky devil tipped his hat and then disappeared back into the elevator.

Not good. Not good at all. Now the bounder knew where we were staying. I would have to sleep with one eye open. If he had followed me here, surely he was on to me. I took a deep breath. If Archie didn't stop Mr. Hugo Schweitzer and his phenol plot, I would.

My resolve strengthened; I stepped inside.

The room was spacious and clean. I appreciated the earthen-colored decor. The two single beds each had their own night table. A dressing table sat across the room. And there was a nice-sized wardrobe for my disguises and Eliza's ample supply of dresses.

I unpacked my large case, slid the empty suitcase into the back of the wardrobe, and then slid my small case—full of my various mustaches and beards—on top of the larger one.

While Eliza ran a bath and commandeered our shared lavatory, I looked out of the window at the busy street below. Our corner room on the seventh floor afforded a fine view of Broadway from one window and 42nd Street from the other. Although we'd started ashore early this morning, it was twilight already. Sparkling snowflakes danced, illuminated by streetlamps.

I sat on the edge of the windowsill and watched as people the size of ants dashed in front of automobiles and horse carriages to cross from one side of the street to the other. A few popped open black brollies, something I associated with rain and not snow.

Until last winter, I'd rarely seen snow in London. Good thing, too. A blizzard anywhere in England wreaked havoc, especially in

London. I would have loved to sit on the windowsill and watch the snow falling, but my eyelids were heavy, and I was asleep on my feet.

Eliza emerged from the lavatory freshly scrubbed. Poppy followed her, dripping on the carpet. Eliza's pretty face was a rosy pink. Poppy, on the other hand, looked like a drowned rat. Obviously, Eliza had shared her bath with the little beast.

"Aunt Fiona, isn't it grand?" The girl was in high spirits.

I smiled. Indeed, it was grand to be on solid land and in a jolly comfortable hotel room. Too bad I was on assignment and not on holiday.

Eliza had a towel wrapped around her torso, but she twirled around as if she were wearing a crinoline ballgown. "Do you think I might try a martini?"

I stood up. "Absolutely not." I was going to have to have a chat with Clifford about putting such ideas into her head. A young girl like Eliza was impressionable, after all.

"What should I wear?" She sat on the edge of her bed. "Where are we going this evening?"

"We are going to bed." I loosened my belt. "You should wear your pajamas."

"Without supper?" She sounded like a young child instead of a young lady.

"I brought some sandwiches from the ship." I fetched my practical oversized bag from the door handle, withdrew a cheese sandwich wrapped in paper, and handed it to Eliza.

Reluctantly, she took it, but glared at me as she unwrapped it. Sulking, she nibbled on the corner of a piece of bread and handed a crust to Poppy, who was sitting next to her on the bed, shivering. Poor thing. I knew how she felt.

A nice cup of tea would have hit the spot, but I was too tired to go in search of one. I made do with a glass of water from the tap.

At least, after I gobbled up half a sandwich, my stomach stopped pestering me for food.

She climbed into bed and hugged Poppy, who snuggled under the blanket.

Completely exhausted, I barely had the energy to disrobe and change into my own pajamas. I needed a good night's sleep to face Fredricks tomorrow... not to mention Mrs. Parker.

The bed was soft and cozy. I crawled in and pulled the blankets up over my chin.

As I drifted off to sleep, I thought of Archie...

Was he thinking of me?

* * *

After a fitful sleep filled with disturbing nightmares about Mr. Schweitzer and romantic dreams about Archie—which were equally disturbing but for different reasons—I woke up groggy and disoriented. Stretching and yawning, I forced myself to open my eyes.

"Finally." Eliza's voice was impatient.

I turned over to see the girl fully dressed and sitting on the edge of her neatly made bed. She was wearing her best hat and gloves and those sweet white buttoned boots. I wondered where she got them. She even had on her coat, a peach woolen number with fur collar and cuffs.

"Can we go out now?" Eliza asked, tapping her little booted foot. From the girl's lap, Poppy lifted her furry head. The pink and yellow bow in her topknot perfectly matched her mistress's striped dress and sailor hat.

"How long have you been there?" I sat up in bed.

"Long enough." Her mouth drew up into a tiny rosebud. "I'm afraid Poppy had a little accident on the floor of the loo."

"Oh dear." I dragged myself out of bed and into the lav, watching where I stepped just in case. We should have changed Poppy's name to Weewee.

As I soaked in the bath, I tried not to think of Eliza tapping her little foot on the other side of the door. Instead, I closed my eyes and wondered if I'd ever discover who—or what—those scoundrels had thrown overboard. The blasted scene was distracting me from my mission.

Anyway, by now, whoever he was had been devoured by fish or sunk to the bottom of the sea. I shuddered. Such dark thoughts —along with my pruny fingers—were surely a sign that it was time to get out of the bath.

As I wrapped the towel around my torso, I remembered the fleur-de-lis button. Who was its owner and how would I find them? Sigh.

Examining my plain face in the looking glass, I reminded myself that I was in New York to trail Fredricks, and not to solve someone else's murder. Trouble was, since none of the passengers was missing, it was no one's murder. And no one, from Captain Stamest to dear Clifford, seemed overly concerned about the man overboard.

Forget about it, Fiona, old girl. My mission was to follow Fredricks and find out if he had anything to do with the delay in American troops landing at the front... along with generally spying on his movements in New York. And I was eager to get started. I was meeting Fredricks for cocktails later and I planned to pump him for information. I would find a way to get him to tell me about his connection to Hugo Schweitzer and the phenol plot.

Fredricks was always going on about ending the war. Perhaps if I crossed my fingers behind my back and promised to help him, he would divulge some intelligence. And if not, there was always Mata Hari's pistol.

10

THE LUNCHEON

To my surprise, Mrs. Parker's luncheon was not at her home, but at the Algonquin Hotel. Why in heaven's name would someone entertain at a hotel? Was she an itinerant?

Not quite as extravagant as the Knickerbocker, the Algonquin was a stately building. Inside, with its mahogany walls and pillars and thick curtains, it had a dark masculine feel. The faint scent of cigar smoke emanated from the heavy upholstery.

In his element, Clifford lit a cigarette as he chatted with the desk clerk. Eliza and I stood a few feet away, waiting to be escorted to the luncheon. After the men had exchanged stories of hunting and then fishing, at last the clerk led us to the luncheon party.

How clever. Although it was indoors, the Italian pergola gave the impression of being outside. A lovely mural of a waterfront with deep blue waves and light blue sky was painted on one wall. And a mirror on the opposite wall gave the impression of spaciousness. The lattice work sported vines, blossoms, and small lights. The tables were dressed in white Cluny lace clothes with scalloped eyelash edges.

A quartet played jazz music—luckily not too loudly. The entire scene was utterly delightful.

"Who is that lovely thing?" Clifford's bright eyes were fixated on an efflorescent redhead standing next to Anna Case. The soprano did not look amused by her lively companion.

Oh no. What was he doing here?

Mr. Hugo Schweitzer appeared out of the woodwork. With him was an elderly gentleman with jowls as wobbly as a blancmange and the stern look of a man who'd just lost a wager. The older fellow slapped Schweitzer on the shoulder and then went to the further table and sat by himself, watching the others.

Schweitzer took Anna Case by the elbow and whisked her off to a table. Her pretty companion tagged along... and Clifford followed after them.

I shook my head. If I knew Clifford, he would have proposed to the *lovely thing* by the end of the cheese course.

The gathering was practically a reunion of people I'd met aboard the ship: Mrs. Parker, of course, but where was Mr. Parker? Margaret Sanger, also sans husband. Anna Case and the odious Mr. Schweitzer. Even the speechifying Emily Hobhouse, who was the wallflower of the bunch. To be polite, I should go and talk to her. Then again, my mother taught me to always pay respects to one's hostess first.

I turned to Eliza, who was wide-eyed and gazing around the pergola. She was the youngest person in attendance and one of the most cheerfully dressed. Apparently, the girl insisted on wearing spring colors year-round. Wrapped in pink and yellow, she looked a bit like a fancy Easter egg.

"I'm just going to pay my respects to Mrs. Parker." I patted the girl on her gloved wrist.

"Isn't it grand?" she squealed, as giddy as a youngster at

Christmas. All her bows and ribbons enhanced her childlike qualities.

"Yes, just howling." The band had picked up the tempo and was playing one of those incomprehensible jazz numbers favored by the young.

Glued to me at the hip, Eliza trailed behind as I wove through the tables toward Mrs. Parker.

Mrs. Parker stood beside the bar, a cocktail in one hand and a cigarette holder in the other. She was surrounded by a group of men in suits, who hung on her every word. There was something about that woman that made men want her and women want to be her. She was attractive, even if her haircut made her look like a newspaper boy.

The men's laughter was a bit intimidating, but I moved as close to the circle as I could without interrupting. I caught Mrs. Parker's eye and smiled.

"Miss Figg." She held her cocktail above her head. "I'm so glad you came." As if attending a funeral instead of hosting a luncheon, she was dressed in black from head to toe, including her pearls. "Please join us." Like Moses parting the red sea, she used her cigarette holder to part the men so I could join the circle. "I was just telling Marc about my in-laws. The only obscenities they don't use to describe me are the ones they can't pronounce."

The circle broke out in laughter again. Mrs. Parker positively glowed in the light of their admiration.

"And no matter what you do, they know a better way to do it." Mrs. Parker was in her element. She soaked up the adoration like a thirsty sponge.

"Where is Mr. Parker?" I asked. "I would like to pay my respects."

"I only require that my husbands are handsome, ruthless, and stupid." Dorothy Parker chuckled. "And Eddie is not... stupid."

"Oh, I'm sorry." My face was hot. "I mean—"

"Two out of three isn't bad," one of her admirers said as he lit her cigarette.

"Depends on which two." Mrs. Parker winked.

"Why stupid?" Eliza asked. "What fun is that?"

My eyes went wide. The girl had some cheek.

"Please give Mr. Parker my regards," I said, looking for an escape route. I was out of my depth with this precious banter. "And thank you again for the invitation... and for including Eliza."

"If he'd only unlock the door to our place, I would." She waved her cigarette. "Why do you think I'm living here?"

"The honeymoon is over," one of her admirers chimed in.

That was quick. "Oh, I see." Flustered, I took my leave of Mrs. Parker and her fan club.

"Isn't Mrs. Parker fun?" Bouncing on her heels, Eliza bubbled over until I thought she might evaporate.

"A regular court jester," I said under my breath and then checked to make sure we were out of earshot of our hostess.

At the other end of the pergola, Margaret Sanger and Emily Hobhouse were deep in conversation. Unlike the circle of crows cackling over Mrs. Parker, the two ladies were serious to the point of forbidding. Since Clifford was engaged chatting up Anna Case and her lovely friend, and I didn't know anyone else in attendance, I screwed up my courage and headed for the dour pair. At least they weren't dressed in all black.

Margaret Sanger's wide white collar hung down the front of her dress like a bib. And Emily Hobhouse's stark frown and harsh gaze warned me not to dare glance at her clothing if I valued my head. When I approached, they were in the middle of a heated debate.

"The true evil is so many babies born into abject poverty." Margaret Sanger pursed her lips. "Birth control should be compulsory, and couples should have to apply for permits to be parents."

I stood blinking at Mrs. Sanger. What about couples who are unable to be parents with or without a permit? I bit my tongue.

Emily Hobhouse gave her interlocutor a stern look. "The true evil is wealthy classes eating oyster cocktails and drinking champagne while their brothers and sisters on the other side of town starve to death." She shook her head.

"My, these two are crabby," Eliza whispered in my ear.

By the sounds of it, too much attention to the state of the world would make anyone crabby. Starving babies. British concentration camps in Africa. Not to mention the bloody endless war. Then again, without some attention, nothing would change.

"If they didn't have so many children, they wouldn't starve—" Mrs. Sanger was working herself into a tizzy.

"They're poor whether they have children or not. Shouldn't we address the poverty first?" Emily Hobhouse interrupted.

She did have a point. Having children was not what made them poor. What of the poverty of spirit that comes of the inability to bear children and a failed marriage as a result?

"The chicken or the egg," Eliza said. "Poverty prevents women from accessing birth control, and having too many children keeps them poor."

I stared at the girl.

Both women turned to us.

"Miss Figg." Mrs. Sanger held out her hand. "Delightful to see you again."

"Good day." Emily Hobhouse scooted past me and then disappeared from the pergola.

I was tempted to follow her out. Between Mrs. Parker's flippant remarks and Mrs. Sanger's provocative ones, I felt quite out of place. Perhaps America was not my cup of tea after all.

As I followed her out with my eyes, I spotted Mr. Schweitzer hanging around behind a potted plant. He glared at me.

My skin crawled. That man gave me the creeps.

Ping. Ping. Ping. I turned to see Mrs. Parker tapping a knife on her wine glass. "Ladies and gentlemen, luncheon is served. If you'll kindly take your places, the Gonk's chefs will tickle your fancy until your spouse cries foul."

A shiver up my spine made me glance around. Mr. Schweitzer had disappeared. I wasn't sure if that was good or bad... or very bad. Maybe he'd just popped off to the lav. Or maybe he was waiting for me behind a fern.

The guests chuckled as they found their seats.

To my chagrin, my place was at the witty Mrs. Parker's table. Clifford was stuck with Anna Case and her evil paramour. At least now I could keep an eye on the suspicious bloke... from a distance. Eliza was stationed next to Margaret Sanger. Spread out among the guests, we could gather information and compare notes—or gossip—after luncheon.

The Algonquin chefs lived up to their reputation. I feasted on canapes, followed by consommé julienne, and for the main course, Virginia ham with potatoes brioche. The meal was one of the best I'd had since the war began. I would love to see what they could do once the war was over. The Americans might not yet have boots on the ground in France, but they too were making sacrifices for the war.

The elderly gentleman who'd come in with Schweitzer appeared at Mrs. Parker's side. "I regret I have to leave early." He bent closer, a jaunty paperboy cap clamped over his balding head.

Mr. Schweitzer had disappeared again. He was a cagey chap.

"So soon, Mr. Edison?" Mrs. Parker feigned regret. "I suppose you have to go invent something." She waved her cigarette holder in the air. "If it's a time machine, I'd like to go back and tell my teenage self she's about to meet the love of her life." She held up her cocktail. "Gin."

Everyone except Mr. Edison laughed. He fumbled with the buttons on his jacket. "Yes, well. I do need to check on an experiment with an electric car."

"An electric car!" Mrs. Parker smirked. "Can you make one with an ejector seat? I'd like to take Mr. Parker for a ride in it."

"I'm also working for the navy." Mr. Edison stood up a little straighter and tugged at the hem of his waistcoat. "Classified."

"If you told us, you'd have to kill us sort of thing?" Mrs. Parker tittered.

"I take killing very seriously." Mr. Edison gave a slight bow. "If you'll excuse me." He marched across the dining room and disappeared.

I didn't blame him. Mrs. Parker's witticisms were fresher than the canapes.

As I watched the famous inventor leaving, I saw Mr. Schweitzer waiting in the shadows. Bloody unnerving. I kept my eyes glued to him until he left. If only he didn't know my room number at the hotel. Tonight, I planned to sleep with a heavy piece of furniture pushed against the door. Once the evil man was no longer in sight and appeared to have left the party, I could breathe easier.

Luckily, the food kept me occupied so I didn't have to join the conversation.

"Benchley and I shared an office so tiny," Mrs. Parker tittered, "if it were an inch smaller, it would have been adultery."

I spit out a mouthful of cranberry ice. Good heavens. The woman really did eat vinegar with a fork.

I was glad when the luncheon was over. Mrs. Parker's flamboyance was giving me indigestion.

When we had finished eating, our hostess suggested we join a parade taking place on Fifth Avenue.

As we filed out of the pergola to fetch our coats, I caught up to Eliza and Clifford.

"A parade." Eliza clapped her hands. "What fun."

"Daft time of year for a parade, if you ask me," I said, as Clifford helped me on with my coat.

"I say, did you meet Mr. Thomas Edison?" Clifford asked. "The famous inventor?"

For the entire walk from the pergola to the lobby, Clifford nattered on about the wonderful Mr. Edison. He was positively electrified by the few minutes he'd spent with the man. For my part, I was more interested in what he'd learned about the suspicious Mr. Schweitzer.

"Schweitzer's a nice enough chap, I suppose." Clifford shrugged.

Clifford was hopeless. He liked everyone.

The rest of the luncheon guests were boisterous as we exited the hotel onto the sidewalk. Snow flurries floated aimlessly, occasionally landing on my nose. Definitely a daft time of year for a parade.

Motorcars honked as we made our way down 44th Street to Fifth Avenue, a long block away. When we arrived at the intersection, I couldn't believe my eyes. Thousands of women wearing long dark coats and large hats carried flags and banners as they marched up the avenue.

Two women passed carrying a large banner between them that read: "We sacrificed our sons to fight for democracy. Democracy owes us the vote."

"What kind of parade is this?" I asked.

"How exciting." Eliza bounced on her heels. "A suffragettes' parade."

"The luncheon party is joining a suffragettes' parade?" I watched as dozens of women marched past.

"So it seems." Eliza clapped her gloved hands. "Shall we?" She pulled at my arm.

"Good Lord," Clifford said. "I'm not marching with a bunch of rabble-rousing women." He clapped his hands too. But I suspected from the cold and not from excitement. "Come on, old girl." He took my elbow. "You don't want to get involved in this."

I was being pulled in opposite directions in a tug-of-war between Eliza and Clifford. In this instance, I was inclined to go with Clifford, but Eliza had a hold of my arm.

"Let's go back... go back... to the hotel," Clifford stammered and sputtered. An army of women was too much for him.

"We'll meet you back there after the parade," Eliza said.

"Will you be alright?" Clifford's eyes were wide with alarm.

"We'll be fine." I shooed him away.

He got that hangdog look and turned to go.

Of course women should have the vote. Of course women were as good as men. But really. Did they need to march in the streets to prove it? In the snow, no less? Didn't we prove it every day by being the best at what we did, whether filing papers or following dangerous spies?

"Votes for women! Votes for women!" A chorus of voices, the cries of the marchers echoed through the street. "Women are people too!"

A group of young men, gathered on the sidewalk, were heckling the marchers. One of them waved a banner that read "Comstock's Crusaders." I recognized another as Mr. John Edgar Hoover from our ship. As we walked past, he shouted, "Women are mothers first."

"Yes, and we've sacrificed our sons to prove it," a woman next to me yelled back. "The least you can do is give us the vote!"

"Women think with their hearts and not their heads," one of the Comstock Crusaders yelled at the passing parade.

"At least we have hearts," a marcher answered.

"Women's votes are squandered votes." John Edgar Hoover's bellowing was unnerving. "Stop vice. Stop contraception."

I was thankful when his thundering receded into the distance. What an odious young man. Although I had to admit there was something compelling about his confidence in himself despite his youth. The newspaper article reported he was twenty-two, even younger than me.

Eliza locked arms with me and joined in the chant. She pulled me into the parade. I couldn't very well leave her on her own. Captain Hall would kill me. Anyway, why not let her have her fun?

The air was brisk and our strides were long. Buoyed by Eliza's excitement and the energy of the crowd, my heart sang with pride. A parade of women stopping traffic and bringing midtown New York to a standstill. It was exhilarating.

Oh, my sainted aunt. Who should I see marching along Fifth Avenue surrounded by the veritable sea of feminine willpower? What was he doing here? None other than Fredrick Fredricks. As usual, Fredricks was wearing his outrageous big game hunting outfit: swagger stick, slouch hat, beige jodhpurs, knee-high black boots, and a heavy woolen hunting jacket. In that pool of dark dresses, he stood out like the Loch Ness monster.

Why was he marching with the suffragettes? There was only one way to find out.

I took a deep breath, detached my arm from Eliza's grip, and dove into the mass of marchers.

At least, in that getup, Fredricks would be easy to spot.

Weaving in and out of the crowd of marchers, I tried to catch up to Fredricks.

As far as I could see up or down the avenue, the street was packed with women of all ages—hundreds marching and hundreds on the sidewalks cheering them on. I'd never seen such a gathering in all my life.

It was exhilarating being carried along by the flock and their repeated chant, "Votes for women." Even the chilly November air couldn't stop these dedicated women.

I'd nearly caught up to Fredricks. His tall, muscular form was just ahead. I could see his broad shoulders and felt hat sticking up above of the crowd.

I felt a hand tighten around my upper arm. What in the blazes? When I swung around, I saw a swarm of constables moving in on the crowd.

"Let's go, lady," the uniformed officer said, pulling on my arm.

"I haven't done anything." I yanked my arm away.

"Disturbing the peace, resisting arrest." The officer shook his head. "Look, lady, don't make this harder than it needs to be."

"Are you threatening me?" I glared at him.

A woman next to me screamed, "Run!"

I glanced around, but there was no clear escape route through the chaos. Constables were dragging marchers into a paddy wagon just off 50th Street. Gasp. I spotted a pink and yellow hat atop a peach coat flying down the street.

Oh no! Eliza.

Run, Eliza, run.

Blimey. The girl galloped and leaped like a gazelle.

"Will you come along peaceful-like?" the officer asked. He held up handcuffs.

Handcuffs? For heaven's sake. "Are those really necessary?"

"Would you prefer the stick?" He waved his Billy club over his head.

Good grief. Did he plan to crack my skull open?

Given the choice between the two, I chose the handcuffs over the stick.

The constable led me to the paddy wagon and pushed me inside... much too roughly, I might add. The hem of my dress caught on the door and ripped. I landed on my bottom in a rather unladylike position.

"Who is your supervisor?" I demanded. I planned to report the ruffian. Not only had he hurt my arm and now my bum, but he'd ruined a perfectly good frock... not to mention interfering with my mission to follow Fredricks.

He scoffed and slammed the door shut, nearly taking my toes off in the process.

I jerked my legs out of the way of the door and in so doing fell into another woman. We both tumbled spout over teapot onto the floor. Winded, I gathered myself as best I could and sat up. "My apologies."

"Miss Figg?" Margaret Sanger was disheveled from her run-in with the law. Her chignon had come loose, and her hair fell over her face. The once white bib of her dress was dotted with mud. And she was missing a shoe.

I probably looked just as miserable.

Good heavens. Talk about reunions. Emily Hobhouse sat on the back bench, staring down at her hands. Perhaps she was praying. I recognized the matronly woman sitting next to her as Jane

Addams, the pacifist I'd met in Vienna at the secret peace talks organized by the emperor and empress of Austria.

At least I was in good company. I would be spending the night in jail with the best and brightest female minds in America.

"Don't let them force feed you." Mrs. Sanger grabbed my wrist. "We must be strong."

"Force feed?"

She held my wrist so tight she was cutting off my circulation.

I stared down at our intertwined wrists. Mine was turning bright pink. And hers displayed a stiff white cuff with one lonely silver fleur-de-lis button and a pin hole where its mate should be.

Blimey. Was Mrs. Sanger involved in the matter of the man overboard?

I swallowed hard and stared down at my sodden shoes.

11

BAILED OUT

"Fiona Figg." The guard's voice startled me. He'd also completely mangled my Christian name. "Fi-noina Figg, step forward. Your bail's been posted."

Thank goodness. Clifford must have come to my rescue at last.

I sat up on the bench where I'd spent the night. I hadn't eaten, slept, or relieved myself since my arrest. My stomach was howling, my eyelids were sagging, and my bladder was screaming. Clenching every muscle in my body, I stepped forward.

"A gentleman's come to fetch you." The guard opened the cell. "Get back, the rest of yous gits."

Good old Clifford. What would I do without him?

The guard led me past a row of cells crammed with women from the march. None of us had been allowed to wash, and as a result, the jail smelled rather ripe.

"Aunt Fiona." The voice came from one of the cells.

Urgently, I scanned the suffragettes. "Eliza?"

"I'm here."

A flash of peach and yellow caught my eye. I stopped in front of the cell.

"Move along," the guard said, shoving me.

"That is my niece," I hissed. "And I will speak to her." After the night I'd had, I was really in no mood.

With both hands, Eliza held onto the bars of her cell. "Oh, Aunt Fiona." Her eyes were swollen and red. "Poor Poppy. I need to get back to poor Poppy."

I'd completely forgotten about the furry little beast. I hated to think of the state of the carpet in our hotel room. We would probably have to pay to have it cleaned.

"Please feed her and kiss her and..." Tears rolled down her cheeks.

"You're in jail and all you can think about is your dog?"

"She's not just a dog," Eliza sniffled. "She's my best friend."

"Yes, well..."

"Come on now, lady." The guard gave me a little shove. "We ain't got all day."

The brute. I was going to find out who was in charge and report these people. Outrageous.

"Please, Aunt Fiona. Tell Poppy I love her."

"Don't worry, dear." I held her hand through the bars. "I will get you out of here and you can tell her yourself."

"Enough!" The guard's shout made me jump.

I waved goodbye to Eliza and followed the guard. As I did, I swore I would liberate Eliza no matter what it took... short of calling her uncle.

When we emerged from the cells into the reception area, I took a deep breath. The smell of freedom was much pleasanter.

Oh no. Not him. "You!"

Fredricks tipped his slouch hat and smiled at me from across the lobby. He strode up to the reception desk. "Yes, that's her, my beloved." He was wearing those ridiculous jodhpurs as usual. He had a book in one hand and his swagger stick in the other.

The guard led me out to the reception desk where Fredricks was waiting for me.

"Fiona, I've missed you." He tucked his book under his arm and held out his hand. "Have you missed me?"

Oh dear. Not this charade again. Every time I saw him, Fredricks claimed to be in love with me. Calling me "his peach" in Paris. Practically asking me to run away with him in Vienna. Inviting me to a royal ball and now an opera. Of course, I knew it was a ruse, or some perverse game he played for his own amusement. It was absurd, after all. Africa's Great White Hunter in love with me? Preposterous.

"Fiona, ma chérie." He chuckled. "How lovely you look."

I stuck my tongue out at him.

He laughed. "Is that an invitation?"

Cheeky devil.

Arms akimbo, I looked him straight in the eyes. "Mr. Fredricks, if you think—"

"Fiona, ma chérie, please, just Fredrick."

"Fredrick, Fredricks, what difference does it make?" Really. What kind of name was Fredrick Fredricks? It would be like my mother naming me Fig Figg. Ludicrous. I stared at his face. Something was different about him, but what?

"That little S, my dear." Fredricks held out his hand. "It can mean the difference between night and day." He winked at me.

Insufferable. I peered down at his book. I always made it a point to find out what Fredricks was reading. Every little bit of information could be useful to the War Office.

"Walt Whitman," I said. "You're reading poetry."

"If you want to get to know a people, read their poetry." Since

I didn't take his hand, he gestured toward the exit. "Shall we? I've come to liberate you."

"My niec—er, friend is still in there." I didn't budge. "I'm not leaving without her."

"Where's that milksop Clifford Douglas?" He glanced around as if Clifford might be lurking behind the door or hiding out in a corner. "What is he this time? Your uncle?"

What an exasperating man. If I didn't have such an immediate need to relieve myself, I would have called the guard and asked him to take me back to the cells. A pang of guilt added itself to my miseries. After all, it was not just Eliza locked up back in those abysmal cells.

"What about the others?" I asked. All those poor women crammed into those tiny cells without proper beds or blankets or toilets. "What about Eliza?"

"Don't worry about them." Fredricks tugged on his gloves.

A ruckus coming from behind the door to the cells made me turn around. The door opened, and a stream of suffragettes rushed by.

"See," Fredricks said, waving his riding stick like a magician's wand. "Free."

"Thank you, Fredrick," one of the women said on her way past.

"Yes, thank you, dearest darling," another said, stopping to kiss him on the cheek.

I did a double take when Anna Case emerged from the back. She stopped and whispered in Fredricks's ear. He chuckled and then kissed her hand.

Even Mrs. Sanger stopped to thank him. As she extended her hand, there it was again. The pin hole where the silver button should have been. I filed the clue away for the time being. Right now, I had more immediate troubles.

Fredricks was especially friendly with Emily Hobhouse. "Keep up the good work, Miss Hobhouse," he said. "You are fighting for our children who are suffering at the hands of the British." He looked at me.

"Thank you, Mr. Fredricks." She smiled weakly. "I will do my best to get the children of South Africa out of those horrid camps."

"I know you will." He patted her hand.

"Aunt Fiona." Eliza dashed up and threw her arms around me.

It must have been the impact, or maybe the strain of a night in jail, for I found myself wiping a tear from my cheek. When I'd pulled myself together, I introduced her to Fredricks. He had, after all, just bailed us out of jail.

Eliza released me and turned to Fredricks. "You're the one who sent Aunt Fiona that marvelous gown."

Fredricks grinned. "I hope you liked it, ma chérie."

Aha. I finally realized what was different about his face. "Your mustache. It's grown."

I'd never seen Fredricks with anything more than a pencil mustache.

"You noticed." Fredricks grinned at me in a most unsettling manner.

"I prefer a clean-shaven man." I averted my gaze.

"I've heard so much about you, sir." Eliza held out her hand. "It's an honor."

Heavens. "Not from me." My cheeks were hot.

"From the other women," Eliza said. "You've been such a friend to the suffragettes. Miss Paul told me about your generous contributions to the cause."

Soon there was a chorus of gratitude—and uncanny familiarity—sounding all around us. Fredricks beamed, surrounded by so many adoring women. Perhaps I should interview some of them later to find out more about Fredricks. I couldn't bloody ask them about the bounder with him standing next to me.

Some of the women stopped to thank Eliza, too.

"I'm going to use that move next time," one of them said.

What move? Did Eliza have a move?

"Those prison guards will regret crossing us," another said as she shook Eliza's hand. "Thank you, dear."

What had the girl done except cry over her puppy? Astonished, I stared as Eliza did some kind of jujitsu move, like I'd seen once in a film. Good heavens. Who was this girl?

"I'll remember that move the next time one of those pigs tries to force feed me," Mrs. Paul winked at Eliza as she passed by. "Thank you again, Fredrick. You are a true friend." She extended her hand to Fredricks.

Women always fawned over Fredricks. Most women found his muscular form and mane of thick black hair irresistible. Not me. I was impervious to his charms. Obviously, even the suffragettes were not.

But why would Fredricks be trying to get into the good graces of these women? And why would a German spy join American suffragettes?

He was up to something. And I was going to find out what... right after I visited the loo.

* * *

Fredricks bustled us into his motorcar. His driver dropped the cigarette he was smoking, ground it under the heel of his boot, and jogged around the automobile to tuck us in. He looked smart in his navy livery, despite a full beard. At least it was neatly trimmed.

Now, Fredricks favored a handlebar mustache, about which, no doubt, he was as fastidious as a monk. The blessed beast was waxed to perfection. In fact, it was too perfect. It didn't look real. Was Fredricks wearing a fake mustache?

I sniffed the air for spirit gum. Instead, I found rosewood and smoky charcoal.

"I waited for you at the Knickerbocker yesterday," Fredricks said, removing his gloves one finger at a time. "Although I should have known you'd be in the clink."

I glowered at him. "Why do you say that?" I inched closer to Eliza and away from him. Since we were three in the backseat, there wasn't much room. Why in the devil didn't Fredricks ride up front?

"I saw you at the march yesterday."

"You did?" How was that possible? I was behind him in the crowd. I was following him.

"Why do you think I slowed down?" He grinned. "So you could catch me."

When he turned to look me in the eyes, I averted my gaze.

"If only those Peelers hadn't shown up." He shook his head. "Miss Chapman and Miss Paul organized such a magnificent march, too."

"How do you know the suffragettes?" Might as well get right to the point.

He laughed. "Why do you sound so suspicious? Can't I support women's rights?"

"You're up to something."

"Why, Fiona, don't you trust me?"

"Not as far as I can throw you."

"Come now." He chuckled. "You know I love women... especially—"

"Eliza," I cut him off. "Are you alright?" We'd best finish this conversation in private and away from the girl.

She nodded. Poor dear looked worse for wear. Her ringlets were sagging, and her little white boots were filthy, as was her woolen coat. And her adorable pink sailor hat was nowhere to be seen.

"I just hope Poppy is okay," she said, so softly it sounded like she was praying.

I patted her hand. "It's only been twenty-four hours. I'm sure she's fine." I hoped I was right. I had no idea how long dogs could go without food and water. I closed my eyes and tried to remember if I'd left the toilet lid up. At least then, the poor beast would have access to water... if her short little legs could reach that high. Good heavens. I was starting to think about Poppy like Eliza did. She was just a dog, after all.

Clifford would know to take care of Poppy. Wouldn't he? Clifford! He must be a nervous wreck wondering what happened to us.

When we arrived at the Knickerbocker, Fredricks escorted us in. We must have looked a sight. I tried not to make eye contact as we walked through the lobby.

Yip. Yip.

Barking. I looked up to see Clifford sitting on a couch with Poppy on his lap. The pup was nibbling on something he was feeding her from his pocket. I let out a great sigh of relief. Clifford may not have rescued us, but he had rescued Poppy.

"Poppy." Eliza flew across the lobby.

A big sloppy smile on her concave face, Poppy leaped off Clifford's lap and met the girl halfway. Eliza scooped up the furball and held it close. Their reunion brought tears to my eyes.

"I had a dog when I was a child." For once, Fredricks's smile was genuine. "Rudo. She was a golden Africanis. Her name means love."

"How touching."

"Your countrymen took her when they disposed of my family." He got an unusually solemn look on his face. "And you wonder why I hate the British."

"That's no excuse to perpetuate suffering and killing. War is brutal, no matter who wages it." I watched Eliza kissing Poppy and smiled.

"I say. There you are, old girl. I've been worried sick." Clifford appeared at my side, a pipe between his teeth. "You girls haven't been marching up Fifth Avenue all night, have you? Good Lord. What is that smell?" He waved his hand in front of his nose. "You two look a mess, especially you, Fiona."

"Douglas, why weren't you at the march?" Fredricks asked. "Don't you believe in votes for women?"

"Well... I don't know..." Clifford stammered. "That puts me in mind of the time we were hunting bush pigs in Limpopo." He chuckled. "Remember when that sow—"

"Suffragettes remind you of wild boar?" I glared at him.

Fredricks raised an eyebrow.

Eliza put Poppy down onto the floor, and the creature made a beeline for Clifford. The dog sat next to his shoe, panting and looking up at him with those pitiful dark eyes.

"Poppy and I have become fast friends." He reached into his pocket and brought out a piece of dried beef. "Haven't we, old bean?" He handed the treat to Poppy, who carefully took it from his fingers and then wolfed it down in one gulp.

"Thank goodness you were here, Uncle Clifford," Eliza sighed. "I can't bear to think—"

Clifford reached down and picked up the pup. "We've been

having a jolly good time." He scratched Poppy's chin and her tail wagged furiously.

"I hate to cut short this lovely reunion," Fredricks said, glancing at his watch. "But the opera is this evening, and I've made us reservations at the restaurant before the performance to make up for the cocktail date we missed."

"Good heavens." I'd forgotten that the opera was tonight. "After a night in jail, our toilette will take twice as long as usual."

"All the more reason you should take your niece and her Pekingese back to your rooms and get some much-needed rest." Fredricks sighed. "I know how difficult it is for you to sleep in prison." He smirked.

"We weren't in prison," Eliza said. "We were merely in a holding cell." Her reunion with Poppy seemed to have reinvigorated her. She'd unburdened Clifford of the pup and was singing and twirling around in her dirty skirts.

"Prison!" The pipe fell out of Clifford's mouth. He bent down to retrieve it. "Not again."

* * *

Busy fussing over Poppy, Eliza asked me to bathe first. I didn't have to be asked twice.

As I ran my bathwater, I was giddy with anticipation. I added lilac-scented bubble bath provided by the hotel. Already, I knew this would be one of the best baths of my life.

I hurriedly stripped off my filthy clothes and dipped my toe into the warm water. When the bathtub was half full, I slid in. What a relief. What a treat.

I thought of the poor boys fighting at the front. They probably hadn't bathed for weeks. I cringed.

Pushing unpleasant images of war from my mind, I closed my

eyes and sank into the heavenly lilac cloud. Sigh. Yes, I might live after all.

Something about the meditative experience of a warm bath always turned my thoughts to my mission. Alone in the quiet of the lav, I had time to make a mental to-do list.

First and foremost, I needed to discern what Fredricks was up to with the suffragettes. Was one of them a double agent? Fredricks was known to dispose of double agents, especially women agents. I suspected he had something to do with the poisoning of at least two countesses, who were coincidentally double agents. Perhaps that was why he was in New York... to kill a German agent who'd turned against the Central Powers.

Was he planning something at the opera? Was that why he invited me? But why? Did the man just like an audience or the thrill of getting one over on me? Anna Case was performing. Did his devious plan somehow involve her? Was this some sick game of cat and mouse? If she was his target, I had to be vigilant tonight. I would not allow him to harm that beautiful young soprano.

Then there was the matter of Mrs. Sanger's missing button and the man overboard. Yes, it wasn't my assignment. Yes, Captain Hall would be livid if he found out I was investigating. And yet how could I let the killer get away?

Surely Mrs. Sanger didn't kill someone and throw him overboard, did she? It was quite unbelievable. Yet her missing button was the same silver fleur-de-lis as the one I'd seen stuck in the ship's railing. And, seeing how I had no other leads, I was determined to follow this one to the bitter end. Anyway, Fredricks was obviously connected to the suffragettes. His plans for sabotage must involve them. So, the suffragettes were the perfect place to start both my investigations. Kill two birds with one stone. Oh dear. What an unfortunate turn of phrase.

A knock on the door interrupted my agenda planning. "Aunt Fiona, are you almost finished?" Poor girl was as impatient for a bath as I'd been.

"Yes, dear." As I exited the bath, I turned my attention to the urgent matter of my wardrobe. What would I wear to the opera?

Fredricks probably expected me to wear the gown he'd given me. And given my assignment from the War Office, it was my solemn duty to oblige. Eliza had been kind enough to repair it for me. The glove that her pup mangled had been beyond repair.

My skin tingled, eager to slip into the lush silk dress again.

I smiled. I had the perfect accessories to go with Fredricks's dress.

My new mother-of-pearl opera glasses and Mata Hari's matching pearl-handled gun.

12

THE OPERA

Carnegie Music Hall was a rectangular eight-story brown-brick building with a black tile roof sitting at the corner of Seventh Avenue and 57th Street. Compared to our hotel, except for the grand entrance, it was downright plain.

The elegant restaurant was abuzz with preconcert patrons enjoying cocktails and canapes. Crystal chandeliers, lace linens, and waiters in dinner jackets created a rich ambiance. As we waited to be seated, I took in the scene.

For someone who'd only been in New York for a few days, I saw quite a few familiar faces. The dubious Mr. Schweitzer was dining with the famous inventor, Thomas Edison, who, I'd learned from Clifford, had invented electricity and sound recordings and many other amazing things. They were joined by the young Mr. John Edgar Hoover, who was animated and talking as if conversation were a race to the finish. I'd never heard anyone talk so fast. I wished I could make out what he was saying.

At the next table, Mrs. Sanger was whispering with a group of women whom I recognized from the suffragette parade and then jail. I gave them a nod. I'd find time to interview them later, after Fredricks and I had parted ways.

As the waiter led us to Fredricks's table, I surveyed the patrons for anyone else I might know and to take in the gorgeous gowns, lovely hats, and incredible jewelry... not to mention the pelts of a menagerie of small mammals. I felt like a film star at a toff banquet.

And to think I was on assignment. What a lucky girl. Then again, if I failed, Fredricks might kill someone tonight. Right under my nose.

Eliza squealed with delight. "Isn't it grand?"

"Yes, quite."

Fredricks stood up when we approached the table. "Where's Clifford? I thought you two were joined at the hip."

I scowled. It's true. Clifford was hard to shake.

"Uncle Clifford stayed home with Poppy." When Eliza smiled, her entire face lit up. She really was a beautiful young woman. And her peaches-and-cream-colored gown underscored her porcelain skin and golden curls.

Luckily, Clifford had fallen in love with the little cur. And he'd do absolutely anything for Eliza. No doubt he was depressed about not getting to play Watson to my Sherlock. I had a better chance at getting gen out of Fredricks without Clifford breathing down my neck.

"Well then, I'll be on my best behavior." He held out my chair.

"That's not an especially high standard," I said as I sat down.

"Now, now, ma chérie." Fredricks grinned. "Let's not bicker in front of the children."

"I hope you don't mean me, Mr. Fredricks." Eliza waited for him to pull out her chair. "I'm hardly a child."

"Hardly." Looking jolly pleased with himself, Fredricks placed himself between Eliza and me.

His face. It was uncanny. But it had changed yet again. "Good heavens," I exclaimed. "You've shaved your mustache." He looked a bit naked without it.

"Your wish is my command." He gave me that unsettling look again.

Business, Fiona. Stick to your assignment.

Before our canapes arrived, I started pumping Fredricks for information. Not that he was ever forthcoming. "Why are you so chummy with the suffragettes?"

"Why not?" He took a sip of the posh wine he'd ordered.

"Principled reasons notwithstanding, you have strategic motives, I'm sure." I resisted saying nefarious motives.

The waiter served a lovely plate of canapes and julienned fresh vegetables.

"Are you suggesting men can't be in favor of suffrage for women?" Fredricks raised his eyebrows. "That's awfully closed-minded of you."

"I'm suggesting that you never do anything without a calculated political motive." I snapped a piece of celery in half.

"Perhaps in addition to believing in suffrage, Mr. Fredricks is a pacificist," Eliza said between nibbles on a canape. "You know most of the suffragettes also oppose the war."

Good grief. *That's it.* Fredricks was using the suffragettes to try to keep the American forces from fighting.

"You're wise beyond your years, dear girl." Fredricks smiled. "For months, I've been trying to convince your *aunt* to join me in my efforts to stop this bloody war."

"So, you're supporting the suffragettes as a way of indirectly supporting their opposition to the war." I could believe Fredricks wanted to stop the war, but only if he were on the winning side, which, given his political alliances, was decidedly the wrong side.

"If America withdraws," Fredricks said, "the British wouldn't have a chance."

"You don't like the British, Mr. Fredricks?" Eliza looked stunned.

Fredricks lowered his head and looked her straight in the eyes. "I loathe the British." He waved his hand at me. "Ask your aunt. She knows why."

Could Fredricks think that if American women were enfranchised, then they would vote to withdraw their sons and husbands from the front lines? And then Germany would win the war?

Clever.

And sneaky.

Very sneaky.

The waiter delivered the first course, a silky vegetable bisque garnished with dill.

As we ate, Fredricks regaled us with tales of his travels. Eliza was enthralled. I was incredulous.

Luckily, I had a perfect view of Misters Schweitzer and Edison, so I was only half paying attention to the tall tales being told at my own table. Given the intense expressions on the two men's faces, I wished I could hear the tales being told at theirs.

Mr. Edison's doughy face had turned bright red, and he seemed to be displeased with Schweitzer. Mr. Hoover was gone. I wondered if their disagreement had something to do with whatever the younger man had been spewing at them earlier.

Edison's apoplectics came to an end when Anna Case appeared. She smiled as she approached their table. Mr. Edison tightened his lips and crossed his arms over his barrel chest. He sat pouting as Anna Case whispered in Schweitzer's ear.

I guess the lovers had made up after their row on the ship.

Miss Case disappeared as quickly as she'd appeared. But her

timing was impeccable. She'd interrupted the men before they got into a shouting match. And her presence—as brief as it was—calmed them down. After she left, they went back to a more amiable conversation, or so it seemed.

We were starting coffee when the bell chimed, signaling the concert was about to start. I stood up to go.

"Relax, ma chérie." Fredricks reached for my hand and gently pulled me back into my chair. "Let's savor these moments together."

Eliza giggled behind her hand.

I dropped back into my chair and glowered at him. After the first heavenly bite of a *langue de chat* butter biscuit, I understood Fredricks's reluctance to dash. Crunchy on the outside and tender on the inside, the biscuit melted in my mouth. I closed my eyes to savor it.

A well-dressed matronly woman with tight curls approached Edison's table. He stood and she took his arm. Mr. Schweitzer stood up too. He shoved his chair in and then stomped off. However amiable the two men had appeared in the end, there was still some tension between them.

By the time the bell chimed again, I'd eaten three biscuits and drank two cups of sweet milky coffee. I couldn't tolerate the dark brew without gobs of milk and sugar.

Everyone else had left for the theater, so we were the last ones in the dining room. We were just gathering our things to go when a different waiter delivered a note for Fredricks. His hand trembled as he held it out. As soon as Fredricks took the note, the waiter disappeared.

Fredricks read the note and frowned.

"What is it?" I asked. Not that he'd tell me the truth. I leaned closer to try to see what it said.

"Edison has asked me to visit him in his box at intermission." Fredricks narrowed his brows. "I can't imagine why."

"Something to do with Mr. Schweitzer, perhaps?" I did my best to sound nonchalant. I'd already discovered that Mr. Schweitzer was working for the Germans.

"Hugo?" Fredricks flushed. "Why ever do you mention him?"

"That hideous fellow from the ship?" Eliza asked.

Heavens. The way he blinked at me, I knew I'd hit on something. *Wait a bloody minute.* What if Hugo Schweitzer had turned? What if he was a double agent and Fredricks was sent to dispose of him?

Blimey. In that case, my job was to protect Schweitzer, even if he was an adulterer and a bounder.

"Shall we?" Fredricks tucked the note into his waistcoat and smiled. "Are you ready to enjoy the concert?" If Schweitzer was his target, of course, he wouldn't let on.

Inside, the main theater was magnificent. The ornately carved ceiling and stage columns reminded me of Schönbrunn Palace. Beautifully symmetrical arches and graceful curves gave the space an elegant yet staid feeling. And the contrast between the ivory walls and the red upholstered wood-backed seats was shockingly delightful.

Fredricks's box was on the first level, stage right, with an excellent view of the audience below. The perfect vantage point for espionage.

I withdrew the opera glasses from my mesh evening bag and surveyed the crowd. Below, tiaras sparkled, and the chatter turned into a symphony. The opera house was nearly full to capacity. I trained my opera glasses on the boxes across from us. What posh people occupied stage-left boxes?

I sucked in air, and my gloved hand flew to my mouth. Archie.

I would recognize his handsome face and fine form anywhere. Was he a fan of opera?

He was staring straight across the theater. I felt myself blush. Did he see me?

No. He was looking at the next box over. Blast. A partition blocked my view. I was dying to know who was in that box.

The lights dimmed.

Eliza—along with a thousand others—clapped vigorously.

The curtains parted.

What the devil?

Mr. Thomas Edison appeared on stage. He held up his hands, and slowly the applause died down. "Ladies and gentlemen." He bowed slightly. "Tonight, you are in for a special treat... and a test."

The audience tittered.

"You shall have a demonstration of my phonographic machine." He waved his hand and a man in full evening kit rolled the machine onto the stage. "But only if you agree to my test." He smiled. "Anna, if you would be so kind as to join us."

Anna Case sashayed onto the stage.

"Ladies and gentlemen, may I present the greatest soprano of our times, Miss Anna Case." Mr. Edison gestured toward the soprano, and she took a bow.

"And now for the test." He wagged his finger at the audience. "I will bet you all that you cannot tell when Miss Case stops singing and my recording of Miss Case begins."

The audience chattered.

"We will turn out the lights in the theater, and I ask you to clap your hands when you hear the recording beginning."

Again, the audience tittered.

"Are your instructions clear?" Mr. Edison crossed the stage to his phonographic machine. "When Miss Case stops and the record starts, you clap." He lifted the arm of the machine. "Are you ready, Miss Case?"

She nodded and smiled.

The lights went out. The auditorium was so quiet you could hear a proverbial pin drop. My heart was racing. I felt like I was back at North Collegiate School for Girls about to take a French test.

A single voice filled the theater, a beautiful voice. It was as if an angel appeared from the heavens and blessed us with a song. Partway through her aria, when she paused to take a breath, there were a few claps that faded as soon as she sang the next note. A couple of minutes later, same thing, a few fading claps. This routine continued until the light went up.

Mr. Edison held both arms in the air above his head. Miss Anna Case took a deep bow. The crowd went wild with applause.

I joined in. I had to admit it was remarkable. Even with everyone anticipating the end of Miss Case's singing and the beginning of the recording, no one could tell for sure where one stopped and the other started. Mr. Edison was a genius.

Mr. Edison left the stage along with his amazing phonographic machine. A pianist took a seat at a baby grand piano behind Miss Case, and the concert began in earnest.

I was enraptured. And judging by the look on her pretty face, so was Eliza. Neither of us could take our eyes off Anna Case. Her voice transported me to another realm. One where there was no war or hunger or strife. A perfect world of perfect peace. If only I could stay forever.

I closed my eyes and floated along with the music... and then Archie appeared in my thoughts. We were dancing. He held me close. My hand touched his shoulder and then his face. His beautiful face.

I'd never actually danced with Archie. In fact, other than a clandestine meeting on behalf of the War Office, I hardly knew him.

Of course, there was that kiss in Austria. I squeezed my eyes tighter and went back to that glorious kiss... and the dancing.

Interrupting my fantasies of off-white weddings and red-hot honeymoons, the intermission came much too soon.

"Excuse me, ladies," Fredricks said. "I'll see what Edison wants and then be right back for champagne. Don't go anywhere." He looked from me to Eliza and smiled, and then disappeared from the box.

"Oh, Aunt Fiona, isn't it splendid?" Eliza asked, clapping her hands together. "Isn't it the most wonderful concert ever?"

I had to admit it was... Most especially for the daydreams prompted by the music.

"Thank you for bringing me." Eliza leaned over and kissed my cheek.

"You should thank Mr. Fredricks. It was, after all, he who provided your ticket."

"I shall." She smiled. "I see why you are so fond of him. And he of you—"

"Fond of him!" I jumped up. "Fond of him." I snapped my fan open and waved it furiously in front of my face. "I can't stand the fiend, but right now, I need to follow him."

"I see," Eliza said with a smirk.

Bang! A loud noise echoed through the theater.

"Good heavens." I glanced around.

"What was that?" Eliza asked.

"It sounded like a gunshot." Shivers ran up my spine. I spun around and urgently freed my opera glasses from my handbag and held it to my eyes, looking for Archie in his box at stage left.

No. No. No. The box was empty. If anything happened to him... I couldn't...

My hand was shaking. I held the glasses in both hands and scanned the other boxes. When my gaze landed back at Archie's box, he stood staring straight at me. He waved. I felt my face flush but waved back.

At least Archie was safe.

The curtain parted and Anna Case appeared on the stage. Mouth open and eyes wide, she was staring up at the stage-right boxes. At the box next to ours, in fact. She must have heard the shot coming from the direction of her lover's box.

Fredricks. Oh dear. He hadn't come back yet. Had someone finally shot him?

Goodness knows he deserved it.

"You stay here," I barked at Eliza. "Don't you dare move."

I dashed out of the box and into the hallway. An usher stood outside the box next to ours, his face ashen and pinched. I ran up to him.

"What happened?"

He shook his head and pointed at a scene inside the box.

What the devil? Fredricks knelt on the floor. He was holding... a gun. Blimey. Next to him, slouched over in his chair, was a man.

I took a few steps closer and bent down to see the man's face. Oh, my sainted aunt.

Mr. Hugo Schweitzer's soulless, dead eyes stared back at me.

"Fredrick, what have you done?"

I had never seen Fredricks so shaken. Usually unflappable even in the most vexing circumstances, at this moment, his face was a mask of incredulity.

A security guard arrived on the scene.

"I... I... I didn't..." Fredricks looked up at me with fear in his eyes.

Fear. Fredricks afraid? I couldn't believe it.

"Fiona," he pleaded. "I didn't do it." He dropped the gun.

"Sir," the guard said. "Please stand up and put your hands above your head."

Fredricks did as he was told. The guard frisked him. Goodness.

I took the opportunity to take a closer look at the weapon. On hands and knees, I bent over the gun and examined it. Odd. The end of the barrel had a golden thread stuck to it. I didn't know much about firearms, but that seemed like an important clue. But clue to what?

"Madam," the guard said. "Please stand up and raise your hands above your head."

"Me?" I scrambled to my feet. "You can't think I had anything to do with this grisly business."

The guard waved his stick at me.

I put my arms in the air. "Really, this is absurd."

"It's a frame-up." Fredricks didn't take his eyes off me. "You have to believe me."

I nodded.

Against my better judgment, I did believe him.

Fredricks was many things—including a bounder and a cad, an enemy spy, and a poisoner, but he was neither a coward nor a liar.

Was he?

13

THE BANGER HYPOTHESIS

As his *friend* and Fredricks's *date* for the evening—ahem—the opera house security guard agreed to allow me to sit next to Fredricks in Edison's box while we awaited the New York constabulary. The guard kept an eye on us and a hand on his gun least we touch anything, or God forbid, make a break for it.

"I did not kill Hugo Schweitzer." Fredricks watched the guard as he leaned closer and whispered. "I was summoned here purportedly to meet Edison. When I got here, Schweitzer had been shot."

"And you just happened to pick up the murder weapon?" I raised my eyebrows.

"I had my reasons." Fredricks sighed. "Schweitzer was not just a chemist." He leaned closer. "He was also—"

"Quiet!" the guard barked at us. "Not another word, you hear."

Sitting in silence, I took the opportunity to survey the crime scene.

Hugo Schweitzer had been shot once in the head at close

range. Judging by the blood splattered on the balcony wall, the bullet had entered from stage right and exited stage left.

The gun still lay where Fredricks had dropped it. The wooden handle with a red number nine carved into it, along with the square housing and long metal rod extending out the back, made it look like a poorly constructed toy.

The guard turned to talk to the police, who'd just arrived.

While he was distracted, I took the opportunity—what might be my last—to question Fredricks. "What kind of gun is that?" I whispered.

"Mauser nine-millimeter. Standard issue in the German Imperial Army."

"Is it yours?"

"Of course not. Do you think I'd bring a gun to the opera?"

"I did." I patted my handbag, which was lying in my lap.

He smiled. "I should have known."

I crossed my legs and my bag fell to the floor. I bent to pick it up.

"What are you doing?" the guard asked.

"I dropped my bag." I held up my bag.

What in heaven's name? One side of my mesh evening bag was covered with ash and paper fragments. I glanced at the floor. On the carpet, around the circumference of a small black burn, were more tan-colored paper fragments and a dusting of ash.

Two men stepped into the opera box.

"I'm Detective Callaway, and this is Burnside." The detective was wearing an evening jacket. Had he been at the opera all along?

"We will need to take you to the station for questioning." Detective Callaway looked down at Fredricks. "If we deem it necessary, we may hold you."

"Me, too?" Wide-eyed, I glanced at Fredricks and then back at the detective. "Surely you don't need to keep me." I didn't relish the prospect of another night in jail.

"We'll see." The detective waved both hands like he was splashing water on his face. "Come on, ladies and gents, let's go."

I followed the detective and Fredricks into the hallway. Good heavens. Eliza. I'd forgotten about Eliza. The poor girl probably wondered where I was. As we passed our box, I peeked in.

Eliza was sitting right where I'd left her. She could be an obedient little thing when she wanted to be.

"Eliza, dear." I motioned her over. "Please tell Clifford to come find me at the nick."

"The nick?" Eliza put her hand over her mouth. "Not again."

I nodded. "I'm afraid so."

"Come on, lady," the detective said. "Quit dilly-dallying."

"Would you be so kind as to tell my niece where you're taking us?" I asked the officer in my most treacly tone.

"Midtown precinct," he snapped. "My supper is waiting. I haven't got all night."

Oh dear. An armed man with an empty stomach. There were hundreds of ways this situation could get worse.

Halfway down the hall, we ran into Archie coming toward us, his face flushed with excitement. "You did it." He looked around and then dropped his cigarette on the carpet and stepped on it.

Cigarettes really were a filthy habit, especially those Kenilworths.

"A-Archie," I stammered.

"You finally caught Fredricks red-handed." He was beaming.

"Lieutenant Somersby, not to dampen your enthusiasm," Fredricks said, "but I'm counting on Fiona to prove my innocence."

"Move along," the detective said, pulling at my elbow.

As the detective pulled me along, I gazed back at Archie.

Please help. I felt like shouting. I'd have given anything to sink into Archie's embrace and forget about Fredricks, and Schweitzer, and that mysterious man overboard.

Instead, I was being hauled off to jail, again.

The detectives put me in the back of their squad car like a common criminal. Fredricks had recovered his composure and was his usual flirtatious self on the ride to the nick.

"Finally, some time alone." He leaned closer. I could feel his warm breath on my neck.

"You're going to get plenty of time alone in prison." I turned my head and stared out of the window.

New York was rather pretty after dark in the snow with its glowing streetlights.

"You know I didn't kill that man." Fredricks laid a handcuffed hand on mine. "I'm not capable—"

I jerked my hand away. "I have no idea what you are or are not capable of."

"Would you like to find out?" he asked, playfully.

Cheeky devil. He was incorrigible, even when being hauled off to jail.

At the nick, the constabulary separated me and Fredricks. Detective Callaway led me to a small room and closed the door.

After sitting in an interrogation room for an hour waiting, finally the detective came back to question me.

I troubled the chain on my mesh evening bag, hoping the detective didn't search me and find Mata Hari's gun... not to mention the paper fragments caught in the beadwork. I preferred to investigate those myself.

The detective asked me what happened several times over, and every time I repeated the same answer.

I heard a shot. I glanced around the theater—I left out the part about Archie waving. I told my "niece" to stay put. And then

I dashed in the direction of the shot to the booth next to ours, where I found Fredricks with a gun in his hand, kneeling near the dead man. Since I'd come to the opera at the invitation of Mr. Fredricks, I stayed with him until the constabulary arrived.

Detective Callaway smirked every time I said constabulary. He seemed to find it amusing.

After recounting the same story several more times, the constable finally decided I was telling the truth, which, of course, I was.

"What will happen to Mr. Fredricks?" I asked on the way out of the interrogation room.

"We are holding him for the time being," the detective said. "He was, as your friend so accurately noted, caught red-handed."

"Yes, but—"

"Don't worry," he said. "We haven't arrested him... yet."

I'd been following Fredrick Fredricks across the continent and now across the Atlantic, waiting and watching to catch him in the act. So why now, when I finally had, did I feel so uneasy? Something wasn't right.

For one thing, Fredricks preferred poisons to firearms for dispensing with double agents. I knew this from my previous assignments.

* * *

"Don't leave the city... or the country," the detective said as he deposited me in the reception area.

Clifford was waiting for me there. Thank goodness.

"Dear Clifford." I patted his arm. "Thank you for coming to my rescue once again."

He grinned. "Happy to, old bean."

"You really are a pal."

"Are you going to tell me what's going on?" Clifford raised an eyebrow. "It's only fair, you know. You leave for the opera and end up in jail... again."

He was right. It was about time to bring him up to speed. I told him about finding Fredricks holding a gun over Mr. Schweitzer's dead body. I told him about the ashes and the thread.

"A gold thread, you say." He puffed on his pipe.

When I stepped out of the nick, the cold night air startled me. The city had a muffled middle-of-the-night sort of sound. Despite the hour, there were still cars and cabs and carriages. But everything seemed to move slower than during the daylight hours... including me.

The dust of the night's events had settled, and I found myself completely knackered. I couldn't wait to get back to the hotel and collapse into bed.

Clifford hailed a cab and then held the door for me. The car was yellow. Only in America would taxicabs be painted the color of overripe corn.

Once inside, I slouched in the seat, relieved to be going home. If only I were really going home... back to London and Northwick Terrace. Sigh. I missed my flat, and my bed, and a decent cup of tea.

"Rum do about Schweitzer," Clifford said. "Although I suppose any man who so brazenly cheats on his wife should not be surprised to meet with a bullet." He chuckled.

"Any man who cheats on his wife *deserves* to meet with a bullet." I thought of poor Andrew. He met with a bullet and mustard gas. Even a cheating husband didn't deserve mustard gas.

"Which one of them do you think did it?" Clifford asked. "The wife or the mistress?"

"The police think your mate Fredrick Fredricks did it."

"Good Lord. You don't say." Clifford tilted his head. "I know Miss Case is too charming for such a stunt. And her lovely friend..." Clifford nattered on about the lovely friend.

I stared out the window and tuned him out. My body was exhausted, but my mind was abuzz. Perhaps Clifford was right. Both the wife and the mistress had a motive. And, as both were at the opera, and the murder happened during intermission, both had the opportunity.

Why was I troubling myself? I didn't owe Fredricks anything. To the contrary. He could rot in prison for all I cared. I fingered one of the argent roses on my dress.

I didn't care about Fredricks. He was a scoundrel and a German spy. But I did care about the truth. If Fredricks hadn't killed Hugo Schweitzer, then the real killer was still on the loose. In fact, for all I knew, the same person or persons who threw the mysterious man overboard on the ship also shot Mr. Schweitzer.

Captain Hall would be none too happy that I'd gotten myself embroiled in another murder case. Then again, this time, the victim was most certainly a German spy, and the suspected killer was a suspected German spy and my target. So, in essence, this murder case was entirely within my purview as a British Intelligence agent.

And, apart from my evening gown, I hadn't worn even one costume... yet.

When I got back to my hotel room, Eliza was sitting up in bed reading a magazine—judging by the way she was turning it upside down and sideways, it would be more accurate to say she was poring over the pictures.

"You're back!" She laid the magazine on the nightstand. "What happened? Why did the police take you? Did Mr. Fredricks really shoot that man?"

I ignored her questions. "Where's Poppy?" I glanced around the room. Unless Eliza had her locked up in the loo, the pup was nowhere to be seen. I pulled on the fingers of my gloves, which were filthy. One pair ruined by the dog and another by finger-prints at the police station.

Eliza lifted her blanket and a little flat face appeared, looking quite put out by the interruption.

Eliza threw off the blanket and sat up in bed. "Tell me, please, Aunt Fiona. Did Mr. Fredricks really shoot Mr. Schweitzer?"

"I don't know." I dropped onto my bed.

"Is it true that you saw him holding the murder weapon?"

"I saw him holding a gun." I tossed my handbag onto the night table. It landed with a thud. Whoops. I'd forgotten about my own gun. "I suppose the police have to confirm that it is in fact the murder weapon."

"Using dactyloscopy?" Eliza's face was flushed with excitement.

I was stunned. My mind raced. Whatever did she mean? *Dactylo*, Greek for finger or toe. *Scopy* meaning observation.

"You know. Fingerprints."

Ah, yes. I'd heard of fingerprinting. "We already know Fredricks touched the gun."

"Maybe someone else did too." Eliza sat up straight. "Maybe they can fingerprint the bullets." Poppy peeked out from under the blankets.

"You think fingerprints would survive a gunshot?" I didn't know much about guns or prints. How did Eliza know so much? The girl surprised me. At the suffragette march, she ran like a gazelle. In jail, she taught the suffragettes jujitsu moves. And now she was talking like a proper detective.

"No. Bullets have their own signatures." She pulled Poppy out from under the covers and cradled the pup like a baby. "Gun barrels make marks on them, or they have imperfections that might give a clue to the casts that made them. That sort of thing."

I sat blinking at her.

"*Toute action de l'homme, et a fortiori, l'action violent qu'est un crime, ne peut pas se dérouler sans laisser quelque marque.*" Eliza tucked Poppy back under the blankets. She picked up my mesh evening bag from the night table, which was between our beds.

"Any action of an individual, and obviously the violent action constituting a crime, cannot occur without leaving a trace," I whispered, translating what Eliza had said. "I didn't know you spoke French."

"Oh, yes." Eliza turned my bag over in her hands. "Mother sent me to a boarding school in Lyon." She examined the handbag and then held it up to her nose and sniffed. Poppy sat up and sniffed too.

"What in heaven's name—" Why was she smelling my bag?

"Potassium nitrate." Eliza picked at a bit of paper stuck in the beads on my bag.

"What are you on about?"

"On your bag. Gunpowder." Between her fingernails, she held a tiny bit of tan paper. "From a banger."

"A what?"

"A banger. You know. A cracker." She looked at me expectantly. Poppy was staring over at me too.

I stared back. My head was as empty as my stomach. I needed either food or sleep or I was going to keel over.

"A cracker." Eliza held out my bag. "This paper is from a cracker."

I blinked.

"What the Americans call a firecracker." She laid my evening bag back on the nightstand. "Bang." She made an exploding gesture with her hands.

Poppy stood up and barked. Obviously, the pup did not approve of bangers exploding in bed. And neither did I.

"Why ever would someone put a banger in Mr. Schweitzer's opera box?" I couldn't sit upright any longer. I fell back on the bed. *Oh, my sainted aunt.* I jolted upright. "To make us think the shot happened later than it actually did. The cracker was rigged to go off *after* the murder."

"It wasn't Mr. Schweitzer's box, though, was it?"

I glanced over at her. The girl was right. Mr. Schweitzer was killed in Mr. Edison's box. But where was Mr. Edison? And Mrs. Schweitzer. Shouldn't they have been in the box when the shot was fired?

"Mr. Fredricks told us he'd been summoned to Mr. Edison's box, did he not?"

Clever girl. "That's right. So where was Mr. Edison?" I rolled over to face her.

"He was on stage for the demonstration."

"Did you see Mrs. Schweitzer?" Eliza asked.

"No." I rubbed my eyes. "She was nowhere to be seen."

"Do you think Mr. Fredricks is a murderer?"

"Eliza, dear." I put my arm across my eyes to shield them from the lights, which seemed to be getting brighter by the minute. "I'm really not in the mood for an interrogation right now. I need sleep."

"The coppers should wax Mr. Fredricks's hands."

I opened my eyes and peeked over at the girl.

Eliza threw her legs over the side of her bed, and slipped her feet into her pink slippers, which perfectly matched her pink nightgown and pink sleeping cap. "But they won't."

I leaned on my elbow. "What's this about fingerprints, bangers, and waxing hands?" Perhaps I was already asleep and dreaming this queer conversation. I shook my head. "Where did you learn such things?"

"I already told you, Aunt Fiona." Eliza went to the mirror and adjusted her cap. "In France."

Blimey. Who was this girl? And what had she done with my ward?

14

THE FALL GUY

At breakfast the next morning, I tucked into the toast and tea with abandon. What I lacked in sleep, I planned to make up for in victuals.

As usual, Eliza picked at her fruit and nibbled on her toast. She chased one particular berry around her plate for at least thirty minutes.

"Good grief." I put my cup down onto the saucer a bit too hard, and my tea sloshed over the sides of the cup. "Just eat the poor thing, don't torture it. You're as bad as a cat."

"Poppy wouldn't like you comparing me to a cat, Aunt Fiona." Eliza smiled. "She absolutely loathes cats. They drive her to distraction." She laughed. "My uncle has a cat, and Poppy terrorizes it something awful."

Captain Blinker Hall had a cat? It was hard to imagine him living with another being, let alone one with fur and whiskers.

"Let's concentrate on the matter at hand," I said, pinching a piece of toast from Clifford's plate while he was up getting another cup of coffee. "Who killed Hugo Schweitzer? We need to make a list of suspects."

Eliza may not be a temporary special agent in British Intelligence, but she was sharp as a tack. And in any case, she already knew enough about Fredrick Fredricks and Hugo Schweitzer to join the investigation. I don't think I could have stopped her if I had wanted to.

"Good Lord, you don't think Fredricks did it?" Clifford joined us again with a fresh cup of coffee. "Not cricket to kill a man at point blank range. What's sporting about that?"

I narrowed my brows. "Is there a sporting way to kill a man?"

"The gladiators—" Eliza said.

"Yes, well, Mr. Schweitzer was not a gladiator." I cut her off before she could continue that line of argument. Although he was a German spy. And Fredricks was a renowned spy-killer, although usually he only killed those spies who'd turned and betrayed his Kaiser. Now Fredricks was caught with a smoking gun, maybe instead of worshiping the "great hunter," Clifford would come around to believing he was no good. It was difficult to tell what Eliza thought of Fredricks. Judging from the way she joined the gushing suffragettes at the nick, she seemed to admire the man.

Judging from the letter in Schweitzer's briefcase, and what Archie had told me about the phenol plot, the chemist had not turned. Far from it. He was in the middle of executing the great phenol plot on behalf of Kaiser Wilhelm himself.

Was it that plot that got him killed? Or was it his philandering with Miss Anna Case? They did have that row on board the *Adriatic*. Then again, maybe his wife decided she'd had enough of his making a fool of her in public. She certainly had a motive to kill the bounder.

I took a slip of paper and a pencil from my bag. I'd brought them from the room for this very purpose. In bold letters, I wrote SUSPECTS across the top.

Number one, Fredrick Fredricks. For some insane reason that

I couldn't fathom, I believed him when he said he was innocent. Yet it was impossible to overlook the fact that he was indeed caught with a smoking gun.

Number two, Anna Case. The opera singer had threatened to throw her lover overboard.

Number three, Mrs. Schweitzer. For obvious reasons.

"Who else might want to kill Hugo Schweitzer?" I asked, holding my pencil at the ready.

"Mr. Thomas Edison seemed rather put out with the old boy at supper last night," Clifford said. "They were having that terrible row until the lovely Miss Case intervened."

"True. The inventor was perturbed to say the least." I wrote the number four and put an asterisk next to it. "But why kill Schweitzer? What's his motive?"

"Maybe he stole one of Mr. Edison's inventions," Eliza offered.

"Maybe Mr. Schweitzer was blackmailing him." Clifford sat back in his chair, crossed his legs, and lit a cigarette.

I scowled at him and dropped a half-eaten piece of toast onto my plate.

"Blackmailing him for what?"

He shrugged. "Deuced if I know. The usual?"

"Which is?"

He shrugged again.

"Mrs. Parker seems none too fond of Mr. Schweitzer," Eliza said. "Remember at the luncheon when she scolded him?"

I added Mrs. Parker's name to my list.

"Does anyone know why she doesn't—didn't—like him?" Clifford asked.

"He didn't laugh at her wit?" I put an asterisk next to her name to indicate motive unknown.

"Surely that's not reason enough to kill someone, Aunt Fiona."

Sometimes the girl was far too serious and at others she was far too silly.

She dipped the corner of her toast into her coffee. "Why don't we go and visit Mr. Fredricks?" With her front teeth, she nipped just the tiniest corner off the bread.

"I suppose you want to bring him biscuits or a pudding with a file in it?" I sipped my tea. "Knowing Fredricks, he doesn't need our help to escape."

"I say. His escape in Paris was a daring feat." Clifford smiled.

My cheeks warmed just remembering how, on one assignment, Fredricks had trussed me up like a Christmas goose and left me lying on that flea-infested mattress in a Paris prison. Stealing my nun's costume to make an escape. What kind of self-respecting gentleman did that?

"Reminds me of the time we were hunting in the Serengeti when a monstrous beast of a lion charged out of the brush." Clifford chuckled. "You should have seen Fredricks. He was as fierce as the lion..."

While Clifford regaled us with stories of the Great White Hunter, I contemplated my next steps.

I had a list of five possible suspects. Two—the wife and mistress—had obvious motives. Another two—Mr. Edison and Mrs. Parker—had been seen quarreling with the victim. And then there was Fredricks left holding the gun.

The least known to me was Mr. Edison. He was possibly the last person to have seen the victim alive. He'd argued with the victim just before he was killed... in his opera box. Perhaps Eliza was right, and Mr. Schweitzer had stolen some invention or secret.

Again, this made me wonder if Mr. Schweitzer's murder had to do with Bayer Aspirin and the great phenol plot. In that case, either one of my five suspects was involved in that scheme, or there was a sixth unknown suspect. Either way, questioning Mr. Edison had to be my next step. He had business with Mr. Schweitzer and might have been the last to see him alive. Could Mr. Edison be involved in the great phenol plot too?

Oh, my sainted aunt! On the ship, Archie and Schweitzer were discussing phenol. I thought I'd misunderstood the German for vinyl recordings. Maybe I hadn't. I intended to find out. Mr. Edison mentioned he was working for the American navy, and rumor had it, he had a laboratory aboard a yacht. I had to find a way onto that boat.

"Aunt Fiona. Are you listening?" Eliza's voice interrupted my thoughts. "Can we?"

"Yes, dear," I said absentmindedly.

"Thank you." Eliza clapped her hands together. "Shall we go now?"

I squinted at her. "Go where?"

"You just agreed that we might visit Mr. Fredricks this morning."

"I did?"

Her golden ringlets bobbed up and down as she nodded. Her mouth formed a perfect little rosebud. She batted her long lashes at me... as if I would fall for her girlish charms.

"Apologies, dear." I drank the dregs of what passed for tea. "I have other plans."

"Please, Aunt Fiona." Eliza smiled sweetly. "You won't regret it."

"Oh, alright." I tossed my napkin onto the table. "What harm will it do?" I supposed starting with Fredricks made some sense. He was, after all, the obvious suspect... either that or the victim of an elaborate frame-up. I revised my plan. Jail first, Edison second. Anyway, perhaps Fredricks knew something about Mr. Edison or the great phenol plot.

"I need to go back to the room and get some supplies." Eliza's eyes danced with delight. You'd think we were on our way to a ball and not a jail.

* * *

I'd been trying without success to persuade the receptionist to allow us to visit Fredricks when the constable who'd detained us at the opera appeared from the back.

"You're the wife, right?"

I may have nodded.

"Let them through." He waved. "Just the wife and the daughter."

"I say," Clifford stammered. "They aren't—"

I may have kicked him in the shin.

"Ouch!" Clifford looked at me like a wounded puppy. "Why'd you do that?"

"Come along, daughter dear," I said, taking Eliza's hand. "Let's go visit Papa."

We left Clifford red-faced and sputtering, and followed the constable to a small, windowless waiting room.

The only furniture in the room was a table and four chairs. It looked more like an interrogation room than a visiting room.

I settled into one of the chairs, and Eliza took a seat next to me. She opened her small bag and pulled out a pair of nail clippers, a magnifying glass, and a round green ring of rubber fabric.

I admired the little bag with its adorable cat sewn in black beads on the pink background. "What is that?" I pointed to the green ring.

"Pressure sensitive adhesive." Eliza arranged her supplies neatly on the table. "It's used in surgeries."

"Are you planning an operation?" I seized the magnifying

glass and examined the adhesive. Humph.

"You'll see." She smiled.

With that oversized pink silk bow in her hair and the frilly blouse under her smock dress, she looked like a schoolgirl setting out her art supplies. I could hardly wait to see what she had planned for Fredricks.

Footfalls signaled the guard's return. Eliza snatched up the nail clippers and hid them in the palm of her hand.

The guard opened the door and escorted Fredricks into the room.

"Fiona, ma chérie." Fredricks grinned. "Have you come to liberate me from this unsavory establishment?" He looked at the guard and gestured toward a chair. "May I?"

The guard nodded.

"We've come, Father dear," Eliza said, holding her hand out across the table. "To make sure you don't have a relapse."

"Relapse?" he asked.

"Of porphyria cutanea tarda." She wigged her fingers. "Please, Father, give me your hand."

"Porphyria cutanea..." I repeated, completely gobsmacked.

"Yes, caused by father's haemchromatosis." She examined his palm and then turned his hand over.

"No touching the prisoner," the guard said, stepping closer to the table.

"But sir, Papa needs this treatment." Eliza batted her lashes. "He's ill, you see. Poor Papa."

"Well, alright." The guard stepped back and stood against the wall. "I'm watching you, so no funny business."

Eliza crossed her heart. "No funny business."

"Haemchro—"

"Caused by imbibing too many spirits," Eliza interrupted me. *What is she on about?* Since the guard was watching us, I kept my mouth shut.

"Daughter, dear." Fredricks chuckled. "Never fear. I've been on the wagon for nearly twelve hours now."

Eliza proceeded to cut strips of adhesive and dab Fredricks's hands. She then examined the strips under the magnifying glass.

I hope she knows what she is doing. Otherwise, we've missed an important opportunity to question Fredricks.

"I found remnants of what may be a banger," I whispered. "Do you have any idea why someone would have set off a cracker at the opera?"

Fredricks tilted his head. "Fiona, ma chérie." He smiled. "I knew I could count on you to investigate." His dark eyes danced. "So, you do care."

"I care about justice, not about you," I sniffed.

Eliza was still busy fussing with her adhesive strips and some chemical drops she just happened to have on hand. *Who is this girl?* You'd think she was Sherlock Holmes the way she wielded that magnifying glass.

"If someone used fireworks," Fredricks said. "Then..."

"Precisely. If someone used fireworks," I interrupted, "then the sound of gunfire we heard was caused by the banger." I grinned. "The firework was a decoy to make us think the murder happened later than it did."

I raised an eyebrow. "I'm betting you heard the shot after you found Schweitzer keeled over."

He gave me an odd look. "After." A sly smile crept across his lips. "Fiona, you're a genius."

I couldn't help but smile in return. "What about Mr. Edison and Schweitzer's wife? Where were they when the real shot was fired? Did you see anyone exit the box before you arrived?"

"No. The box was empty except for the corpse." He lowered his voice. "From what I've overheard in this human zoo, Edison left shortly after the tone test, and Mrs. Schweitzer was called away to the telephone just before intermission." He smirked. "She was the last person to see him alive. Suspicious, no?"

Suspicious, yes. This was a task for Clifford. He could chat up a turnip and find out what lay beneath its roots. While I spied on Mr. Edison, I should send him to interview Mrs. Schweitzer. Afterall, I couldn't take Fredricks's word for anything.

Eliza glanced at the guard and then leaned over and whispered in my ear. "Mr. Fredricks fired the gun."

"How do you know?" I sat blinking at her.

"Mr. Fredricks is guilty," she announced. "There are signs of potassium *nitrite* and potassium *nitrate* on his hands."

"What?" I asked. "And how does that signify?"

"Miss Eliza, with all due respect, you've misread your test." Fredricks examined his hand.

Good heavens. Fredricks was guilty. I should have known. And yet, something didn't sit right. A niggling in my gut told me he was innocent.

"I did not shoot Mr. Schweitzer." Fredricks leaned back in his chair and folded his arms over his broad chest. "The banger was used to frame me. And your test proves conclusively that I'm innocent."

"Guilty," Eliza said, gathering up her "supplies" and tucking them back into her pink beaded cat bag.

There was more to the girl than puppies and bows.

"Fredricks, my worthy opponent—" I cleared my throat. "Er, husband." I glanced over at the guard, who was grinning at some magazine wrapped in brown paper. "Either you are the fall guy or you're a cold-blooded killer."

"Can't I be both?" Fredricks grinned.

"Indeed." This case was not closed yet. As much as I wanted Fredricks behind bars, I wanted justice more.

15

THE GOLDEN CUSHION

Back at the hotel, over an early luncheon, we told Clifford what had transpired in our interview with Fredricks.

"Good Lord." If his vigorous chewing was any indication, he was enthusiastic about the case. "Is Fredricks innocent or guilty?"

"Precisely what I aim to find out." I reviewed my list of suspects. "Who had the motive, means, and opportunity?" I put brackets around Fredricks's name.

"Guilty," Eliza said, poking her fork at a boiled potato.

"Anna Case was on stage." I drew a circle around her name.

"The jilted lover," Clifford said with his mouth full of sandwich.

"We need to get back to Carnegie Music Hall and determine if she could have left the stage, killed Mr. Schweitzer, and then returned to the stage all in the first few minutes of the intermission." I underlined Anna Case.

"Mrs. Schweitzer was at the bar at the time." Eliza gave up on the potato and picked up her spoon.

"And how do you know that?" I asked.

"I saw her there."

I scowled. "Didn't I tell you to stay put?"

She shrugged and lifted a spoonful of soup to her mouth. "What does it matter since your Mr. Fredricks is guilty and already in jail?"

I ignored her question and continued my own. "What about Mrs. Parker?" I pushed my plate aside. "She joked about killing Mr. Edison. Perhaps she had it in for Mr. Schweitzer, too."

"I saw her leave with a bartender." Eliza stirred her soup.

"When?" What in heaven's name was the girl doing at the bar? Sigh. She was a handful to say the least.

"At the bar. Just after you left our box." Eliza avoided my glare.

"Well, then. Could either woman have killed Schweitzer and gotten back to the bar in time to be seen by you?" I really had better keep an eye on that girl. She was sharper—and sneakier—than I'd given her credit for.

We needed to get back to Carnegie Hall and determine how long it took to get from the box to the bar... and from the stage to the box. Could either the lover or the wife have killed Mr. Schweitzer during intermission after Mr. Edison left the box and before the banger went off? Hopefully, my investigation of Mr. Edison would yield some answers too... if I ever got to carry it out. With my attentions on the jealous women, Mr. Edison would have to wait.

Luckily, I'd fetched my Valentine's guide to New York from my room. I thumbed through the guidebook until I found Carnegie Music Hall. "Look here." I pointed to the page. "The music hall offers tours every afternoon at one." I glanced at my watch.

"I know where *we're* going after lunch." Clifford smiled as he chewed.

"If we hurry, we can just make it." I set my napkin on the table. "Ready?"

"I haven't had my pudding," Clifford pouted.

"You can stay and have pudding while we go on the tour." I stood up. "Coming, Eliza?"

She dropped her spoon into her uneaten bowl of soup. "I'd love to go." She dabbed her mouth.

"Oh, no, you don't." Clifford threw his napkin on the table and stood up. "You're not going sleuthing without me."

I knew Clifford couldn't pass up the chance to play detective. After all, he fancied himself a regular Sherlock Holmes.

* * *

During the daytime, the music hall lost some of its charm. Without the sparkling chandeliers and warm illumination from wall sconces, the red upholstery was dull, and the ivory balusters had lost their luster. The sound of the tour guide's booming voice echoed through the empty theater. "Since opening in 1891, the music hall has set the standard for international excellence."

We trailed behind the guide as he dispersed tidbits of history. "Andrew Carnegie was inspired to build Carnegie Hall by his new wife, Louise, who sang with the Oratorio Society of New York."

I hung back and, when no one was looking, I broke away from the tour.

As I tiptoed toward an exit, the guide was telling the group that the hall was designed by William Burnet Tuthill, a professional architect who was also a cellist.

"Any questions?" The guide's booming voice followed me out into the lobby.

Yes. Actually, I did have a question. Was it possible for Anna Case to get from the stage to Mr. Edison's box, shoot Hugo Schweitzer, and then return to the stage to peek out the curtain? I was certain it was her I'd seen shortly after hearing the shot—or should I say banger—at the beginning of intermission. Seems unlikely she would have time since she was singing on stage just prior to intermission... unless she did the deed during Mr. Edison's tone test when the lights were out and the recording was singing in her stead. Would she have had time to exit the stage, get to the box, kill her lover, and get back to the stage all while Mr. Edison was playing her voice on the phonograph? Again, Mr. Edison was a key witness.

Anna Case had argued with Schweitzer. She'd threatened to throw him overboard. She was having an illicit liaison with him. But did she kill him?

Glancing around the lobby to make sure I wasn't seen, I darted through a door marked "Employees Only." Following a long hallway that wound around the theater, eventually I found myself backstage. Good.

Thinking back to the gunshot, I'd say at most, three minutes had passed from the time I heard the shot to when I saw Anna Case peek out from behind the curtain.

If Eliza was right and the paper on my handbag was from a banger, then what I thought was a gunshot was really a fire-cracker. So, Anna Case could have run off the stage after her performance, killed Schweitzer, set up the banger to go off later, and then intentionally parted the curtain so she would be seen to have an alibi.

I had to admit, it was jolly clever.

Still, since both Mr. Edison and Mrs. Schweitzer saw Hugo Schweitzer alive at intermission, the soprano would not have had much time to finish her song, dash off to the box, shoot her lover, and then get back on stage... Unless she wasn't actually singing.

I positioned myself in the center of the stage where Anna Case had been when she sang, and then wrapped the chain of my handbag around my wrist. Glancing at my watch, I set off for Mr. Edison's box as fast as my legs would carry me.

There was no way to get there except by retracing my steps down the long winding hallway back to the lobby and then climbing the marble stairway to the second floor. Surely someone would have noticed a woman in red running through the lobby, especially since she'd been the woman they'd just seen on stage.

By the time I arrived at Edison's box, I was panting faster than Poppy. I bent over with my hands on my knees to catch my breath and glanced at my watch. It had taken me eight minutes running at top speed, one way. She still had to shoot him and then run all the way back.

No. It was impossible. I unwound the chain from my wrist, removed my small notebook and a pencil from my handbag, and crossed off Anna Case from my list of suspects.

I looked down into the orchestra pit just in time to see the group disappear under the stage. I took a deep breath and raced back down to catch them up.

I was quite overcome by the time I got there. The group was nowhere to be seen. So, I flopped into one of the chairs set up for the orchestra.

Closing my eyes, I rehearsed my list of suspects: Mrs. Schweitzer, who, Eliza said was at the bar when her husband was shot. Mrs. Parker, who apparently left at intermission with one of the bartenders. Mr. Edison, whom I'd seen arguing with the victim right before the performance.

My money was on Edison, in spite of the fact Eliza—and everyone else—insisted it was Fredricks.

The sounds of chatter made me open my eyes. The group appeared out of a panel in the wall behind the orchestra. I jumped up and went to investigate. A secret door?

"Aunt Fiona." Eliza burst out of the group. "Where have you been? You missed the best part of the tour." She was practically squealing with delight.

Clifford appeared by her side. "You're going to regret sneaking off, old bean." He grinned like a hyena.

What in the world? Why were they both acting so barmy?

The tour guide led the rest of the group out of the orchestra pit. "And now to the apartments," he called back to the group. "Over the years, many celebrities have lived above this very theater."

"Did you know the subway stops directly below us?" Clifford sounded chuffed, as if he personally was responsible for such a feat.

Eliza clapped her hands together. "And below that is a secret passage."

"What?" I stood blinking at her. "A secret passageway to the stage?" Perhaps there was another route Anna Case could have taken from the stage to the box, a shorter route, one that allowed her enough time to commit murder and then get back to open the curtain... One that gave her an alibi. "Show me."

"I say." Clifford looked longingly toward the rest of the group as they marched up the center aisle of the theater. "We'll miss the rest of the tour."

"Eliza, my dear." I took her hand. "You'll take your aunt Fiona to the secret passage, won't you?" I glanced at Clifford out of the corner of my eye.

He was pouting again. "What if there are more secrets to be learned *above* the theater?"

I hadn't thought of that. "Good point." I pursed my lips. Indeed, there could be another secret passageway or some other piece of information crucial to the case. "Clifford, you do reconnaissance. Follow the rest of the tour."

His face fell. "I'd rather—"

"You know, you could track down the waiter who delivered the note from Edison."

He beamed. "Jolly good."

I knew he'd jump at the chance to play detective, especially if it involved chatting people up. He so loved to meet new people and regale them with his stories, which, I had to admit, put them at ease and encouraged them to reciprocate. Clifford did come in handy when he wasn't breathing down my neck.

"We will meet back at the hotel for tea after." I patted his arm. "As always, your info will be vital to the case."

"Yes, well." He smiled. "I suppose you're right." He gave my hand a squeeze and then bounded the stairs and trotted up the center aisle.

I watched after him until his lanky form blended into the rest of the group. "Now, let's see this secret passageway, shall we?" I marched up to the panel in the wall out of which the party had appeared a few minutes before. Looking the piece up and down, I couldn't for the life of me find any doorknob or handle or latch of any sort.

Eliza skipped in front of me. "Here, Aunt Fiona. Let me." She stepped on a small button on the floor, and the panel popped open. "Voilà!"

Jolly clever.

She led me into a long narrow electrical room with a mammoth generator that looked like a mechanical octopus with all the tubes coming off it. The smell of dust mixed with a metallic odor so tart I could almost taste it. A humming sound vibrated through my bones.

As we walked, she repeated everything she'd learned on the tour. "You can access this tunnel from the orchestra pit and from behind the stage."

A hissing noise gave me a start.

"The generator is so powerful," Eliza pointed at the monster, "that on days when there is no performance, the hall sells energy to the city."

At the end of the room was a door. A strange door like what you might see on a submarine. Heavy and metal and a foot up off the ground. I reached for the handle and yanked. Nothing. The blasted thing wouldn't budge. "Are you sure this was part of the tour?" I asked.

Eliza nodded. "Allow me."

Right. The girl was half my size. I stepped out of her way.

With a little grunt, she jammed on the handle, and the door squeaked on its hinges.

"We're in!" She pumped her fist.

The mite was stronger than she looked. She pulled a torch out of a bracket next to the door.

"Oh, my." Now *this* was a tunnel. The uneven walls were whitewashed rough stone that jutted out over the walkway in places. The tunnel extended underground as far as the eye could see.

Blimey.

Flashing the torch as she went, Eliza continued in tour guide mode. "We're under 7th Street."

The closeness of the walls made me a bit queasy. And why was it so blasted hot down here when it was freezing outside? I put my hand against my forehead. Perhaps I was coming down with something.

"Are you alright?" Eliza asked.

I nodded. "Where does this tunnel lead?"

She smiled. "To the other side of the theater." She shone the light straight ahead onto another submarine hatch.

Aha. So, someone would not have to run around the circumference of the theater to get from one side to the other. Either from the orchestra pit or stage left, the murderer could have used this tunnel to make his—or her—escape.

Perhaps it was possible that immediately after her performance, Anna Case could have ducked backstage, run through the tunnel, killed her lover, and then made it back in time to open that curtain.

Wait. What is that? "Stop." I pointed to a recess in the stone wall. "Shine the torch over there."

Eliza obliged.

What in heaven's name? A square object sat up against the wall.

I scooted past Eliza and went to the spot. I lifted the object. "Give me more light."

"It's a cushion from the box seats," Eliza said examining it. "Remember? We had them at the back of our seats."

"Yes, a golden cushion." I turned it over. The faint scent of citrus. Was I imagining things? I sniffed the pillow. It smelled familiar. Archie. How odd. Probably lots of men wore that same cologne.

"Powder burns." Eliza stuck her finger in the center of the pillow. "A golden cushion with a bullet hole in it."

I examined the hole. She was right. "That explains the golden thread on the barrel of the gun. The pillow was used as a silencer... or perhaps along with a silencer."

16

USS SACHEM

Americans didn't know how to do proper tea. Instead, we got watery tea, no biscuits, sweets slathered in icing and nothing to nibble on except peanuts.

"Cocktails are the thing here," Clifford said. "I think the Americans are onto something." He sipped his martini. "Try it." He pushed the cocktail in my direction.

I scowled.

"Come on, be a sport." He tilted his head. "If you try it, I'll tell you what I found out about the waiter."

"Oh, alright." I took a sip. Egad. Disgusting. It was all I could do to swallow it instead of spitting it out. I pushed the glass back. "I'll stick to watery tea, thank you."

"May I try it, Uncle Clifford?" Eliza batted her lashes.

Clifford passed the glass to her.

"No," I intervened. "Cocktails in the afternoon are not proper for young ladies."

"In France, gentlemen offer drinks to young ladies—"

"They also give the French disease," I interrupted her.

"Mrs. Parker drinks cocktails." Clifford raised his glass. "Drinks for women and all that rot."

"Precisely." I removed my notebook from my practical over-sized bag where I'd transferred my spy gear for the day's adventures. Enough chitchat. "Let's get down to business, shall we?" I turned to Clifford. "Your turn. What did you find out about the waiter?"

Clifford flashed a conspiratorial grin. "Well, you'll never guess. You know I went back to the restaurant, and first, I talked—"

"The waiter?" I tapped my pencil on the table.

"Ah, yes." He cleared his throat. "I had a look around, you see, and—"

"Clifford." I narrowed my brows. "Get to the point."

"The waiter doesn't exist." He took a sip of his cocktail. "Seems he appeared out of the woodwork and disappeared just as fast."

"Interesting." I made a note. "So, the note was probably from the murderer and not from Edison... unless..." Edison was the murderer.

"What about the gold cushion with a bullet hole?" Eliza was munching on some overly sweet concoction the Americans called a cookie. At least the girl was eating something. "Mr. Fredricks must have used that cushion to silence the shot."

"Then why did we find it in the tunnel?" I broke the edge off one of Eliza's cookies and tasted it. Ack. Too sweet indeed. I dropped the rest back onto her plate. "Fredricks didn't have time to get from our box to Mr. Edison's box and visit the tunnel before I found him with the murder weapon in his hands." The scent of citrus came back to me. I pushed thoughts of Archie from my mind.

"And if he disposed of the pillow in the tunnel, then why not the gun too?" Clifford stabbed the air with his finger.

"Right." I made another note in my book. "The killer used the pillow to silence the gun, threw us off track with the banger, and framed Fredricks."

"Unless Mr. Fredricks is guilty." Eliza munched her cookies.

My investigation of Edison could wait no longer. Only he could tell me whether he sent the note to Fredricks and when he last saw Schweitzer alive. Indeed, he might be able to shed some light on Schweitzer's involvement with the great phenol plot if I was right about the phonographic records requiring phenol for their manufacture.

"I say. Devilishly ingenious." Clifford drained his cocktail, leaving only the hideous olive languishing in the bottom of the glass. "Whoever killed Hugo Schweitzer used the pillow and then hid it in the underground tunnel."

"Indeed." I recircled Anna Case on my list of suspects. "Taking the long route from the stage to the box, Miss Case could not have committed the deed and gotten back to the stage to open the curtain and seal her alibi. But using the shortcut she could have."

"You think she had the gun concealed in her opera gown?" Eliza asked.

"And the pillow?" Clifford stabbed at the olive with a toothpick. "Surely Miss Case couldn't have concealed a seat cushion in her gown." Clifford huffed. "That beautiful creature is no more capable of murder than sweet Eliza here."

"She could have used a cushion from the box seats." Eliza took another cookie. My, the girl had a sweet tooth. "But since we already know Mr. Fredricks is the killer, this entire conversation is superfluous." Poppy made a little growling sound.

The girl's insistence on Fredricks's guilt was getting old; obviously Poppy agreed with me.

"I didn't notice any pillows missing from Mr. Edison's box." I closed my eyes and recreated the scene in my memory. Although my photographic memory was more reliable on paper, it was also imprinted with a spatial grid, a sort of geometrical memory. No. In my mind's eye, all the cushions were accounted for. Anyway, I'm sure I would have noticed if any were missing as I sat in that bloody box with Fredricks, waiting for the constable to haul us down to the nick.

"Who else is on your list?" Clifford asked.

"If we cross off Fredricks, that leaves Mr. Thomas Edison and Mrs. Dorothy Parker." I shrugged. "Neither has an obvious motive." Although given the row between Mr. Edison and Mr. Schweitzer right before the murder, he was the more likely suspect. He was working for the navy. Perhaps he'd found out Schweitzer was a German spy and disposed of him. And then there was the great phenol plot. I shook my head. It just didn't add up.

"In addition to the murder, we have the frame-up." I drew a square around Fredricks's name. "Who would want to frame Fredricks?" Then again, who wouldn't want to frame Fredricks? Even I wanted to frame Fredricks.

Someone sent him a note conveniently asking him to come to Mr. Edison's box at the very moment the banger went off and he'd been caught red-handed. Had Mr. Edison sent that note? In which case, was Edison the murderer? Or had someone else forged the note? Yes. I really had to interview Mr. Edison as soon as possible.

"Do you think Mr. Hoover could be a suspect?" Clifford asked. "He seemed like a nice enough chap, but you never know."

"You really think so, Uncle Clifford?" Eliza asked. "I found him insufferable. All he talked about was immorality and insuring women don't get the vote... as if suffrage caused venereal disease."

"Really, Eliza!" Of course, I knew soldiers were returning home with the French disease. And surely the girl was right. Votes for women had nothing to do with it. "Is such coarse language necessary?"

Poppy barked. I reached over and patted the dog's head.

"Sorry, Aunt Fiona." She bit her lip. "I'm just repeating what Edgar said." She shook her head and gazed down at her plate. As usual, she'd barely touched her food.

"He did appear to upset both Mr. Edison and Mr. Schweitzer." I held the pencil in the air ready to write. "What motive could he possibly have?"

"Perhaps Mr. Schweitzer had more vices than we know." Clifford grinned.

"If John Edgar Hoover plans to eliminate every man with a vice, there won't be a man left alive." I wrote his name on my list and added an asterisk.

"Yes, I suppose men do have more vices than women," Clifford said, thoughtfully.

"If women succeed and get the vote," Eliza said, "perhaps we will be allowed more vices." She chuckled. Poppy sat up and licked the girl's chin.

Really. Dogs at tea. What would be next?

I squinted at her. "The world doesn't need any more vice from either sex." I closed my notebook. "What we need is a plan." I slid my notebook back into my bag. My plan was to lose Eliza and Clifford tout de suite and then visit Edison's laboratory on my own and in disguise. Yes, I had the perfect costume. My pulse quickened just thinking about my mustache collection.

Like Captain Hall, Clifford found my disguises laughable. So,

I needed to get rid of him somehow. Then, once again, I would prove him wrong. My disguises were quite effective.

"If you'll excuse me." I laid my napkin on the table. "I will be back in a moment."

Clifford gave me a knowing smile. He supposed I was off to the loo. If he only knew.

* * *

For a secret mission, it didn't take long to find out where Edison was working for the navy. The hotel concierge was only too happy to tell me about the USS *Sachem* and Edison's invention of smoke-screens to camouflage ships.

Between coughs and some wheezing—poor chap—the little man nattered on about Mr. Edison, including some hideous stories of experiments with electrocution involving stray animals around his Menlo Park laboratory.

I shuddered.

When the concierge started a story about the electrocution of an elephant to prove the dangers of Mr. Edison's rival's form of electricity, I held up my hand to stop him. I guided him back to the matter of Mr. Edison's naval experiments.

It was known all over the city that Edison had a special laboratory aboard the private yacht, which was anchored in Long Island Sound. The helpful concierge explained that he was a navy man himself before his lungs gave out on him.

I tipped the little man, an American custom as per instructed by Valentine's guidebook, and then went back to the table.

When I arrived, Clifford was extolling the virtues of red meat for the health of the blood. Eliza was chasing a piece of potato around her plate with a fork.

"I think I might take a nap," I said.

"I bought the new issue of *Vogue*," Eliza said. "I'll join you in the room."

I frowned.

"I promise not to make a peep." Eliza put her finger to her lips. "And neither will Poppy." She lifted the puppy and kissed her wet little nose. "Right, Pop-pop?"

Sigh.

The most difficult aspect of getting aboard the USS *Sachem* was shaking loose Eliza and Clifford. The pair were glued to me like two strips of adhesive tape. I'd gotten rid of Clifford... now for Eliza.

While Eliza was enjoying her fashion magazine, I took the opportunity to slip out of the room. "I need some aspirin from the gift shop." I held my hand to my forehead.

"I have some." Eliza dropped her magazine on the bed and jumped up.

"Thank you, dear." I smiled. "I think I'll just go down and get some juice."

"We'll come with you." She scooped up Poppy.

"That's not necessary." I waved her away. "I'll be back in a jiffy. You and Poppy enjoy your pretty pictures."

* * *

Decidedly naughty, I sought out the help of Mr. Billy Buck. Turns out, he had left several messages for Eliza with the front desk. Apparently, she had refused to read them.

Being a dutiful "aunt," I read them for her. And I took the liberty of answering them too. Within the hour—after several trips back and forth to the lobby—I'd arranged for an outing to the famous Metropolitan Museum of Art for late this afternoon.

It was all set. Mr. Buck would pick up Eliza at the hotel. And

Clifford would go along to chaperone. Now, all I had to do was persuade Eliza and Clifford to go along with my scheme.

Back in the room, I presented my idea to Eliza.

"You contacted Billy?" Eliza's mouth fell open. "Why?"

Poppy let out a little yelp. If I didn't know better, I'd say the furry little creature was jealous. Whenever Eliza even mentioned a lad, the pup objected.

"I thought you liked the boy." A little matchmaking in the service of espionage seemed warranted.

"I can manage my own love life." Eliza's ringlets danced when she shook her head. "Really, Aunt Fiona."

It was jolly odd that Eliza was so keen on him one minute and now couldn't care less.

"This will give you a chance to make up." I smiled.

"Oh, alright, if it will make you happy." Eliza caressed the pup, who was curled up on her lap. "I'll go to the museum with Billy."

"And Clifford will chaperone." I clapped my hands together. "Perfect."

Clifford was happy enough to make the trek to the museum. When the hour arrived, and Mr. Billy Buck was waiting in the lobby, I begged off the excursion with a headache.

"But Aunt Fiona," Eliza said. "The museum was your idea."

"I know, dear." I patted her little gloved hand. "You go and enjoy yourselves." I glanced at Mr. Buck, who was gazing at Eliza with that look only first love can muster.

"I'll take good care of her, Aunt Fiona," Billy said.

I forced a smile. I wasn't keen on his calling me "Aunt Fiona." Seems the girl had started an infelicitous trend.

The warm glow of Eliza's cheeks suggested that she was happy to see Billy. Hopefully, he would keep her distracted for the rest of the afternoon, while I snuck aboard Mr. Edison's yacht... incognito. Before I left London, I'd purchased the perfect outfit from Angel's Fancy Dress. And I couldn't wait to try it out.

After the trio was safely tucked into a bright yellow taxicab, I went in search of the wheezing concierge. With his help, I secured passage on a water taxi to carry "a friend" out to the USS *Sachem*... but only after I endured a veritable lecture on the origins of the yacht's name, from the chief of the Lenni-Lenape tribe, Tammany Sachem, after whom New York's influential Tammany Society was named.

"Tammany Hall. A true American institution," the concierge said with a cough. "The ultimate patriots."

I bit my tongue. As a schoolgirl, I could swear that I learned the first colonists in America had massacred native peoples like Chief Tammany. Oh, the irony.

As soon as I extricated myself from the chatty concierge, I dashed back to my room to change.

I assembled my costume: white trousers, starched shirt, white tunic with gold crown and anchor buttons, and polished black men's shoes—the smallest I could find—and a white cap with an officer's red, gold, and black anchor badge. My pulse quickened as I examined my outfit. Yes, this would do nicely.

Since my first assignment, I hadn't had the opportunity to grow my hair out. My once fine auburn locks were shorn stubble on my head. I looked a bit like a hedgehog. At least for the outing I had planned for this afternoon, I would not need a wig.

Good thing, too. I had a nasty rash on my scalp from wearing wigs for the last two months. It was a relief to air out my scalp.

I retrieved my handlebar mustache from my small case. My favorite. Spirit glue. Not exactly my favorite. The smell was like a pungent old friend... one who did not bathe regularly.

I slipped off my day frock and slid into the persona of Captain Rathbone of the Royal Navy, research division, on his way to inspect the progress of our allies on naval camouflage. At the dressing table, I applied the glue, pressed on the mustache, and then admired my reflection in the looking glass.

White pressed, shipshape and Bristol fashion. I smiled. Yes. This would do quite nicely indeed.

Blast. When I stepped outside into the brisk November wind, I changed my mind. I'd forgotten to purchase a men's overcoat. Now what? Perhaps my friend the concierge could help.

Hugging myself and shivering, I returned to the lobby in search of my wheezy friend. If I could convince him to let me into Clifford's room, I could borrow one of his overcoats.

The concierge was sitting at his desk reading a newspaper.

"Excuse me." I smiled. "Could I trouble you again?"

He looked up from his paper.

"You see, my husband locked me out and I need to get back in our room." I was becoming so accustomed to posing as someone's wife that the prevarication came all too easily. "I'm hoping you might help me out one last time."

"I'm sorry?" he said, his eyes wide.

"I appreciate all you've done for me. But if you could just let me into our room, I'll never bother you again." I tried Eliza's trick and batted my lashes at him.

"I'm sorry, sir." He squinted at me. "Do I know you?"

Bloody hell. I put my hands on my head, which was covered in a navy captain's cap. My mouth fell open. I stood blinking at him, absolutely speechless. The risk of becoming too accustomed to charades was forgetting when you were playing a part.

"Pardon me." I turned on my heels and restrained myself from running to the nearest exit. With all the control I could muster, I walked across the lobby. When I was well out of sight of the bell desk, I leaned against the wall to catch my breath. *Golly, what an idiot.*

Plan B. I went back up to my own room, fetched my own coat, and changed into my own hat. What to do about the blasted mustache? It couldn't be helped. I stuffed the captain's cap into my largest handbag and then went back down to the lobby for round two.

As the doorman hailed a taxicab for me, I stood stock still, my bag in one hand and my other hand across my upper lip. Once I was safely seated in the back of the taxi, I let out an audible sigh of relief.

I really did have to learn to be more careful. I had to stop dashing off half-cocked. If only I wasn't always in such a hurry. The life of espionage was not for the faint of heart.

The advantage of being British was that I'd learned from my father at a tender age to keep a stiff upper lip whatever the circumstances. I touched my bushy upper lip. It was, after all, the English way.

By the time I arrived at the docks, the sun was already low in the sky. I would have to hurry if I wanted to get back to the hotel before dark. I asked the driver to wait for me. To ensure that he did, I promised him three times the fare with half up front and the other half when I returned.

I quickly changed my hat and left my practical bag in the taxi. I considered going without my overcoat, but I couldn't bear the thought of the trip across the water without it. I would have to leave it in the water taxi and bribe the driver with triple fare to come back and get me.

It was a dodgy business. But it couldn't be helped.

17

EDISON'S LABORATORY

A midshipman—or some such person in a naval uniform—met the water taxi. He was as crisp and smart as a folded flag.

I, on the other hand, had just crossed Long Island Sound with gale force winds in a motorboat the size of a dinghy. A bit queasy and nearly frozen, despite my overcoat, I was eager to get this mission underway. "Permission to come aboard," I said, conjuring my deepest tenor. I peered at his name tag. "Sailor Weston."

"Private first class, sir." He saluted. "And you are?"

I returned his salute, and then glanced down at my chest to see if I too had a name tag. I did. "Arbuthnot." I read the plate aloud.

"Rear Admiral Arbuthnot." He gave another salute.

Oh, my. *I'm a rear admiral and not a captain.* In my defense, the uniforms were similar. Still, I needed to brush up on my military hierarchy.

"I'm sorry, sir." He stood as straight as a statue. "But I have no record of your visit."

"Surprise visit," I said. "Lower the gangplank, if you please."

"But sir—"

I cut him off. "Or should I report you to your superiors?"

He gave me an apologetic look but didn't budge.

"I'm from the Royal British Navy, here to learn about Mr. Edison's progress with ship camouflage." I scanned the length of the yacht, which was considerable. "May I speak with Mr. Edison?" If he was here, I would interview him. If not, I would find some excuse to search the vessel. Whichever, I knew Rear Admiral Arbuthnot would be more successful than Miss Fiona Figg. If I'd learned anything from my short career in espionage, it was that whatever the hierarchy, military or otherwise, women were always at the bottom.

Either Mr. Edison had some wealthy benefactors, or the American navy commandeered jolly nice private steamers. The two-story yacht had two towering masts and a massive steampipe in between them. From the water, the bowed shape of the hull echoed in its roof made the yacht look like it was smiling.

"Yes, sir." Although he still stood erect, his stance relaxed somewhat. "Is Mr. Edison expecting you, sir? I don't think he's here today, but I can check."

Aha! The name Edison was the key.

"Yes, I met with him recently at the opera, and he invited me aboard."

"The opera?" His eyes went wide.

"Indeed, Carnegie Music Hall, Saturday evening." I shivered. Without my overcoat, I was deuced cold. *Hurry up, man. Let me on this blasted yacht.*

"The night that man died." Sailor Weston's gaze was miles away.

"Indeed, the very night." Perhaps he knew something. "Did you know the man, by chance? He was a chemist friend of Mr. Edison's."

He jolted into action and lowered the gangplank.

About bloody time, too. I was half-frozen. I nodded to the water taxi driver, who already had extorted triple fare to keep my overcoat and return for me in forty minutes.

"Apologies, Rear Admiral." The sailor helped me up the plank. "I didn't realize you were a guest of Mr. Edison's." His fair cheeks colored.

I narrowed my eyes, assessing his countenance. Ever since I'd mentioned the opera, he'd changed. "Did you know Mr. Hugo Schweitzer?" I asked. "Perhaps he visited Mr. Edison here?"

The sailor nodded but avoided eye contact.

I suspected there was more to the story. Still holding onto the chain railing of the gangplank, I stepped down from the plank onto the yacht. My teeth were chattering, and my blasted mustache was blowing in the wind.

"Might we go inside?" I was desperate for a nice hot cuppa and worried my mustache might fly off.

"Yes, sir." The sailor gestured toward a door. "Of course, sir. This way, sir."

Obviously, being a rear admiral had its advantages, especially one who was a personal friend of Mr. Edison.

He led me to a small reception area. "If you'll wait here, I'll fetch someone... else."

"Just a moment, sailor." I stood, arms akimbo, and gave him a stern look.

"Yes, sir." He stopped in his tracks and then turned back to face me.

"Was Mr. Hugo Schweitzer a regular visitor here?" I used my most authoritative tone.

"Yes, sir."

"And his business?"

"I couldn't say, sir." Again, he gazed into the air over my head instead of making eye contact. "You would have to ask Mr. Edison, sir." Maybe soldiers were like dogs—the betas didn't make eye contact with the alphas. "Unfortunately, Mr. Edison is not aboard now. But I'll fetch someone to give you a tour. If you'll just wait here, sir."

"Thank you, sailor." I saluted him. "At ease." After all my fibbing, it was a relief Edison wasn't here. And now, a look around the lab could prove enlightening.

The sailor stared at me for a few seconds before darting out of the room.

While I was alone, I took the opportunity to snoop. The interior of the yacht was made of lovely carved wood. Even fitted out for war, underneath, the USS *Sachem* was still a luxury boat.

Unfortunately, there was not much to explore in the reception area. The small room was sparse, with only a desk and two chairs. The surface of the desk was bare except for a small lamp. I tried the top drawer. Locked.

Glancing around, I removed my lockpick set from my jacket pocket. I slipped the tension wrench from the leather pouch and slid it into the lock. The lock gave, and I quickly opened the drawer. I tucked my wrench back into the kit and popped the kit into my pocket.

The drawer contained only a pencil and a large notebook. Upon examination, the notebook proved to be a guest book. I flipped through the pages, taking note of the visitors. I didn't have time to digest the information, so I filed it away in my memory for later recall. I did notice that Hugo Schweitzer's name appeared several times in the recent past.

The sound of footfalls encouraged me to drop the notebook back in the desk drawer. My heart jolted when another sailor appeared in the doorway. I shut the drawer with my hip, stepped away from the desk, and smiled innocently.

The new sailor wore a blue and white uniform much like the first chap, only this fellow had more stripes on his shoulders. Perhaps I was climbing the chain of command.

"I'm told you would like a tour of the laboratory." His form was too bulky to stand as straight as the first lad, but he did his best. "Mr. Edison is out for the day, but I can show you some of what we're doing here." He stepped forward and held out his hand. "I'm Lieutenant Commander Washington."

"Rear Admiral Arbuthnot." I took his hand and gave it a manly shake. His palm was sweaty. Cringe.

His lips tightened, and he withdrew his hand. "Please follow me." His spectacles had slid down his nose and he pushed them back up.

After he'd turned his back on me, I wiped my hand off on my trousers.

Lieutenant Commander Washington led me down a narrow windowless hallway. He stopped halfway down, pulled a key from a ring hanging off his belt, and opened a door. "This is the camouflage research laboratory." He held the door for me. "Mr. Edison is a genius."

As I stepped into the laboratory, my nostrils were assaulted by a strong acrid smell. So strong, in fact, my eyes burned. "Smoke-screens?" I asked with a cough.

"The idea is to create enough smoke around the ship that the enemy can't find it." The Lieutenant Commander's voice was full of excitement. He had to be involved in the research to be this passionate.

"You work with Mr. Edison?" I squeezed tears out of my eyes and then wiped my cheeks with the backs of my hands. The horrible smell was eroding my composure. "What is that smell?"

"Titanium tetrachloride." He loped across the room to a set of bubbling beakers. "We restrict air to the boiler, which produces thick black smoke. But because it's black, it absorbs heat from the sun and rises and leaves the ship visible. By adding titanium, we produce a white low-lying cloud." He beamed with pride.

"I see." I had no blooming idea what he was talking about. "Brilliant." Starting to get used to the smell, I circled the room, taking in the contents.

Long tables were covered with tubes, jars, notebooks, boxes, and an assortment of other unidentifiable paraphernalia. An occasional hissing sound came from something in the corner that looked like an oven.

I had no clue what I was looking at... or looking for. "Is—er, was—the chemist, Mr. Schweitzer, involved in this research?" The very dead chemist.

Lieutenant Commander Washington gave me a quizzical look. "Did you know Hugo?"

"Mr. Edison introduced me to him at the opera," I lied through my teeth.

"Tragic." He fiddled with a tube leading to a beaker full of orange steam. "No." He turned to me. "Hugo was more interested in our projects at Menlo Park."

"You work with Mr. Edison at Menlo Park?" Electrocuting stray animals, from what I'd heard. Hideous. What kind of men did such a thing?

"I've worked with Mr. Edison for years." He smiled. "Long before the navy and this war."

"How interesting." I twirled my mustache for effect. "Electricity, alternating currents, and all that?"

"Oh, no." He stepped closer. "Mr. Edison is a champion of direct current. It's Westinghouse and Tesla who propose alternating current."

"The war of the currents," I said under my breath. "Like Mr. Schweitzer's chemists' war."

"Chemists' war?" He pushed his spectacles up his nose again.

I tacked away from the chemists' war. "What was Mr. Schweitzer's business at Menlo Park, if I may ask?"

"Mr. Edison makes recordings." His hands danced as he talked. "Perhaps you saw his tone test at the opera." He smiled. Luckily for me, unlike the first chap, Lieutenant Commander Washington was eager to chat about his work with Mr. Edison.

"Indeed." I nodded. "Jolly impressive." I held my hands behind my back, trying to imitate the posture of the seaman who had greeted me.

"Those phonographic recordings require a substance called phenol—"

I gasped and my hand flew to my mouth.

The great phenol plot. Was Mr. Edison involved too?

"Are you quite alright, Rear Admiral?"

"Yes, quite." I cleared my throat. "You were saying about phenol?"

"Very clever, actually." A beaker in hand, he walked over to a small sink. "Mr. Edison devised an ingenious way to make carbolic acid, phenol, from coal tar and—"

"And Mr. Schweitzer needed phenol to make Bayer aspirin," I interrupted before he took me into the briars of chemistry again.

"Why, yes." He emptied a beaker into the sink. "Mr. Edison made arrangements to sell surplus phenol to Mr. Schweitzer."

"How ingenious." Edison was making phonograph records out of the stuff. And Schweitzer was making aspirin out of it. What in blazes did that have to do with the war or the Kaiser? "What about the navy?" I asked.

"The navy?" He stopped scrubbing at the sink and looked over at me.

"Isn't the navy interested in phenol?" I noticed I'd been troubling the name plate attached to my jacket and abruptly dropped my arms to my sides. "For explosives."

"Yes, but phenol is in short supply and—"

"Didn't you just say that Mr. Edison has a surplus?" Practicing interrogation, I was developing a nasty habit of interrupting.

"Not after selling to Bayer Aspirin." He tilted his head. "Mr. Edison can't really spare any more than he already has—"

"Why not sell to the American navy?" I asked. "Surely it's his patriotic duty."

"Mr. Edison isn't a pacificist by any means." His face was flushed. "But he would rather his phenol treat soldiers' ailments than kill them."

"No matter what side they're on?"

A beaker slipped out of his hands and broke onto the floor. An orange cloud spread throughout the room. Suddenly, I felt like I was breathing in razor blades.

Coughing, I backed out into the hallway.

Lieutenant Commander Washington dashed out behind me. "Apologies. How clumsy of me."

The noxious smell had snuck out behind him. He slammed the door shut. "Let's get some air." He coughed.

I followed him down the hallway, through the reception area, and back out on deck.

The water taxi was a black silhouette against a rust-colored sky. The cold breeze stung my cheeks. But I was glad for the fresh air. "Thank you for the tour, Lieutenant Commander." I held out my hand. "It was most enlightening."

"At your service, Rear Admiral." He stood erect and gave me a parting salute.

I returned the salute.

Quickly, he set down the gangplank.

The water below churned and swirled.

I shuddered, remembering the poor chap thrown overboard at sea. I hoped he was dead before he went in.

I held the chains as I slid along the plank, doing my best not to fall into Long Island Sound.

18

ESCAPE ARTIST

At least the taxicab was warm. I pulled my overcoat tight around my torso and stuffed my frozen fingers between the folds of the wool fabric.

The sun had set. A violet twilight provided the backdrop for streetlamps, their light sparkling against the snowy streets. The contrast between the beautiful tableau of the city at twilight and the jumbled sounds of horns and horses was jarring.

I needed to concoct some story for Clifford and Eliza, but my mind was occupied with what I'd just discovered at Edison's floating laboratory.

I chuckled to myself, chuffed with how well my disguise had worked. My theater teacher was right. I really did make a jolly good man.

This was no time to bask in the glory of my success. I had a killer to catch... and an adversary to liberate.

Sigh. Why in the world was I helping Fredricks? I still couldn't fathom the hold he had over me. I shivered. No. He had no hold over me. It was only my commitment to the truth that drove me to prove his innocence... if he *was* innocent. If not, I would prove his guilt.

Either way, on behalf of all women, I was determined to solve the case and *prove myself* to Captain Hall.

I wondered if Fredricks knew what Hugo Schweitzer had been doing with Edison. Certainly, Fredricks would have known if Schweitzer was a German spy. For all I knew, they'd been working together. I thought of those rings they both wore, the ones with the panther insignias. A secret fraternity of German spies?

I would make another trip to visit Fredricks and ask him. Not that I would get a straight answer. He might not lie, but he never told the truth either.

The taxicab dropped me in front of the hotel. I handed the driver the last of my American money. The way he grinned at me, it must have been more than enough.

At this point, I was so knackered and cold, all I wanted was a warm bath and a clean upper lip. My blasted mustache was itching something awful.

Hugging myself, I dashed into the hotel and out of the frigid New York winter. Give me dreary old Blighty any day.

I'd only taken a few steps when I heard an uproarious commotion coming from the lounge. What in the world?

My curiosity got the better of my exhaustion, and I had to investigate. A handful of men stood just outside the lounge peering in. I joined them to see what they were gawking at.

I peeked around the shoulder of a rather bulky gentleman. My gaze fell upon several familiar faces, including Mrs. Sanger and her co-conspirator, and Miss Anna Case and her redheaded friend. Mrs. Parker sat at the bar, holding a sign that read "Drinks for Women."

Good heavens. The suffragettes had occupied the hotel lounge.

One of the men slapped me on the back. "Have you ever seen such a gaggle of silly geese?"

Stunned, I took a step back. I was about to give the bloke a piece of my mind when I recognized his broad nose and crooked mouth. Mr. John Edgar Hoover. The young man from the *Adriatic*, and ringleader of the hecklers at the women's march.

"You show a great deal of interest in the suffragettes, Mr. Hoover." I met his gaze. The way he looked at me gave me the queerest feeling. I had to look away.

"Have we met?" he asked. "You seem to have me at a disadvantage."

Of course, he didn't recognize me, and all the better for it. "Rear Admiral Arbuthnot."

"How did you know my name?"

"From the newspapers." I cleared my throat. "You have an unforgettable face."

"I never forget a face." He smiled. "Especially one as nice as yours."

And I thought Mrs. Parker was fresh.

"What do you have against the suffragettes?" I changed the subject.

"Those radicals will be the undoing of the country." He shook his head as if clearing water from his ears. "It's my job to protect this great country from the likes of those subversives."

"Do you have sisters, Mr. Hoover?" I felt like ripping off my mustache and revealing myself. "I know you have a mother."

"My dear mother knows right from wrong," he smirked. "Guns and tanks are not the greatest threat to our security." He jabbed the air in the general direction of the lounge. "It's these damned women."

"I don't think you'll get far with that attitude." I shook my finger at him. "Women are the future. Where would you be without them?"

"I'd be just fine, thank you." He adjusted his tie. He was well-dressed, I'd give him that. He had excellent personal hygiene. His moral hygiene was another story.

"I say. What's all this?" Clifford's familiar voice sent a chill up my spine.

Ever since he'd discovered my disguises, he'd been harder to deceive. Not impossible. Still, I didn't want to take the chance of ending my triumphant mission in embarrassment, especially in front of Mr. Hoover. Then again, maybe he'd change his tune if he knew he was speaking with a "damned woman." Harumph.

"Votes for women!" The chant echoed through the lobby.

"Good Lord." Clifford stuffed his hands into his trouser pockets. "Not this again."

"If I have my way," Mr. Hoover said, "I'll clear the country of this sort of scourge."

"How do you plan to do that?" I couldn't resist.

"Records." He smiled. "Never underestimate the power of paper and an immaculate filing system."

Speechless, my head jerked back of its own accord. Blimey. I couldn't have said it better myself.

"Depends," I said when I regained my composure. "Vindictive and mean-spirited gossip is never worth the paper it's printed on."

I thought of the society pages of the New York newspapers.

"You're English," he said.

At that, Clifford turned to face us. Blast.

I stared down at my shoes.

"Have you heard of the game of fox and hounds?" Mr. Hoover sniffed and put his nose in the air.

"Righty ho." Clifford smiled. "We used to play fox and hounds at Harrow. It was great fun and I—"

Mr. Hoover held his hand up. "The fox always leaves a trail," he sneered. "And I am an excellent bloodhound."

Weasel, more like. "Good evening, gentlemen." I gave a crisp salute and left them to their jeering.

In the lift, I peeled off my mustache and stashed it in my pocket. After all, I didn't want to give Eliza a fright. Ouch. The blasted thing stung like the Dickens. I removed my captain's cap, which I'd learned was actually a rear admiral's, and tucked it under my arm under my overcoat.

Funny. Mr. Hoover never commented on the fur collar or pearl buttons on my coat. Hopefully, he didn't notice. And since the coat was long, perhaps Eliza wouldn't notice I was wearing trousers.

I knocked softly to warn her of my arrival, and then opened the door.

She was lying on top of her bed, reading a fashion magazine. Poppy was curled up beside her.

When she saw me, she let out a shriek. Poppy jumped up and barked.

Good heavens. What had I forgotten? I'd removed my mustache. I'd removed my cap. What had I missed? I looked myself up and down.

Eliza laughed. "Aunt Fiona, what happened to your hair?"

I touched my head. Right. The poor girl had never seen my shorn head. I'd been diligent in wrapping my head in a scarf or wearing a wig.

"You look like a porcupine who's had a fright," she laughed. "Or stuck its paw in an electrical socket." Tears rolled down her cheeks.

"Come now." I scowled at her. "Calm down." I bolted into the lavatory and shut the door.

Finally, I could relax and be myself again. I removed my overcoat and turned on the tap. Just the sound of the bath running was soothing. I removed Rear Admiral Arbuthnot, folded him neatly, and laid him on the toilet lid.

As I sank down into the warm water, I let out an audible sigh. What a relief.

I'd survived the streets of New York on my own, a trip to the docks, a water taxi ride, and a broken beaker of foul orange gas. Not to mention Mr. Hoover's insults to womankind. I hoped he wasn't further corrupting dear Clifford with his retrograde notions.

Sigh. I closed my eyes, emptied my head, and became one with the water.

The only sounds were the water dripping and the sound of my own breath. I inhaled the scent of lilac soap. Heavenly.

With every breath, the smell of rosewood and charcoal grew stronger. My eyes flew open. My pulse quickened.

No. He couldn't be here. I must be imagining things. Of course, he was in jail... unless they'd let him out. But then why would he be in my room?

"Eliza," I called out.

"Yes," she answered.

Shuffling noises on the other side of the door put me on high alert.

"Is everything okay, Aunt Fiona?" Her voice was louder now.

"Yes, dear." I cleared my throat. "And you? Are you alone?"

"Alone?" she repeated.

I waited. Silence.

"No. Poppy's here too."

Since I could no longer enjoy my bath, I climbed out of the

tub. After a bracing towel off, I wrapped a dry towel around my torso and ventured out of the lav.

Eliza was back on her bed with her furry companion glued to her side. It must be nice to have such a loyal friend. As long as she had Poppy, she'd never be alone.

I grabbed my robe and stood in front of the wardrobe, staring at my clothes.

A recurring dilemma presented itself. Food or sleep? I really needed both but had energy enough for only one.

"Can we go dancing, Aunt Fiona?" Eliza looked up over her magazine. She was wearing her overcoat and adorable pink sailor hat.

"Do you have an invitation to a ball?" Sleep. Definitely sleep. I slid my nightgown off its hanger.

"They have dancing clubs—"

"No, absolutely not." Captain Hall would sack me tout de suite if I said yes.

"But Billy—"

"Proper young ladies do not frequent dancing clubs." I slipped my tired feet into my slippers.

"Dancing strengthens the body and frees the spirit." She closed her magazine. "Or do you think young ladies shouldn't have strong bodies and souls?"

Sigh. I shook my head. "Of course young ladies should be strong." I didn't mention that I'd lifted ten-pound bags of flour to gain muscle for my first assignment and my Dr. Vogel disguise. "There are more wholesome ways to nourish body and soul." I shivered. I couldn't continue this conversation wearing only a towel. "Exercise and reading, my dear."

She held up her fashion magazine. "I am reading."

"Good." I left her pouting and returned to the lav to change into my night clothes. It had been a long day and I was completely exhausted.

When I stepped out of the lav, I got the cold shoulder from Eliza. Still in her coat and hat, she was lying on her bed, facing the wall, cuddling Poppy. The dog looked at me and snarled. Obviously, she was angry with me too.

So be it. I'd been entrusted with the girl's safety, and I took it seriously... and more to the point, I didn't want to lose my job at the War Office.

I slipped into bed and closed my eyes. My head was pounding. "Do you mind if we turn off the lights, dear?"

No answer. Shuffling noises. The room went dark. Thank goodness. Sigh.

Was she going to sleep in her clothes and that coat? She might do just out of spite.

As my muscles relaxed, my mind rehearsed the day's events. I'd already experienced them once. Did I really need to obsess over every detail again? I took a deep breath.

I did find that meditating on the day's problems right before sleep often engendered new and creative solutions... remembering the next morning was the trick. I'd been told that writers kept notebooks next to their beds for just such nocturnal inspiration.

I was too tired for notebooks, and my head hurt too much for light or movement. With my hand over my eyes, I lay perfectly still, hoping sleep would come soon and put me out of my misery.

Unfortunately, my mind was not as obedient as my body. I could put my body to bed, but my mind continued to wander.

If Fredricks was innocent, then who killed Hugo Schweitzer? And how was his murder connected to the great phenol plot? Indeed, if Schweitzer was buying phenol from Thomas Edison to make Bayer aspirin, how did that help the Germans? I'd seen the letter from Kaiser Wilhelm. I knew phenol was key. Could it all be a plot to keep the Americans from supplying their troops with explosives? A kind of roundabout way to keep them out of the war?

The scent of citrus stung my memory like a wasp. Archie. Surely Archie wouldn't have killed Schweitzer. Would he? He did vow to stop him no matter the cost. But I saw him waving from across the theater right after the shot was fired. Crikey. Right after the banger went off. No, I wouldn't let my mind go there. It was all too terrible.

No. It was Fredricks. Eliza might be right. Fredricks was guilty. In any case, he had something to do with this mess. And why was he supporting the suffragettes? If he hoped women's votes would mean American withdrawal from the war, then that was a long shot. Was Fredricks playing the long game? If Eliza was right, he was playing both long and short.

Although the Americans had entered the war last April, they had yet to fire a shot. Could the suffragettes have something to do with that? And could Fredricks be counting on them to stop the American war effort?

Perhaps the Kaiser's strategy was to defeat the Americans indirectly. Get them out of the war. Cut off the supply of phenol for explosives by diverting it to aspirin.

I rubbed my temples. Yes, aspirin was key. I got up to fetch some. A dose of phenol was just what I needed.

Stumbling around in the dark wouldn't do. Poppy must have felt the same way. She started barking. If Eliza had been asleep, she wouldn't be now. I might as well turn on the light.

I felt for the switch on the dressing table lamp and twisted it on. It took a second for my eyes to adjust to the light. I glanced over at the barking dog.

Holy Mary, mother of God.

The girl was gone.

I quickly threw on the first frock I found, and then dashed down the hall to Clifford's room.

When Clifford opened the door, he gasped. "Good Lord, what's happened?" He was wearing a plaid bathrobe and house slippers.

"The girl." The words caught in my throat. "She's gone."

"Your hair." He stood staring at me. He was a fine one to talk. What little hair he had was sticking straight up.

Heavens. He'd seen me without my wig before. You'd think he'd be used to it. Still, I'd best grab a wig before we went out searching for Eliza.

"And what about your hair?" I reached out and smoothed a wayward strand. "Get dressed. I'll be right back."

I sprinted back to my room, tugged on my blonde bob, and threw my coat over my clothes. I didn't have time to match my hat to my dress, so I had grabbed the first one I saw, a pink cloche with ruffled ribbons... one of Eliza's frilly numbers.

On the way out the door, I ran into Clifford. He was dressed in full evening kit with his overcoat slung over his arm and a fedora in his hand.

"Where did she go at this time of night?" he asked, frantically.

It must have finally sunk in that the girl was AWOL.

19

CURTAIN CALL

Clifford and I had searched every inch of the hotel looking for Eliza.

My friend, the wheezy concierge, was on duty. When I approached his desk, his eyes filled with alarm—no doubt a mirror of my own.

I must have looked a sight.

"Have you seen my niece?" I wound my glove around my finger. "She's gone missing."

"Pretty girl," Clifford said. "About... how old would you say she is?" He turned to me.

"Eighteen." I glanced around the lobby to see if I could spot her. Where could the girl have gone? "She was wearing a peach-colored overcoat and a pink sailor hat."

"You mean Miss Eliza." He smiled. "I called a taxicab to take her to Carnegie Music Hall." He leaned closer and whispered. "I think she's meeting her fella there."

Oh no. "It's my fault." I shouldn't have encouraged Billy Buck. What was I thinking? "Please call us a taxicab." I realized I was wringing my hands and stopped.

"Carnegie Music Hall?" He coughed.

I nodded.

"We aren't dressed for the opera," Clifford said, looking me up and down.

"You mean *I'm* not dressed for the opera." After the day I'd had, I was lucky to be dressed at all. I touched my head. At least I'd remembered to tug on a wig and grab my bag.

* * *

I was in such a state, I didn't remember how we'd gotten to Carnegie Hall. I knew we'd taken a taxicab, but my thoughts were a tornado of worry and regret. I should have kept better track of the girl. I shouldn't have been so concerned about myself, and more concerned about her. I was going to throttle her when I found her.

Clifford purchased tickets, which turned out to be free. An usher handed us programs and clicked her tongue as she showed us to our seats in the very back of the orchestra section.

To my surprise, there was no concert at Carnegie Music Hall. Instead, the suffragettes were having a series of lectures. The fancy gowns and evening jackets of opera night were replaced with red, white, and blue sashes and placards proclaiming "Votes for Women."

"Good Lord." Clifford dropped into his seat. "You can't get away from them. Like carpet beetles, they're everywhere."

I ignored the infelicitous comparison to insects and scanned the audience for a pink hat.

Luckily, I still had my opera glasses in my practical bag... along with Mata Hari's gun, my lockpick kit, my spy lipstick... and the strange thing Poppy had found on deck.

Miss Carrie Chapman Catt was on stage, lecturing passionately on why suffragettes should not be violently force-fed or treated like common criminals. "They are political prisoners and should be treated as such."

"Lock them up for good!" a small group of men heckled from the sidelines.

I whipped my opera glasses out of my bag and peered at the group. Sure enough, Comstock's Crusaders, again. And the leader of the pack was Mr. John Edgar Hoover.

It figured.

They had matching uniforms of blue suits, white shirts, and red ties with gold tie clips sporting tiny American flags. Obviously, they fancied themselves the patriots here.

The auditorium lights dimmed, making it deuced difficult to tell one silhouette from another. With my opera glasses glued to my eyes, I scanned the crowd for Eliza. Where was that girl?

If anything had happened to her, I would... I would... I wiped perspiration from my forehead. I would... be sacked for sure.

It was no use. I couldn't get a clear view from my seat. I scooted past Clifford and then tiptoed up the aisle, stopping at every row to peer at the patrons. As I continued my journey toward the stage, women in the audience glared at me, shushed me, or whispered for me to "sit down."

I swear, they were more tolerant of the Comstock Crusaders than they were of me.

The speaker fell silent, and I felt all eyes turn to me. I must have caused such a distraction that Miss Catt decided to put a stop to it. The house lights went up and ushers from both sides of the auditorium rushed toward me.

Jerking my opera glasses to my face, I took the opportunity of illumination to scan the crowd again, this time aiming the glasses at the balcony and the side boxes.

Good heavens.

There she was. Eliza. In the same stage-right box we'd had last Sunday afternoon. She leaned over the balcony wall, smiling and waving at me. What in heaven's name?

An usher shone a torch in my face. "Miss, you'll have to sit down, or we'll have to ask you to leave." I recognized him as the usher who'd found Fredricks holding the gun next to Schweitzer's dead body.

I took my opportunity as it came. "The night of the, ahem, death, did you see anyone enter or leave the dead man's box?"

He stood blinking at me.

"I was there, remember?"

A look of recognition crossed his face. "I wasn't up there until right before intermission when the lady left."

I nodded encouragingly. "Did you see anyone else?"

"No one, except you, and the man with the gun."

Another usher came up behind me and shushed us.

Cheeks pink with chagrin, the first usher took my elbow. "Please take your seat, ma'am."

I was surrounded. I had no choice but to take my seat until intermission... either that or be forcibly removed from the theater.

"Your ticket, please?" The second usher held out her hand.

"Why don't you remove those rowdy crusaders?" I pointed to the group of hecklers, and then rummaged through my handbag for my ticket.

"Freedom of speech." She examined my ticket.

"Don't I have freedom of speech?"

"You were approaching the stage." She handed me back my ticket. "Words are one thing. Deeds another. We have to protect the speakers." She gestured toward my seat. "No more interruptions, please." She held her finger to her lips like a prickly librarian.

At least I'd found Eliza. Why was she in our box? Had she found something?

Listening to one speaker after another extol the virtues of votes for women, I chomped at the bit. *For goodness sake, give women the vote and let's get on with it.*

Now that I knew where she was, I kept my glasses trained on Eliza. She sat on the edge of her seat with a pair of opera glasses glued to the stage.

I fanned myself with the program, waiting for the blasted thing to end so I could find out what that girl was up to. She'd found something. I knew it.

The next speaker—one Miss Dorothy Payne Whitney Straight Elmhirst—was wearing the most astounding hat, a billowy mauve meringue sitting atop a woven bucket adorned with flowers. I trained my glasses on her for a closer look. The heart-shaped diamond brooch at her throat was precious.

My, but she droned on.

Yes. Women have the right to control their own bodies. Yes. Women have the right to education. They also have a duty to be more concise and get on with it.

I couldn't wait for her to finish.

Thank goodness. The last speaker was announced. Nurse Margaret Sanger. Despite her huge bib collar, Mrs. Sanger's lecture about birth control couldn't keep my attention. "Women should have a say about the future of this country and about the future of their own lives." She bowed slightly.

Finally. The lectures were finished.

Clapping vigorously, I stood up. I couldn't wait to get out of this cramped seat and find Eliza.

"Sit down!" The women behind me were at it again.

I dropped back into my seat lest I be dragged from the theater in handcuffs.

What now? Sigh. Miss Carrie Catt announced a musical number by a special guest soprano. Would this program never end?

Good heavens. I sat up straighter and peered through my glasses.

Miss Anna Case took center stage. Again, she was wearing her flowing red gown and white pearl necklace, as if she intentionally dressed to match the décor of the theater. And there he was. Mr. Edison, wheeling his famous phonographic machine onto the stage.

Like a magician with a trained monkey, Mr. Edison gave his mesmerizing spiel and then commanded the theater lights be dimmed.

Mr. Edison. Ah. Good. At intermission, I would catch him up and ask about the note sent to Fredricks. With any luck, I could determine whether the summons was really from Edison or some impostor planning to frame Fredricks... and, so far, succeeding.

Miss Case's pure unwavering voice pierced the darkness. Seamlessly—for I couldn't hear it—the performance moved back and forth between live voice and the recording.

Thud. A loud noise rocked the theater.

I flinched.

The thud was followed by an uncanny high-pitched scream like the air escaping from a balloon.

Good heavens.

Even the loud thud and high-pitched screech didn't interrupt the singing.

What in the world was happening? Heads turned and the crowd chattered.

The lights went up.

The singing continued. It was most definitely *not* live.

The audience gasped.

For Anna Case lay sprawled out on the stage, smashed under a curtain boom.

My hand flew to my mouth. Had it been an accident? Or... another vile murder.

"Bloody ghastly." Clifford's ruddy cheeks paled. "Poor thing."

If it wasn't an accident, and Anna Case was the victim of foul play, then she no longer topped my list of suspects for the first murder. Could she have known something about her lover's murder that provoked the killer to strike again?

I jumped up and sprang into action. If Anna Case was murdered, then the killer was probably still in this theater. Patrons were fleeing the building. I nearly was trampled trying to move against the herd to get to the stage.

Mr. Edison was kneeling near the body. If it turned out the soprano had been electrocuted, he would be the prime suspect.

"I say," Clifford called after me. "Where are you going?"

I ignored him and continued pushing against the swarm. Grasping the handle of Mata Hari's gun through the fabric of my bag, I dashed into the orchestra pit. I pushed my shoulder against the secret door panel.

Right. The foot button. I stomped on it. Presto. The panel popped open.

I was confronted by the whirring of the generator and that metallic smell... along with an undercurrent of something else. Something acrid. Something familiar. Familiar and foul. The smell of cigar. Stale cigar smoke would cling to men's clothes for all eternity.

I hurried through the machine room, my hand never leaving the gun. I knew from the golden cushion that Hugo Schweitzer's killer had escaped through the tunnel. If we had the same killer, then he might be traversing the tunnel at this very moment.

As I approached the heavy submarine door, my pulse quickened. I threw my body weight into the handle. It wouldn't budge. I dropped my bag on the floor so I could use both hands. I gripped the bloody handle and pushed with all my might.

I thought the veins in my neck might explode. I took a deep breath and jammed on the handle again. The door gave way and I tumbled into the tunnel. I jumped up, brushed myself off, and fetched my bag... and, more to the point, Mata Hari's gun.

Stumbling, I concentrated on seeing in the dark. My eyes hadn't adjusted. The only light was coming from the door I'd left ajar. Right. The torch. I went back for the torch.

Even with the torch, I stumbled along the uneven surface of the tunnel. My heart was racing faster than my feet.

The sound of footfalls stopped me in my tracks. Someone else was in the tunnel. I held my breath and listened. The sounds were getting louder. Was the killer doubling back? Had he heard me too?

Should I turn around and run? Or keep going and face a murderer on my own in the dark underground where no one would hear me scream? I swallowed hard and withdrew the gun from my bag.

Here goes. I extinguished the torch and laid it on the ground. My hand trembled as I held the gun out in front of me. Slowly, I tiptoed toward the footfalls, which continued to get closer.

Gun first, I rounded a corner. "Stop, or I'll shoot."

A bright light shone in my face. The killer was blinding me with a torch beam.

"Aunt Fiona?"

Oh, my word. "Eliza?" I shielded my eyes with my hand.

She lowered the torch and trotted to my side. "Great minds think alike."

Forgetting all about my earlier vexation, I wrapped her in a tight embrace. "I don't know what I would have done if something had happened to you."

"Don't worry about me," she said into my shoulder.

"I'm worried about my job." I held her at arm's length and examined her. "Your uncle would have my head—and my job—if I let any harm come to you."

She giggled and pointed at my hand.

"And stop that incessant giggling." I followed her gaze. Mata Hari's gun. Quickly, I tucked the weapon back into my bag. "Oh, that."

As the gun went in, the unidentified thing popped out. It landed on the ground.

I snatched it up before Eliza could ask me what it was. Not only didn't I know, but also, I didn't want her involved in yet another murder investigation... not that she wasn't capable.

"Oh, Aunt Fiona." Her giggle turned into a laugh. "Where did you get that?"

Should I tell her the whole story of Mata Hari and the pearl-handled gun? "In France," I said... she'd used that line on me often enough.

"You went all the way to France to get a diaphragm?" she asked, still giggling.

"A what?"

She was laughing so hard she had to suck in air. "You'll have to ask Mrs. Sanger."

"Did you hear that?" I perked up my ears. Was someone else in the tunnel?

Eliza stopped laughing and stood as still as a statue.

The noise was barely audible. There was definitely someone —or something—in this tunnel with us.

I stepped back against the wall. Eliza did the same.

The stone wall was cold against my back. I shivered—whether from the cold or the approaching danger, I didn't know.

Slowly, I pulled Mata Hari's gun out of my day bag.

I hoped it wasn't a rat. My aim wasn't good enough for such a small target.

20

JAIL BIRD

"Ladies." A familiar baritone echoed through the tunnel. "Fancy meeting you here." A waft of rosewood and smoky charcoal followed his voice.

"Bloody hell." I stepped into the path. "What in blazes are you doing here?"

It was a rat... of the large human variety.

"I could ask you the same," Fredricks said, shining a torch in my face.

I shielded my eyes with my hands.

"I expect..." He lowered the torch. "We are all endeavoring to clear my good name."

I scoffed.

"When did they let you out of jail?" Eliza stepped out of the shadows. "And why?"

"I let myself out," Fredricks grinned.

"You mean you escaped?" I gasped.

"It is my forte." He tugged at the hem of his evening coat. He'd managed to escape and dress for the opera.

"Have you found any evidence to prove my innocence?" He

moved closer... too close. I could smell his sandalwood cologne. The warmth of his breath on my neck made me shudder.

"To the contrary," I said, taking a step backwards.

Eliza yelped when I stepped on her toes.

"Your presence here makes you a suspect in the murder of Anna Case." It couldn't be just a coincidence that Fredricks was present at both murders. And to think I'd fallen for his story. To think I was actually trying to help him. "I'm taking you to the police." I lifted the gun.

He chuckled. "Are you going to shoot me?"

I waved the gun at him.

"Now, now, ma chérie." His tone was hushed, as if singing a lullaby. "You know how upset I get when you shoot at me."

I gripped the weapon with both hands and pointed it straight at him. "I'm taking you to the police," I repeated.

"No need, ma chérie." He tipped his slouch hat and disappeared back into the darkness.

I stood there with my mouth open like a daft idiot, sputtering after him.

* * *

None of the constables at the opera house would give me the time of day. I had to wait to phone the nick when I got back to my hotel.

As soon as I pushed my way through the entrance to the Knickerbocker, I went to track down a telephone. The telephone at the front desk was too public for my comfort, so I went to the bell desk to see if my wheezy concierge friend might allow me to use his telephone. He was only too happy to oblige. Trouble was, he stood there watching me... and eavesdropping.

"Mr. Fredrick Fredricks has escaped," I whispered into the receiver as soon as someone answered.

"How do you know that?" the constable asked.

I recounted my meeting with Fredricks at Carnegie Hall—leaving out the parts about the underground tunnel and Mata Hari's gun.

"We've had no reports of a jailbreak," the constable said.

"I saw him with my own eyes," I insisted.

"Alright, calm down, Miss." He sighed into the receiver.

"Go and check," I huffed. "You'll see he is quite absent."

"Okay, lady." He sighed again—this time even more exaggerated than the last. "If you insist, but I'm telling you—"

"Just do it," I said forcefully.

"Okay. Okay. Don't get your panties in a twist."

What kind of way was that for a constable to talk to a lady? "I'll report you—"

"What was the prisoner's name again?" His tone was more serious now.

"Fredrick Fredricks."

"Fredrick or Fredricks?" he asked.

"Both." I tapped my foot.

When I glanced over at the concierge, he flashed a knowing smile as if we were co-conspirators in some secret plot.

I turned my back on him and waited for the officer to return to the telephone.

"Nope." His gruff voice startled me. "Mr. Fredricks is tucked away in his bunk."

"What?" I nearly choked on my words. "But I saw him. That's impossible."

"Look, lady, quit wasting my time. Good night." The line went dead. The copper had hung up on me. What nerve!

I joined Clifford and Eliza at the bar.

"There you are, old girl," Clifford said cheerfully. "We've been waiting for you to order." He waved the bartender over and ordered a martini.

"Fredricks is back in jail." I dropped onto a chair.

"What?" Eliza's eyes went wide. "How?"

"He's as sneaky as a weasel."

After the night we'd had, I allowed Eliza a brandy. I had one too in hopes it would settle my nerves.

Since I'd set sail from England, I'd witnessed three murders. Well, maybe not witnessed directly—nonetheless.

First, there was the poor soul thrown overboard by those two men in black. Then there was Hugo Schweitzer, shot at the opera. And now Miss Anna Case, smashed by a curtain boom.

The question was, were the murders connected? If so, how? And if not, then there were two, or three, or even four killers on the loose. The first one could not have been committed by Fredricks since he wasn't on the ship... or was he? He'd had that bloody gown delivered to me with his card. But I hadn't seen him during the entire voyage. Still, he was a tricky devil.

As soon as the bartender delivered our drinks, I took a big swig of brandy. Gulping it down proved more than I bargained for, and I was lucky not to cough it out.

Eliza sipped her brandy with more delight than was warranted.

"Young lady, why did you run off without asking?" I asked in what I hoped was a stern yet maternal tone.

"I had a hunch." Eliza smiled sweetly.

"You worried us to death on a hunch?" The brandy stung my throat. "What sort of hunch?"

"The murderous sort." She smirked.

"Eliza, really—"

"Rum do." Clifford used the olive-laden toothpick to stir his martini. "Tragic accident. Poor lady, so lovely and her voice—"

"But *was* it an accident?" I cut him off before he delivered a eulogy.

"You think it was intentional?" Clifford dropped the toothpick back into the glass.

"I know it was," Eliza said.

Clifford and I both stared at the girl.

"What do you mean you *know* it was?" I asked. "How?"

"You're not the only one with spy glasses." She pulled her opera glasses out of her beaded cat handbag. "I saw someone running from the catwalk right after the lights went up and Miss Case went down."

"Who?" I asked.

"Fredricks." Her ringlets bobbed. "He did it."

"Why would anyone want to kill Anna Case?" Clifford asked. "Especially Fredricks. He doesn't even know her."

I thought of the newspaper picture of Fredricks and Miss Case. He did know her. And by the way they'd gazed at each other in that photograph, I'd say they knew each other quite well. She had probably succumbed to Fredricks's charms. Most women did. I, of course, was quite immune.

"Good question." I opened my notebook to my list of suspects in the Schweitzer case. I crossed Anna Case off the top of the list. Although... it was possible that she'd killed her lover and then someone else had killed her. "We need to get back to Carnegie Music Hall and investigate that catwalk." *And we need to go back to the nick and find out what Fredricks is really up to.*

"Perhaps we should leave that to the police, old girl." Clifford drained his glass.

I scowled at him. If, as I now knew, Hugo Schweitzer and Thomas Edison had some shady business with the phenol, business that affected the American war efforts, then—no matter who committed them—these murders were a matter for the War Office, and, subsequently, for me. "Captain Hall will certainly want to know if these murders are related to espionage," I said, more to myself than to my friends. Especially if they were committed by a renowned German agent and my assigned target, one Fredrick Fredricks, aka the panther.

"Espionage." Clifford scoffed. "Why, Fiona, you say the darndest things."

Blast. I should be more careful in front of the girl.

Over the top of her brandy snifter, Eliza gave me a knowing look. She might be a very silly girl, but she had the sensible instincts of a spy... and it was those instincts that would undoubtedly get me sacked.

"Mrs. Sanger was the last person on stage before the soprano sang." I wrote her name and circled it. "We need to interview Mrs. Sanger. She may have seen something suspicious." I rummaged through my bag for a card she'd given me before we left the ship. "Tomorrow morning, we can visit her clinic."

"In Brooklyn?" Eliza chimed in.

"How far is Brooklyn?" I squinted at her. "Isn't it in New York?"

"It's a world away." Her voice drifted off and she stared into space.

How in heaven's name could she know anything about Brooklyn or how far it was from New York? "How do you know?"

"I read the newspapers." She smiled. "You should try it sometime, Aunt Fiona." Something about her face had changed. Her countenance seemed more self-assured and considerably less... silly.

Maybe it was the brandy. *Hers or mine?*

21

BROOKLYN

The next morning, Eliza and I made the trek to Brooklyn. Clifford stayed behind to babysit Poppy. That man melted into a puddle of mush in front of the little pooch.

Eliza had borrowed my Valentine's New York City guidebook and plotted our course. We took the IRT railway to the Manhattan Bridge. Then we caught a tram on the Three Cent Line to cross the East River. Next, she had us taking another railcar and then changing onto a bus.

As we'd already been traveling for an hour, I vetoed her plan and hailed a yellow cab. Turns out, yellow was a jolly practical color because it could be seen from afar.

Finally, we arrived at 46 Amboy Street and the Brownsville Clinic, a white three-story building that stood out from the red brick buildings around it. On either side of the dark wooden front door were two floor-to-ceiling windows covered with long white sheer curtains.

Shawled and hatless, their chapped red hands holding the hands of their children, women of various ages waited in a long queue to get in. Blimey. So many women willing to brave the cold to get what Margaret Sanger had to offer.

Wasn't the clinic open yet? I glanced at my watch. It was well after ten.

Eliza stepped to the back of the queue. I didn't know whether to follow or not. After all, we were here to interview Mrs. Sanger and not to get birth control.

A pang deep in my chest reminded me of Andrew and my inability to conceive a baby. Unfortunately, I was one of the few women who didn't need birth control. My body had decided to provide its own.

Despite my heavy overcoat, fur hat, and woolen gloves, I found myself shivering. I leaned closer to Eliza. "Do you really think we need to wait in the queue?"

Eliza shrugged and broke out of the queue.

I followed her to the front door.

A woman shouted at us in a foreign language, Russian, maybe. I didn't know what she'd said, but I could tell it wasn't nice.

Inside, the clinic was clean and bright and looked like a doctor's surgery, a very busy doctor's surgery.

The waiting room was packed and stuffy from so many bodies crammed together. Some women sat with children on their laps. Others stood, shifting from foot to foot, with babies on their hips. Some had holes in their shoes. Many wore coarse cloth skirts and heavy blouses. Most looked weary beyond their years.

No one spoke. It was as if they shared a great secret.

Moving as efficiently as an assembly line, uniformed nurses ushered the women into back rooms, women made patient by desperation.

Unfazed, Eliza hummed and occasionally shimmied, at some imaginary ball in her mind. The closeness of the room and the heat sent me outside for fresh air several times before it was our turn.

A courteous but cold nurse led us to a room in the back. She bade us to sit and wait.

The room was even colder than the nurse. It was sterile and white and had very little heating. Cold in every sense. Still, it was a welcome change from the crowded waiting room. I dropped into a chair.

Although I was used to hospitals from my time volunteering at Charing Cross, I was not used to being a patient. Technically, of course, I wasn't a patient now. Still, it was unsettling to be waiting in a clinic.

I had to remind myself that I was here to interview Mrs. Sanger, nothing more. I certainly was not here for birth control.

As the last person on stage before the *accident*, she may have noticed something out of the ordinary... someone lurking on the catwalk, perhaps?

She may have thrown a body overboard. She may even have been involved in Anna Case's murder. I was glad the waiting room was full of potential witnesses in case Mrs. Sanger was a heinous killer.

Eliza paced the room, stopping to pick up a plastic model of the female reproductive system. "Fimbria." She brought the model over to me. "Don't they look like daisies?" She pointed to the ends of the fallopian tubes.

"Hmm." I was more interested in the placard illustrating common pathologies of the reproductive organs: endometriosis, uterine fibroids, interstitial cystitis, and of course the French disease. I wondered if my insides harbored such an interloper and if that was why Andrew and I never had a baby.

The door opened. Mrs. Sanger entered, followed by another woman, whom she introduced as her sister, Mrs. Byrne. I recognized her from the ship. I hadn't heard her utter a single word the entire voyage.

"First, I want to assure you that anything we discuss is completely confidential." Mrs. Sanger took a chair opposite mine. "Women—all women—have the right to contraceptives. It's nothing to be ashamed of."

"Oh, no." I fanned myself with my bag. "We're here to ask about last night at Carnegie Hall."

"Tragic." Mrs. Sanger closed her eyes. "There are those who would stop at nothing to thwart women's rights."

"What do you mean?" I asked. She must not think it was an accident either.

"Those horrible Comstock Crusaders, for one." Her lips tightened. "And the prison guards, for another."

"But the prison guards weren't at the opera," I reminded her.

"I was ready to die for the cause," Mrs. Byrne said. Her voice was soft and even, just like her complexion.

"She went without food for eight days." Mrs. Sanger was obviously proud of her sister's achievement.

"Until those beasts force-fed me. Holding me down and pushing tubes down my throat until I gagged." Her eyes hardened. "I was the first but unfortunately not the last woman to be subjected to such punishment."

"How dreadful." Eliza left the female anatomy behind to join us.

"Did you notice anything odd or suspicious on or around the stage before the accident?" I asked, removing my notepad and pencil from my bag.

"Those Comstock men constantly threaten us." Mrs. Sanger shook her head. "Sadly, I'm not surprised they went this far." She sighed. "But poor Anna. Why her? She was just singing, for God's sake."

"Do you know anyone who would want to kill her?"

"Anna?" Mrs. Sanger scoffed. "Everyone loved Anna."

"Perhaps someone loved her too much?" I offered.

"She always did have men chasing after her." Mrs. Sanger spit out the word "men" as if it was poison.

"Were you going to show Mrs. Sanger what you and Poppy found on the ship?" Eliza asked with a sly smile.

"Right." I withdrew the object from my bag. "The dog found this strange object on deck near the spot where that poor man was thrown overboard."

"Oh, my," Mrs. Byrne said, taking the thing out of my hands. "Don't use this, dear. It has a hole in it."

"The dog chewed it," I said. Why in blazes was everyone so concerned with the blasted hole?

Mrs. Sanger paled. "Near where the two figures dressed in black threw something overboard?"

I nodded. "At Mrs. Parker's luncheon, I noticed you were missing a button on the sleeve of your blouse, a silver fleur-de-lis button."

Mrs. Sanger bit her lip.

Mrs. Byrne put her hand on her sister's shoulder.

"And we found a matching button stuck in the ship's railing in the very spot where the body went overboard." I raised my eyebrows. "Coincidence?" I waved the rubber disk at her. "And what exactly is this?"

Mrs. Byrne grabbed it out of my hand. "Why, that's a diaphragm." She turned it over to inspect it. "A method of contraception, but it won't work with a hole in it." She tossed the holey diaphragm onto the counter.

"They aren't legal here," Mrs. Sanger added. "So, we bring them over from France and drop them in the harbor to avoid the customs agents."

"You smuggle contraband contraception into the country?" *Oh, my sainted aunt.* It wasn't a body they'd thrown overboard. It was a shipment of diaphragms from France.

"Do you see all those women out there?" Mrs. Sanger stood up and paced the length of the room. "Haggard at thirty because they've born a baby a year for a decade. Every woman deserves to control her own body." She stopped and stared down at me. "Turn us in if you must."

"We've survived jail before," her sister said, defiantly. "No matter how many times they lock us up, we won't stop."

"Why did you throw your cargo overboard so far out to sea?" How would they collect them so far out?

"That damned Hoover boy was on to us." Mrs. Sanger shook her fist. "He and his damned crusaders. If men could get pregnant, there would be contraception on every corner."

What a thought. Not all women could get pregnant.

"Pregnant men," Eliza giggled.

"Are you going to turn us in?" Mrs. Sanger asked. "We're trying to help all these poor women."

"I'm just relieved you're not murderers." I gave a nervous chuckle.

"Some people consider contraception murder," Mrs. Sanger said. "They care more about a collection of unformed cells than thinking, feeling women." Her voice trembled. "It's not right."

"Be that as it may." I dropped my notepad back in my bag. "You should be more careful with your cargo drops."

Mrs. Sanger nodded.

"Your secret is safe with us." I stood and extended my hand.

"Don't worry," Eliza said. "We won't turn you in."

She gave it a hearty shake. "Thank you."

Eliza picked up the diaphragm off the counter.

"I don't think we need that anymore, dear," I said, buttoning my overcoat.

Eliza smiled. "Might I get one without the hole?"

"Captain Hall will put a hole in Billy Buck if he finds out."

Not to mention, I'll get sacked.

I glanced at my watch. "If we hop it, we have time to visit Fredricks before you have to report to school."

* * *

The constable ushered us into the visiting room. The windowless chamber was even more depressing—and stuffy—than I'd remembered it.

Eliza and I sat on one side of the small table and waited for the guard to deliver Fredricks.

"Ladies, how good of you to come." Fredricks entered the room with his usual flourish. Even in prison garb, he exuded charm... and that smoky rosewood scent. It must be his confident air, or his mischievous smile, or maybe his mane of black hair. For some reason, Fredricks always managed to transcend his circumstances, no matter how bleak.

Fredricks sat across from us.

"I'll be outside if you need me," the guard said.

Thank goodness. We could interview Fredricks in private.

As soon as the guard had left the room, I leaned over the table and hissed, "What game are you playing at?"

"Why, Fiona," he grinned, "I'm happy to see you too."

"What were you doing at Carnegie Hall?" I fanned myself with my bag.

"I told you. I was trying to clear my name." He feigned a hurt expression. "Don't you believe me?"

"Why did you come back to jail?" Who escaped from jail and then went back? Fredricks must be up to something.

"Your little gun is very persuasive." He smiled. "And I knew if I came back, you would too."

Eliza squirmed in her chair.

"Mademoiselle Eliza, surely you can prove my innocence." He extended his hands to the girl. "You must have learned something useful in Locard's laboratory."

She gave a start and jerked her hands away. "Whatever do you mean?"

"Locard's laboratory in Lyon." He flattened his palms on the tabletop. "You were a student there, were you not?"

"What are you talking about?" I remembered the girl had mentioned boarding school in Lyon. "And who is this Locard chap?"

"Edmond Locard is the preeminent criminologist in the world." Fredricks withdrew his hands. "He has consulted with police in Paris, London, Vienna, and New York."

"Criminologist?" What in the world is a criminologist?

"The study of criminalistics," Eliza said. "New ways of collecting evidence and catching criminals." She glared across the table at Fredricks.

"Is it true?" I asked the girl. "You studied in France with this criminologist?"

She blushed and nodded.

Good heavens. Who was this girl? "We'll talk about it later." I shook my head to clear my mind. "Right now, we must figure out who killed Hugo Schweitzer and Anna Case… and what does Fredricks have to do with all of this?" I knew he had to be involved somehow.

"Nothing." Fredricks leaned back in his chair. "I have nothing to do with it."

"You knew Hugo Schweitzer and Anna Case," I said with perhaps too much accusation in my voice. I must have been as red as a beet. My cheeks were on fire.

"I know a lot of people." He smiled. "I'm a very popular fellow. Ladies' man, man's man, man about town, don't you know."

Eliza giggled behind her hand again. Even if she was trained by a world-famous criminologist, she was still silly.

"If you want me to help prove your innocence, then you'll have to tell me what you're doing in New York and how you're involved with these murders." I slouched out of my woolen overcoat.

"You should talk to Edison about Schweitzer." Fredricks's expression was serious now, finally. "Edison is—was—supplying Schweitzer with a key ingredient for the Bayer Aspirin factory."

The great phenol plot. "Why is that important?"

"Phenol is an ingredient also used in explosives—"

"But Schweitzer is making aspirin and not bombs," I cut him off.

He stroked his strong chin. "If the entire American supply goes to making aspirin and Edison's records, then none is left for the armaments to blow up my friends and allies." He flashed a snide grin.

So, it really was as simple as diverting the supply of phenol away from the American military. Perhaps the lack of explosives had kept the Americans from the front? They must have bullets, for goodness' sake.

"How does Anna Case fit in?" I pulled my notebook from my bag and reviewed my notes.

"She's a beautiful woman." He shrugged. "Why shouldn't I know her? And she's a friend of the suffragettes."

The blasted suffragettes again. "Did you kill her?"

"How could you even say such a thing?" The tone of his voice made it obvious that his incredulity was feigned. "Don't you trust me, ma chérie? After all we've been through?"

"Oh, come now, you've poisoned countless countesses and—"

"You have your duty and I have mine." He pushed his chair away from the table. "Regardless, we'll need to work together to stop this bloody war."

"How do you plan to stop the war from inside a prison cell?" Eliza said.

Sometimes the girl surprised me with her harshness. I glanced over and gave her a disapproving look. "I don't like this bloody war any more than you do—"

"But you do like a certain lieutenant." He stood up. "Why don't you ask your beloved Lieutenant Archie Somersby who killed Hugo Schweitzer?" He paced the length of the tiny room. "Why don't you ask him who summoned me to Edison's box?" He stopped, stared down at me, and ran his hand through his thick hair. "Or who telephoned Mrs. Schweitzer?"

"Are you suggesting... do you believe..." I stuttered. Fredricks was always trying to put me off Archie. *Well, it wouldn't work.* I tightened my lips and glared up at him. Not my darling Archie. Right?

"No, ma chérie." He knocked on the door to signal the guard. "I don't believe."

The guard opened the door.

On the way out, Fredricks turned back, a steely glint in his eyes. "I know."

The door clicked shut.

"Who is Lieutenant Archie Somersby?" Eliza asked.

"My... a... just a friend." I stumbled on the words.

Who was Lieutenant Archie Somersby, indeed?

22

THE MISSING CUSHION

Eliza insisted on accompanying me to Carnegie Hall for one last sleuth fest before she was delivered to her school. She chattered in the yellow cab all the way from the nick to the music hall. Preoccupied with thoughts of Archie, for the life of me, I had no idea what she nattered on about. Her cheerful spirits were diametrically opposed to my own.

In the past, Fredricks had insisted that Archie was a double agent. I refused to believe it. Like me, Archie worked for British Intelligence. He was a lieutenant in the British army. He'd been wounded in battle fighting for England. And he'd been dogging Fredricks around the globe much longer than I had. Perhaps that's why Fredricks hated him so.

As the taxicab dropped us in front of Carnegie Music Hall, I vowed to prove Fredricks wrong. Forget about proving him innocent. He could rot in prison for all I cared. In fact, he deserved to rot in prison. *He* was the German agent, after all. Not Archie.

I paid the entrance fee, and we joined the tour. As soon as the group entered the secret underground tunnel, Eliza and I snuck away.

"Shall we split up?" Eliza asked. "We could cover more ground that way."

A sensible plan. "I'll revisit Edison's box." *And Archie's box.*

"I'll take the catwalk." She stripped off her overcoat and laid it on a chair in the back of the orchestra pit. "Whoever was up there must have accidently left a clue. They always do."

"Is that what they teach girls in boarding schools in France?"

She smiled and nodded.

"Be careful." I hated to think of the girl crawling around up there but given my fear of heights—and my mission to prove Fredricks wrong about Archie—it was for the best. After all, someone had to find out how that boom dropped onto the soprano.

Glancing around to make sure no one was watching, I scurried out of the orchestra pit, down the aisle and up the stairs to the stage-left box where I'd seen Archie the night of Schweitzer's murder.

At the time, I'd been relieved Archie was alive and the shot I'd heard hadn't been for him. He'd been in his box immediately after the shot, so it never crossed my mind that he could be the killer. Anyway, why would it? I knew Archie. He wasn't a killer.

Now that I'd learned the sound wasn't from a gun but a banger, and the killer used the golden pillow to muffle the real shot, it was possible. And the hidden tunnel made it possible to get from one side of the theater to the other in a matter of minutes. The scent of citrus... Archie's cologne. I shook my head. It had to be a coincidence. Didn't it?

The killer could have shot Schweitzer at any time he was alone in the box and then placed the banger to go off later. He would have needed a long fuse. The ashes I'd found under the seat proved that... thanks to Eliza's forensics training and examination of the bits stuck to my mesh evening bag.

The murderer killed Schweitzer, lit the fuse to the banger cracker and then escaped. By the time the "shot" echoed through the auditorium, he was already long gone.

According to Fredricks, Mr. Edison left immediately after the tone test demonstration, which was long before intermission. And Mrs. Schweitzer was called away to the telephone just before intermission. So, the shot had to have been fired during the time between when Mrs. Schweitzer left the box just before intermission and when Fredricks found the body during intermission.

Right, Fredricks had been summoned to the box. If Edison hadn't sent the note, then who had? I had to find that waiter, the one who delivered the note. Whoever killed Schweitzer had intentionally framed Fredricks. Who wanted Schweitzer dead and Fredricks in prison... or worse, executed?

You finally caught Fredricks red-handed. That's what Archie said when I passed him in the hallway the night of the murder. *How did he know that?* I shuddered to think.

No. No. No. I would prove it wasn't him.

But how?

I must find some evidence in this music hall—something the police missed.

On my hands and knees, I crawled around every inch of the floor of Edison's box. Obviously, the theater had been cleaned since that fateful night.

The ashes were gone.

The banger was gone.

Only the faded bloodstains remained.

Still, there might be something the coppers and cleaners had missed. Just some little speck to prove Archie had nothing to do with this murder.

I searched every inch of the box and found nothing. If only that constable hadn't been watching me like a hawk the night of the murder, I could have conducted a proper investigation while the crime scene was still fresh. By now, the killer's tracks were as stale as war-rationed bread.

I gave up on Edison's box. Maybe I'd find something in Archie's box. I cringed. Something to prove his innocence. Like what?

I stood up and brushed off my frock. Just because the box had been cleared of evidence didn't mean it was clean. As I stepped into the hallway, I spotted Eliza running toward me.

"Aunt Fiona." She was waving at me.

I quickened my pace.

"Look what I found," she beamed. She waved her closed fist over her head.

She slid to a stop right in front of me and held out the object on the palm of her hand.

Blimey. A tiny American flag from one of the Comstock boys' tie clips.

"Where did you find that?"

"On the catwalk." She smiled. "It was wedged between two ropes."

"So, the murderer was one of those dreadful Comstock Crusaders." Poor Anna Case. Did one of those horrible blokes kill her just because she was in favor of women's right to vote? She wasn't even one of the suffragette ring leaders. If the killer wanted to kill suffragettes, then why not Mrs. Sanger or Miss Carrie Catt?

"Let's nail those dreadful crusaders!" Eliza did a little dance. "Mr. Fredricks and Mr. Hoover's bunch. It's a red-letter day!"

While I shared her dislike of those overly zealous men, her performance was a bit much. I glanced at my watch. "The tour will be ending soon."

Eliza proudly popped the pin into a pocket on her skirt. "Should we rejoin them?"

"I want to check one more box first." *Archie's box.* I wished I'd done it before Eliza found me. I didn't want to put any more suspicions in her mind. But I had to do it. I had to know. The thought of Archie committing cold-blooded murder was bringing me around to Eliza's conclusion. If, as Eliza insisted, Fredricks did kill Schweitzer, then he would be locked up, and my mission would be completed. Better Fredricks than Archie.

Sigh. Even Fredricks didn't deserve to be hanged for something he didn't do.

I looked at my watch again to time the trip from Edison's box to Archie's. If *someone* from Archie's box had murdered Hugo Schweitzer, then they had to have been able to move quickly from one side of the theater to the other, from stage right to stage left.

The usher hadn't seen anyone enter or leave the box after intermission started, except for Fredricks... and then me. And I'd seen Archie standing in his box waving right after the banger went off. So, even if he'd set up the cracker as a decoy gunshot to frame Fredricks, and the real shot was earlier, it couldn't have been much earlier or either Edison or Schweitzer's wife would have seen him.

Given the timetable I'd worked out, that left him approximately ten minutes to get from one side of the theater to the other, kill Schweitzer, and then get back again.

I set off at a good clip—not fast enough to attract attention, but still jolly fast—urgent need to use the lavatory fast.

Eliza trailed close behind.

At the end of the balcony hallway, I searched the floor for the trigger switch I suspected must be there. Another secret passageway would explain how someone could get from stage left to stage right and back again in a matter of minutes. As I ran the toe of my shoe across the carpet, I hoped to heaven I was wrong.

"It's a dead-end, Aunt Fiona." Eliza stared at my awkward tap dance as I searched for the hidden switch.

Finally! I tapped the switch with my toe and the wall panel popped open. For all my faffing about, I deducted thirty seconds from my time. Presumably the killer would have known exactly where to find the switch.

Eliza gave a little squeal of delight and clapped her hands together. "It leads to the secret tunnel."

A rickety wooden staircase descended to the ground floor and then another set of stairs took us to the underground tunnel. From there, we easily made our way under the stage, across the theater, and back up to the first-floor boxes, only now on stage left.

As soon as I stepped into the box, I saw it. *Oh no!*

"Fredricks *is* innocent," I whispered.

"Aunt Fiona, are you okay?" Eliza stared at me. "You're as white as a sheet."

Gutted, my heart sank. There it was, as painful as a kick in the shin... a bare wooden back on one of the seats where a lovely golden cushion should have been.

Dearest Archie, what have you done?

* * *

After what seemed like an eternity, the yellow cab pulled up in front of the Institute of Musical Arts, a boxy brick building that sat across from the sprawling campus of Columbia University.

It was hard to believe that after only five days aboard the ship and almost a week together on land, I'd grown quite fond of the girl. Still, considering the revelation about Archie, I was glad to get her safely out of the way before I confronted him.

"Please write to me, Aunt Fiona." Eliza kissed my cheek. "Promise you will. And take good care of Poppy."

Clifford would be taking care of the little beast until Eliza got permission to bring the creature to campus.

I nodded. "Take care of yourself, my dear." I pulled her into an embrace. "And be a good girl."

She pulled out of the embrace and smiled sweetly. "I'm always good."

I chuckled. If her uncle only knew what she'd been doing. Despite my bad influence, he would be pleased to know she was delivered safely to school.

She hopped out of the taxi and put her hands together as if in prayer. "Thank you."

"You're welcome, dear." I waved.

"I almost forgot." She stuck her head into the backseat and held out her hand. "The murderer's American flag."

"I'll take it to the police." I tucked it into my bag.

"I'm glad we solved the murders," she said as if discussing a word puzzle instead of grisly murders.

"Yes, dear." Had we solved the murders? We'd solved the mystery of the man overboard. And we knew the soprano was killed by one of the Comstock Crusaders. But which one? And then there was Hugo Schweitzer. Who did Eliza think was the killer? "Except for Mr. Schweitzer. We still don't know—"

"Mr. Fredricks," Eliza interrupted. "You caught him red-handed."

Odd. That's what Archie had said. I wasn't about to contradict her at this point.

"Mr. Fredricks will be tried for the murder." A ray of winter sun hit her golden hair. "I hope you meant it when you said you didn't fancy him."

"Of course I don't fancy him!" I shielded my eyes with my

hand to get a better look at the girl. "But suppose he is innocent..."

"He's a rotter, a scoundrel, a cad, and a German spy." She grabbed her small suitcase from the floor of the taxicab. "You said so yourself."

"Don't you care about justice?"

"Why, Aunt Fiona, you do fancy him!" She squealed and clapped her hands. "He does have good taste in evening gowns."

"Hey, lady," the cab driver interrupted us. "I haven't got all day."

"Please make sure to send the rest of my luggage. And kiss Poppy for me and tell her Mummy loves her." Eliza blew me a kiss. "And remember, Aunt Fiona, the worst form of injustice is the pretense of justice." She dashed off.

I watched as she skipped across the grass toward the administration building. She was an enigma, but a sweet enigma... a philosopher, criminologist, and pretty schoolgirl all rolled into one. I was going to miss her. I dabbed at my eye with my handkerchief. *The worst form of injustice is the pretense of justice.* Whatever could she mean?

"Where to, lady?" the driver asked gruffly.

"The Knickerbocker Hotel." I stared out of the window and wished I was back home in Northwick Terrace. I'd give anything for a nice cuppa, a hot bath, and a good night's sleep in my own cozy bed.

* * *

Snow devils danced in the wind. Women scurried up the street, holding their hats on with one hand and holding their shopping bags in the other.

Even in the hushed tones of winter, New York was vibrant

and wild. Unlike my staid and stoic London. Not unlike the difference between Eliza and me. I wondered how the girl would settle in. No doubt she'd make scads of friends before supper.

I need not worry about that girl. She could more than take care of herself. Anyway, at the moment, I had bigger fish to fry.

As soon as I landed at the hotel, I dashed off to find a telephone.

At least with Eliza safe at school, I could attend to my investigation without her interference. There was still a chance I could prove Archie innocent. Maybe the seat cushion missing from his box was just a coincidence. Or maybe someone was trying to frame him, too.

Heart racing, I hurried across the lobby in search of the wheezy concierge. Not stopping, I dug in my bag for the number. As I'd done so many times before, I slipped it out of the little pocket inside my bag where I kept it as if it were a love note. The paper with Archie's telephone number was worn and creased from the many times I'd fingered it.

I'd wanted to call him so many times since I'd left the ship, but I'd always stopped myself. Now, I had to call him, and I dreaded it more than anything I'd ever had to do. What if he had killed Hugo Schweitzer? What if Fredricks was right?

Breathe, Fiona, just breathe.

Fredricks had repeatedly warned me Archie Somersby was not what he seemed. But I'd refused to believe Archie was a double agent.

I brushed tears from my cheeks with the backs of my hands.

I couldn't let my feelings get in the way. I was a British agent. I had a job to do. *If Archie is a double agent, I'll treat him like any other traitor.*

I quickened my pace.

My wheezy friend was only too happy to lend me his telephone. The catch, of course, was he stood nearby, eavesdropping.

My hand shook as I read off the number to the switchboard operator.

"Lucy Lemon speaking," a woman answered.

Was she Archie's paramour? My stomach roiled. For all I knew, she could be his wife.

"Is Lieutenant Somersby available?" My voice trembled.

"Who?" she asked.

"Archie Somersby?" Was he using a code name?

"Who is calling?" Her voice was stern. Maybe she didn't expect him to have a lady caller.

I hesitated. Should I give my name? I didn't know what to do. Sigh. I closed my eyes and tried not to cry. "I... I..."

"What's your number, honey?" she asked, softer now.

"I'm at the Knickerbocker Hotel." I read the number off the telephone.

"If I see him, I'll tell him." Click. The line went dead.

Now what?

I paced back and forth in front of the concierge desk.

"Something wrong?" my wheezy friend asked.

I shook my head and wiped my cheek.

"You sure?"

I nodded and sniffed.

As I removed a handkerchief from my bag, my hand grazed Mata Hari's gun. Guns were no help now. All the spy gadgets in the world couldn't help me with this. Even my photographic memory was useless against the imprint of Archie on my heart.

I dabbed at my eyes. *Oh, Archie. Where are you?* He could be halfway across the world. How could I feel so much for someone about whom I knew so little?

I sat on a divan a few feet from the concierge desk, close

enough to hear if the telephone rang. Wringing the handkerchief with both hands, I forced myself to breathe. I closed my eyes again.

When I did, I saw Archie's smile with that one adorable crooked tooth. I thought of the way he'd called me "my love" and how he'd made me promise to stay away from Hugo Schweitzer. Was he protecting me? Or did he merely want me out of the way?

I put my head in my hands. Had every tender moment we shared been a lie? Had he been manipulating me all this time? A sharp pain stabbed at my chest like a dagger through the heart.

Bloody hell. I'm in love with Archie.

23

THE FINAL INVESTIGATION

I jumped up as if to flee the very idea. *In love with Archie?*

No. No. No. I had to resist such fantastic ideas.

I paced back and forth in front of the concierge desk. What now? How long should I wait for Archie to call me back? Where was he? How would I find him if he didn't call?

The wheezy concierge followed me with his eyes. I was beginning to wonder if the privilege of using his telephone was worth being watched like a hawk.

"There you are." The familiar voice startled me. "Are you alright, old bean?"

I turned around and was greeted by Clifford's reassuring face.

I nodded and sniffed.

"You look like a raccoon." He wiped my cheek with his thumb.

Blimey. My eye kohl must have run down my face.

Clifford took my elbow and led me to the divan. "Did you get Eliza delivered to the Institute of Musical Arts?"

"Yes. She's at school, finally." I dropped back onto the divan.

"I say, what instrument does she play, anyway?" he asked.

How odd. I'd never thought to ask her. Come to think of it, I didn't know much about the girl.

I shrugged.

"What about your investigation?" He pulled his pipe from his jacket pocket, looked at me, and then put it back. "Did you crack the case?" He sighed. "Good old Fredricks rotting away in that cell. Poor chap."

Poor chap, indeed. He didn't deserve to be in that cell *this time*, but that didn't mean he was innocent.

I sighed. So much had happened. Where to start? "Eliza found evidence on the catwalk implicating one of those horrible crusader boys." I shuddered, imagining a heavy boom falling out of the sky and smashing me like a bug. "Someone tampered with the boom."

"So, it wasn't an accident?" He retrieved his pipe again.

I gave him the evil eye.

He held the offending instrument between his teeth but didn't light it. "John Edgar Hoover and his lads?" Clifford narrowed his brows. "Are you sure? They seem like jolly good chaps to me."

"Yes." I shook my head. "They would." I retrieved the tie clip flag from my bag. "I need to call the police." I headed back to the concierge desk.

Clifford jumped up and was hot on my heels. "The police!"

The constable on the other end of the telephone was incredulous. He didn't believe we'd found evidence his colleagues had overlooked. Finally, he agreed to send someone over to fetch the tie clip flag.

Clifford and I went back to the divan to await the arrival of the police.

"What did Fredricks have to say for himself?" Clifford asked, lighting his pipe.

I didn't have the heart to tell him not to smoke, but I wasn't about to tell blabbermouth Clifford anything to incriminate Archie. Fredricks had suggested I should find out if someone forged the message from Edison and who called Mrs. Schweitzer away from the opera box. "I need to use the telephone again." I was up and down so much, I felt like a bandalore on a string.

"Suit yourself." He took the opportunity to blow out a huge cloud of foul smoke.

The concierge found the number, and I telephoned Mr. Edison's Menlo Park laboratory first. When I was aboard the navy yacht, the sailor mentioned that Edison was at the Menlo Park laboratory... electrocuting strays or inventing household appliances.

A man answered. It was not Mr. Edison. After asking me my name, he left the phone for a few seconds and returned to tell me Mr. Edison was not available.

With the help of the concierge, I tracked down a number for Mrs. Schweitzer. She was weepy on the other end of the telephone. "Why would anyone kill darling Hugo?"

I could think of several possible reasons: He was a womanizer and adulterer. He was a German spy. He had swindled Edison.

"Who called you away from the opera box that night?"

"I already told the police," she sniffled.

"Might you tell me too?" I glanced over at Clifford who was happily puffing away.

"Just before intermission, an usher came to tell me I had a telephone call." She sighed. "When I got down to the box office and picked up the receiver, no one was on the other end."

"Did you go straight back to your box?" I knew from Eliza's account that she hadn't.

"Ah... no. I went to get a glass of wine." She cleared her throat. "By the time I got back to the box, the police were there."

So, she was gone from before intermission until long after the murder. Presumably, the killer had called her away from the box. Clever.

I had to find out if the message to Fredricks was really from Edison. I had an idea.

I telephoned Menlo Park again. This time, I introduced myself as Rear Admiral Arbuthnot.

Sure enough, Mr. Edison took my call. Fiona Figg, a mere file clerk and woman to boot, hadn't been important enough, but a rear admiral and a man... that was a different story.

"As I told the police..." He sighed into the telephone. "I did not send a message to Mr. Fredricks. I did not summon him to a meeting in my opera box. No. I had nothing to do with it." That's why no one knew the waiter who came out of the woodwork and then disappeared again. He wasn't a waiter at all, but a co-conspirator, or more likely just a dupe, or paid unwitting accomplice. As I recalled, he was young and nervous.

"What was your relationship with Hugo Schweitzer?" I asked since I had him on the hook.

Silence.

"You collaborated with him, did you not?"

"No!" he growled. "I am not a collaborator."

Obviously, I'd hit a nerve. "You were selling phenol to the Bayer Aspirin company, were you not?"

"Schweitzer tricked me, damn him." I heard papers shuffling on the other end. "Look, I've already told the Attorney General and Mr. Hoover I didn't know I was trading with the enemy. It was aspirin, for God's sake."

"John Edgar Hoover?"

"Yes," he huffed. "J. Edgar Hoover from the Justice Department. I told him everything I know." Click. He'd hung up on me.

Blimey. The Hoover boy was working for the American Justice Department. How could someone so opinionated when it came to women's rights oversee justice? Perhaps I needed to have a chat with Mr. J. Edgar Hoover.

I couldn't wait here all day for Archie to telephone. I had to act. Given Mr. Hoover's opinion of women, I was sure he wouldn't have the time of day for Miss Fiona Figg. But Rear Admiral Arbuthnot was a different story.

I waved to Clifford, who jumped up and happily came to my side.

"Will you stay with Poppy?" I knew I could distract him with the pup. He was smitten with the little beast. "I have an errand to run."

"I could come with you." He smiled. "Are you sleuthing again?"

Yes. He loved to play Sherlock Holmes, *play* being the operative word.

"It won't take me long." I patted his arm. "Let's go fetch Poppy so you can take her for a nice walk, shall we?"

After a bit more cajoling, Clifford obliged. He was jolly pleased to see his furry little friend again, and the two of them trotted off down the hall.

With those two out of the way, I slipped out of my frock and into Rear Admiral Arbuthnot.

Now, where to find Mr. Hoover? Wherever the suffragettes gathered, Mr. Hoover appeared nearby, heckling from the sidelines. I just needed to find out where the suffragettes were marching or meeting. Perhaps my wheezy friend at the concierge's desk could help. He seemed to know everything going on about town.

The concierge eyed me with suspicion as he told me the suffragettes often rallied outside their headquarters in Union Square. It was a long shot, but I was frazzled and didn't know what else to do or where else to go.

"If Lieutenant Archie Somersby telephones... ahem, for Miss Fiona Figg, please tell him Miss Figg would like to meet him at his earliest convenience."

"What is your relationship to Miss Figg?" he asked. He really was a nosy bloke.

"I'm... her... brother," I stammered.

"Why didn't you say so?" The concierge smiled and nodded. "Yes, sir. I will, sir." At least he was loyal. And jolly helpful to boot.

By the time I arrived at Union Square, light snow was falling. Despite the precipitation and chilly breeze, a couple of dozen women were gathered in the square, listening to a woman with a bullhorn. Most of the women wore long woolen skirts, white shirts under dark woolen jackets, and oversized felt hats. From a distance, it looked like they had matching outfits, but once I got closer, I saw all sorts of variants in textures and patterns.

I recognized the woman yelling into the bullhorn as Miss Carrie Catt. She'd been speaking at the music hall the night Anna Case was killed. I was surprised the horrid Comstock boys didn't target her instead of the poor soprano. Not that I thought they should, mind. To the contrary. I just didn't understand why they would target Miss Case, who was only a weekend suffragette, unlike so many of the others.

I scanned the crowd. A group of hecklers shouted and guffawed from the sidewalk. Taking my longest strides, I made my way across the square and joined the men. If Mr. Hoover was here, this was where he would be. Even if he wasn't, one of these men could be Anna Case's killer.

Under long wool overcoats, the men wore matching navy suits, with starched white shirts and red ties. So patriotic. And yes, there they were—the gold tie clips sporting tiny American flags.

Infiltrating the men, I scrutinized ties as I passed on the

chance that I might find someone missing a flag from their tie clip. A few broken soldiers saluted me. I returned their salutes. My eyes darting from ties to faces, I saw fear behind the mocking countenance of these men. What were they afraid would happen if women got the vote?

Women were already running the country while they were away fighting, even more so back at home in Britain than here in America. Were they worried women wouldn't want them back bruised and broken... damaged goods?

"Rear Admiral." Someone tapped me on the shoulder. I turned around to the smiling face of John Edgar Hoover.

"I was hoping we'd meet again." As usual, he was well-dressed and freshly pressed.

"Me too." I tugged at the hem of my jacket and adjusted my voice. "In fact, I was hoping to find you here fighting the good fight."

He beamed with pride. "What can I do for you?"

Good heavens. Did he just wink at me?

"What do you know of Edison and Schweitzer and the great phenol plot?" Might as well get right to the point.

He narrowed his brows. A practiced inscrutability replaced his smile. "What do you know about that?"

"I've been briefed by British Intelligence." Since Archie was the first to tell me about the great phenol plot, and he worked for British Intelligence—double agent or not—I was telling the truth, more or less.

"It's classified—"

I cut him off. "I have clearance," I said in the cockiest voice I could muster.

He pulled a cigar from the pocket of his waistcoat and offered it to me.

I nodded.

He unwrapped it, snipped the end off, and handed it to me.

Disgusting. I took it, hoping to cajole information out of him.

He took out another cigar for himself. "Then you know Schweitzer was a German spy diverting phenol from the Americans." He unwrapped a cigar. "Edison was duped into making it for him." Using a pretty little ivory knife, he snipped the end off the foul thing. "And your countrymen sent an assassin to take care of the problem." He flashed a smug grin and then clamped the cigar between his teeth. "End of story."

An assassin. Was Archie an assassin?

He flicked the flint on his gold-plated lighter and raised his eyebrows.

I stuck the foul cigar in between my lips and grimaced.

He lit my cigar and then his own.

Trying to imitate his gestures, I puffed on the thing. A raging cloud of razor blades raced down my throat and I succumbed to a violent coughing fit.

"Are you okay?" Mr. Hoover chuckled and rubbed my back. "I'd love to give you a brandy back at my room."

Was he suggesting what I thought he was?

I shook my head and willed myself to stop coughing. "You've been most helpful."

"Anytime, lover." His hand traveled further down my back.

Cheeky devil.

"Thank you." I moved out of his reach. "But no, thank you." I took another step and trod on someone's foot. "My apologies."

Under a heavy overcoat with a hotel insignia on the lapel, the man was wearing the *uniform* of the Comstock Crusaders, along with a top hat and white gloves. Doorman was my guess.

The doorman saluted me. "Sir."

I glanced down at the nameplate on his overcoat. "At ease, Campbell."

That's when I saw it. His tie clip had a nub of glue where the tiny American flag should have been.

"What's your Christian name, sir?" I asked as calmly as I could—given I was likely face to face with the man who killed Anna Case.

24

THE SHOWDOWN

Back at the hotel, I used the concierge desk telephone once again. This time, I had a name for the police. Mr. Christopher Campbell, doorman at the Union Square Hotel, and rabid Comstock Crusader. He'd broken down in tears as he admitted that he didn't mean to kill anyone, especially not the lovely Miss Anna Case. He only meant to "scare" those other "crazy whores."

I shuddered to think of such an ordinary man with an excess of hatred for half of humankind.

"Did anyone call for me?" I asked my wheezy friend.

"No, sir, Admiral, sir."

Oh, right. "Did anyone call for Miss Figg?"

"No calls for your sister either."

I tipped my hat and thanked the concierge.

He held out his hand, waiting.

Oh, right. The tip. Funny. He never asked Miss Fiona Figg for a tip.

I dug in my trouser pockets. Of course, I didn't have any coins in my pockets. I shrugged and apologized and promised a tip on my next trip to the lobby.

When I got back to my room, I shucked off Rear Admiral Arbuthnot and ran a hot bath.

Ahhh. I sank into the water, closed my eyes, and slid down in the bathtub until I was completely submerged. Holding my breath, I listened to the watery sounds of my own limbs moving... the drip of the tap... the pounding in my head. Gasping, I emerged, gulping for air.

What if Archie never returned my call? Why didn't I ask him where he was staying in New York that night on the ship... when we were alone in his cabin? Alone with Archie, sitting on his bed, shoulder to shoulder. If he had killed Hugo Schweitzer, maybe he'd skipped town. He could be halfway around the world by now.

I lathered my arms with lilac-scented soap, scrubbing the living daylights out of my hands, as if I could wash away the last week. The man overboard turned out to be contraband contraceptives. The soprano's death was a scare tactic gone wrong. And what of Hugo Schweitzer? He was without a doubt a German spy with orders directly from the Kaiser to win the "chemists' war" by siphoning off phenol, the main ingredient in TNT.

A knock at my door startled me. I sat up in the bath.

"I say, Fiona, are you in there?"

Clifford.

"Just a minute," I shouted.

Bark. Bark. Bark.

And Poppy.

I hopped out of the bathtub, grabbed a towel, and hurriedly dried myself. Blast. The only clothes ready to hand were Rear Admiral Arbuthnot's. Even though Clifford was in the hallway, I was embarrassed to go into my room to fetch some proper clothes.

Feeling vulnerable in just a towel wrapped around my torso, I dashed into the room, went to the wardrobe and grabbed the first frock I saw. It was a pink, frilly number, one Eliza had forgotten to pack. As I was a good six inches taller than Eliza, my long limbs stuck out in every direction. I stuffed my bare feet into my Mary Janes, tugged the blonde bob onto my head, and answered the door.

"Good Lord." Clifford laughed. "Who are you supposed to be?" He nearly doubled over in glee. "The bearded lady?"

My hand flew to my chin. "What beard?"

Clifford pointed at my upper lip.

Horsefeathers. I'd forgotten to remove Rear Admiral Arbuthnot's mustache.

"What mischief have you been up to now, old bean?" He covered his mouth, but I saw the laughter in his eyes.

Poppy jerked the leash out of Clifford's hand and ran into the room. She sniffed every corner and ran in circles looking for her mistress.

"You might as well come in." I left the door ajar, went to the dressing table, and sat down in front of the looking glass. Ouch. The blasted mustache stung when I ripped it off. And it left my upper lip bright red. I picked off residual pieces of spirit glue.

"Spill the beans, old thing." Clifford came into the room and shut the door. "You've been sleuthing again, haven't you? What did you find out?" Clifford sat on Eliza's neatly made bed. "You look jolly pretty in pink, by the way."

I didn't know if he was having me on or not. Although my dress and my cheeks were equally rosy.

Clifford rubbed his hands together. "Devilishly cold out there." He gazed lovingly at the little dog, who'd curled up by his feet. "Poor pup misses the girl, and so do I."

I had to admit, I did too. "We all do. But we'll adjust." I looked down at the little beast curled up on Clifford's shoes. I wasn't keen on inheriting the furry creature. But Clifford had promised he'd take the dog if Eliza wasn't allowed to have her on campus. "Stiff upper lip and all that."

So as not to incur any more of Clifford's ridicule, I tugged my blonde bob over my damp hair. I did look absurd in Eliza's frilly dress, especially since it was two sizes too small. At least with the wig, I looked like a poorly dressed doll instead of a man in drag.

"Enough stalling, Fiona." Clifford removed his pipe from his pocket but then thought better of it. "Tell me what you know."

I told him about my investigation on Edison's yacht and the great phenol plot.

"Good Lord." He stiffened. "That's treason. Is Edison in on it?"

"No. I don't think he is." I fussed with my wig. "What have you been doing?" I was distracted by thoughts of Archie, so I changed the subject, hoping Clifford would take the bait. Sure enough, he did.

While Clifford nattered on about everything the dog had done on their walk, down to the last infelicitous detail, I took stock of my equipment: spy lipstick, lockpick set, and Mata Hari's gun. Moving them from evening bag to practical bag and back again made it deuced difficult to keep track.

Bang. Bang. Bang.

Someone was banging on the door. Clifford and I looked at each other in alarm.

"Fiona, darling. It's me."

I knew that smooth tenor voice. I jumped up and flew to the door.

When I opened it, I stood face to face with... Lieutenant Archie Somersby.

My cheeks warmed. I was expecting him to return my telephone call, not show up at my door. My heart skipped a beat.

"Has something happened?" he asked, coming closer... too

close. He put his hand on my arm. "Are you alright? I came as soon as I got the message."

"How did you know it was me?" My heart was racing.

"You're the only person I know at the Knickerbocker Hotel." He glanced over at Clifford, who was tamping tobacco into his pipe.

"Did you do it?" I whispered, my voice trembling. "Did you kill him?"

"Can we talk?" He peeked inside the room. "In private."

"I say, what's going on here?" Clifford came to my side. "Is the lieutenant bothering you, old girl?" He tugged at the hem of his jacket.

Outranked, Archie gave a crisp salute. "Captain Douglas."

"Captain Douglas was just leaving." *Breathe, Fiona. Just breathe.*

"I say..." Clifford stammered. "Is that quite cricket? Inviting a man—"

"The lieutenant and I have business to discuss," I cut him off. Anyway, wasn't Clifford a man? He'd been alone with me in my room for the last half an hour. "Why don't you take Poppy for a walk?"

"We've already been—" Clifford frowned. The little dog was sitting at his feet looking up at him.

"Take the dog for another walk." I wasn't in the mood for pleasantries or cajoling.

Pouting, Clifford gathered up the lead and the pup. Poppy snarled at Archie on the way past.

"Thank you, Clifford, dear." I softened my tone. He really was trying to help. But I needed to talk with Archie alone.

"Are you sure you're alright, old bean?" His blue eyes searched mine.

I nodded. "Just go."

"Yes, ma'am." Clifford took a step backwards into the hall.

When he was finally out of my hair, I invited Archie inside and shut the door.

"Well?" I paced the length of the room. "Did you do it? Did you kill Hugo Schweitzer?" Just in case Archie was a cold-blooded killer, I snatched up my mesh evening bag off the nightstand. My fingers tightened around Mata Hari's gun inside.

"Schweitzer was a German spy." Archie took a step toward me. "He knew you'd been in his berth on the ship." He took another step. "He planned to kill you."

"Golly." I stood blinking at him.

"I couldn't let him do that." Archie reached out and took my free hand.

A spark of electricity traveled up my arm. I shivered and withdrew my hand from his. "Was it necessary to murder him?" I desperately wanted to kiss him. *Come on, Fiona, get a grip.*

"He diverted the entire phenol supply from the American army to Bayer Aspirin on orders from the Kaiser." Archie tapped a cigarette out of a packet of Kenilworths. "You found the evidence in his briefcase." He lit the cigarette.

"So, you killed him?" I looked him straight in the eye and stifled a cough. Blasted cigarette smoke.

"I had to—" He reached for my hand again.

I jerked my hand away. "You murdered him."

"I did it for you, Fiona." He gave me a quizzical look. "Don't you think you should be a little bit grateful?"

"Grateful you're an assassin?" I held my bag behind my back. "I never asked you to murder anyone."

"Calm down. Darling." He gave me a reassuring smile, but I could tell he was worried. "Fiona. Please."

"Did you frame Fredricks?" I took a step backwards, still grasping the gun through the fabric of my bag.

"No." He smiled. "You caught Fredricks red-handed." When he took a step in my direction, I took another step backwards.

I was pinned up against the nightstand. Slowly, both hands behind my back, I withdrew the gun from my handbag.

"Come on, Fiona." He shook his head and a lovely chestnut lock fell over his forehead. "Fredricks deserves to hang, and you, my love, deserve a commendation."

"Is that why you framed him?" My hand trembled as I dropped the handbag on the night table. "So I'd get a promotion?"

"You know Captain Hall doesn't take you seriously." He grinned. "With your adorable mustaches and beards." He chuckled. "Why not kill two birds with one stone?"

"Literally." Nonchalantly, I brought my gun hand around and dropped it to my side. "Schweitzer is dead and Fredricks will hang." I lifted the gun. "A man shouldn't hang for a crime he didn't commit."

"Whoa." He held up his hand. "Calm down, Fio!" His tone changed from cajoling to demanding. "Give me the gun."

No one ever called me Fio, except my late ex-husband, Andrew. It was unnerving to hear Archie using that nickname.

"You need to go to the police," I said through my tears, holding the gun with both hands to steady my aim. "Fredricks shouldn't hang for your crime."

"It's war." His countenance hardened. "Fio, give me the bloody gun."

That nickname again. I wished he'd stop calling me that. The last time I heard it was on Andrew's deathbed in Charing Cross Hospital.

"And all is fair in love and war?" Tears flowing down my face, I shook my head. "If we don't stand on principles, then what are we fighting for?" My nose was running, and my hands trembled.

Still, I didn't let go of the gun. "If we become cold-blooded killers, then we are just as bad as our enemies." I quickly wiped my cheek with the back of my hand. "Aren't we fighting for justice and truth?"

"We're fighting for old Blighty." He took a drag of his cigarette, blew out a cloud of smoke. He smiled at me, but I sensed fear in his eyes.

"England stands for truth and justice." I took a deep breath, which I immediately regretted when I got a lungful of smoke. "If we give up our values in wartime, then we give up our reason for fighting." Through my tears, the room was a blur and so was he. My hands trembled as I pointed the gun straight at his heart.

"Don't be naïve, Fiona." He wiggled his fingers at me. "Now give me that damned gun before someone gets hurt." He dropped the cigarette on the floor and ground it out under the heel of his shoe.

His tone scared me, and his words stung. *Naïve.* Patronizing from Clifford or the men in Room 40 was one thing, but from Archie, the man I loved? I couldn't take it. I waved the gun at him. "I'm taking you to the police."

"Look, Fiona." He ran his hand through his hair. "I was following orders."

"Explain that to the police." I bit my lip but held the gun steady.

"The War Office wanted me to get rid of Schweitzer before he did any more damage." He held out both hands as if inviting me into an embrace.

Oh, Archie. Why did you do it? Why did you kill a man and frame another? Please tell me you didn't do it for me. I just stood there, crying.

"It's better this way." He ran his hand through his hair again.

"Don't you see? Two German spies out of the way and you'll get the credit."

"I don't want the credit." The collar of my dress was wet with tears. I glanced down. Good grief. I'd forgotten I was wearing Eliza's ridiculous dress. What must Archie think?

"Fio, I'm helping you get ahead."

I couldn't tell if his eyes were pleading with me or accusing me.

"I don't need your help!" I waved the gun at him.

He held up his hand again. "Okay, okay. I'll go to the police." Without missing a beat, he lunged at me.

I jumped sideways, just escaping his grasp. "I'll shoot." I steadied the gun.

He let out a nervous laugh. "You wouldn't shoot me."

"Try me." I let the tears flow down my cheeks. I didn't dare take my hands off the gun to wipe them off.

"You're making a mistake." He shook his head.

The tears were hot and streaming now. I stood there, speechless, pointing the gun at him. Oh, Archie, how could you?

"I know you won't shoot me," he whispered, taking a step backwards.

I stood there blubbering. If he took another step, I'd shoot. I aimed for his leg.

He stopped and gazed at me, his green eyes soft.

I took a deep breathe to strengthen my resolve.

"Come away with me." He held out his hands again. "Give me the gun and we can go away together."

I blinked the tears from my eyes. He was trying to cajole me into giving up. Maybe Fredricks was right, and Archie was a double agent. How could I know? Which side was he on? "I can't," I sniffed. "I can't trust you."

His shoulders sagged like a two-ton weight had dropped on him. He sighed and bit his lip. "I love you, Fiona."

I dropped the gun.

His eyes shone. "Goodbye."

I watched in awe as he walked out of the room.

25

THE TEAM

Thirty minutes later, my hands were still shaking. My cheeks were stained with tears. He loved me. Archie loved me. Or was he just saying that to keep me from shooting him?

I sat on my bed, hugging myself and rocking back and forth. On my lap, Mata Hari's gun was tucked back into my handbag.

Would I ever see him again? Had Archie just walked out of my life for good?

I shouldn't have threatened him with a gun. Of course I couldn't shoot him. But he'd killed a man... in cold blood. And he'd framed another. I thought he was one of the good chaps. He was a British soldier. Didn't that mean he was on the side of right, and good, and justice?

I buried my head in my hands.

He'd done it for me. To protect me. *Oh, Archie.*

I couldn't stem the tide of sobs.

I was a puddle of grief and regret when Clifford returned from walking the dog.

"Good Lord." Clifford sat down on the bed next to me. "What did that bounder do to you?" He put his arm around my shoulders. "Come on, old girl." He pulled a handkerchief from his breast pocket and handed it to me. "Chin up and all that."

Poppy stood on her hind legs and pawed at Clifford's trousers. Magically, he produced a bit of dog kibble from his pocket and fed it to the little beast. No wonder she was begging.

"You're teaching her bad manners." I put my hand down to shoo the creature away. She licked my hand. So much for discipline.

"She's a jolly clever pup." Clifford stood up. "Watch this." He tied a knotted rope onto the lavatory door handle. "Poppy." He dug in his pocket for another treat.

That got the little dog's attention. She sat alert at his feet.

"Do you need the loo?" Clifford asked her in a silly hyper-excited voice. "Go to the loo. Go on."

The creature stood on her hindlegs with her paws against the door. Then she grabbed the knotted rope in her mouth and pulled the door handle down. The door popped open, and she trotted inside.

I clapped my hands together and laughed. "Jolly clever."

"I keep a pad on the floor of the loo and if I'm not there to take her out, she can go in on her own, and Bob's your uncle." He beamed with pride.

Disgusting. But it was better than the beast doing her business on the floor.

Tap. Tap. Tap.

Another knock at the door.

My heart leaped into my throat. Had Archie come back? If he had, that meant he was turning himself in. I almost hoped it wasn't him.

I opened the door. "Eliza, what are you doing back so soon?"

Poppy came running and leaped into her mistress's arms. The

girl cooed at the squirming furry ball. When Poppy licked her face, Eliza giggled in delight.

Eliza carried the pup into the room and plopped down on *my* bed... probably because Clifford was sitting cross-legged, smoking, on hers.

"I saw him leaving," she said coyly.

"Who?" I asked, closing the door.

"Your lieutenant." She smiled up at me. "Is he the one?"

My breath caught. "The one?" Were my feelings for him that obvious? "Whatever do you mean?" Staring down at my shoes, I fiddled with the strap on my bag.

She put Poppy on the floor. The little beast ran straight to me. When I patted the creature on her furry little topknot, she licked my hand again. Was the beasty motivated by sympathy or the residue of my lunch?

"The one who shot Mr. Schweitzer." Eliza lay back on my bed.

Alarm bells went off in my head. "Why do you say that?" I forgot that I was holding my handbag and I must have let it go. It dropped to the floor with a thud. Mata Hari's gun.

Poppy pounced on it, clamped her steel jaws around my bag, and ran off. Horrid little creature.

"He was at the opera that night." Eliza kicked her shoes off. "In the box with the missing seat cushion."

The blasted girl didn't miss a beat.

Poppy jumped onto my bed and delivered my evening bag to her mistress. "Good baby." Eliza retrieved my poor bag from her pup's maw. A quizzical look crossed her face as she wiped dog slobber off my handbag. "Does your lieutenant smoke?"

"Unfortunately." I nodded. "And he's not *my* lieutenant."

"What brand?" She sat up, holding up my handbag to examine it.

"Disgusting Kenilworths." I crossed the room to grab my bag out of her hands.

"Kenilworths are fine cigarettes," Clifford said. "Lots of Tommies smoke them." He puffed on his pipe.

"Why do you ask?" I ignored Clifford and scrutinized my handbag.

"Look at this." With her fingernail, Eliza held out a fragment of paper with tiny letters on it.

I bent down to take a closer look. Blimey. The letters "Ken" were imprinted on the paper. "A piece of cigarette paper."

"Your lieutenant must have used a cigarette as a delay fuse to light the banger." Eliza smiled. "Very clever."

"Good Lord." Clifford came to my side. "Are you saying Lieutenant Somersby set off the banger cracker using one of his cigarettes as fuse?" He bent over to examine the paper fragment. "That bounder Somersby should be arrested, and poor Fredricks should be freed."

Fredricks. Right. He was still in jail. "We should go and see Fredricks and clear his name." As soon as it was out of my mouth, I regretted saying it. How could I clear Fredricks's name without sullying Archie's? I didn't want Archie to hang. Archie was a British solider. Fredricks was a German spy. Where was the justice in that?

I wish I'd never come to America.

I dropped my handbag—with its incriminating evidence. The final nail in Archie's coffin.

If Schweitzer was a German spy, then Archie was just doing his duty. America was our ally. Surely they wouldn't execute a British soldier for doing his duty... would they?

I wish I'd never met Lieutenant Archie Somersby.

"Brilliant." Clifford ambled to the door. "I'll just fetch my coat and hat and then I'll meet you in the lobby." Of course, he was eager to free his mate, the great South African huntsman. After all, they'd killed half the species on the continent together, which made them blood brothers... at least from Clifford's perspective.

Eliza was down on the floor playing with Poppy. Not very ladylike, not to mention unhygienic.

"Where did you learn about bangers and cigarette papers and gunpowder residue?" I dropped back onto my bed. "And all that gen about crimes and criminals?"

"I've told you." She didn't look up. "At the boarding school in Lyon." She threw a balled-up piece of newspaper. Poppy barked and chased after it. Eliza's laughter was pure and bright. From looking at her, you'd think she was just an innocent schoolgirl. But I suspected there was more to the girl than met the eye.

"Where did you grow up?" I asked, staring out of the window. It was snowing again. I should bundle up to go outside, but the weight of the world pressing down on me was paralyzing. Maybe if I stalled, we wouldn't have to spring Fredricks and tell the police about Archie.

Eliza glanced up at me but didn't answer.

"Have you always been close to your uncle, Captain Hall?" *Good heavens. Captain Hall.* How was I going to explain everything to him? The great phenol plot. Hugo Schweitzer, the German spy. Lieutenant Archie Somersby, the assassin. The murder of Anna Case and those immoral moralists, the Comstock Crusaders.

Trying to parse right from wrong was making my head spin. The spy, the assassin, the moralist. Who was right? Each of them would swear on their life they were good, and their opponents were evil. Both Archie and Fredricks claimed to be doing their duty. Hugo Schweitzer probably thought he was too. Even the rabid Comstock boys probably thought it was their duty to stop the suffragettes and women's reproductive rights.

"He's not really my uncle." Eliza's voice jolted me out of my reveries.

"What?" I perked up.

She leaned over and picked up my handbag. "He's my bene-factor... and my commander." She pulled Mata Hari's gun from my bag.

I sat there, blinking at her.

"He sent me on this mission..." She turned the gun over in her hands. "To make sure you captured Fredricks. All those invita-tions to royal balls and operas, he was worried you were courting instead of spying."

Captain Hall never had trusted me. I knew it. I was constantly trying to prove myself to him. He wouldn't have sent me on *this* mission except for Fredricks taunting me with opera tickets and invitations. The War Office merely used me to get to Fredricks. I'd been so close to catching him red-handed. So many times. But the slippery eel always managed to escape.

But Eliza? She was just a schoolgirl here on a music scholar-ship. What did she mean she was sent on this mission? Was it all a ruse? I pressed my hands into my temples. I needed some headache powders.

What about Poppy? Was the pup a ruse too?

"Are you okay, Aunt Fiona?" Eliza stood up. She still had the gun in her hand.

"We shouldn't keep Clifford waiting." I rubbed my forehead. "He's eager to liberate his friend."

"Mr. Fredricks is where he belongs." Eliza held the gun in her right hand as casually as she held Poppy's lead. "Let's leave well enough alone, shall we, Auntie?" She slipped her feet into her shoes.

"We can't let an innocent—"

"Fredricks is far from innocent. He is an enemy of England.

He is a German spy and collaborator." She smiled sweetly. "We've accomplished our mission."

"Our mission?" What did she mean *our* mission? I went to the wardrobe to fetch my coat and hat.

She nodded and her blonde curls bobbed up and down. "We make a brilliant team."

My cheeks burned. "Team?"

"You won't need those." She waved the gun toward the lavatory. "Why don't you take a seat on the toilet while I go inform Uncle Clifford you've gone to bed with a headache."

I stood staring at her. Had Captain Hall sent her to spy on me? Or was she working for the Germans too? My head was spinning again. I felt quite faint.

"Why don't you sit down, Auntie?" Eliza took me by the elbow and led me into the lav. "You don't look well."

"What is going on here?" I sat on the edge of the bathtub. "I take it you didn't come to New York for a music scholarship."

"Lieutenant Somersby is right." She laughed. "There's no pulling the wool over your eyes for long."

Bloody hell. Was Archie in on this too? My stomach flipped.

"What about Clifford?" I asked. "He's waiting for us... for me."

"Uncle Clifford is not as clever as you are, Auntie dear." She smiled. "I can take care of him." Poppy barked, obviously not keen on her mistress bad-mouthing her new friend.

"What do you think you're doing?" *Can I get the drop on her?* I kept my eyes trained on the gun in her right hand.

"Nothing. And neither are you." She sat down on the commode. "In an hour, Mr. Fredricks will be on a ship headed back to England, where hopefully he will be executed for his crimes against Britain."

"Even if he did do it, Schweitzer was a German spy killed in America." Fredricks wouldn't be executed. Would he? Then again, I was pretty sure he'd killed an English countess and a Russian one too. "More to the point, Fredricks didn't do it. He's innocent and you know it."

"But no one else needs to know." The sweetness had disappeared from her smile. "Agreed?"

"You want me to agree to lie when a man's life is at stake?" If push came to shove, I rather liked Fredricks, even if we were on opposite sides. "You lied about the gunpowder test. It proved Fredricks was innocent, didn't it?"

"We have a mission to complete." She smirked and stood up. "Our mission is to bring Fredricks to justice."

"And what of the pretense of justice being the pinnacle of injustice?" I wasn't about to let a man die for a crime he didn't commit.

"I'm going to give you some time to think." With one hand, she pulled a length of rope out of her skirt pocket.

Resourceful little minx.

"It's not that I don't trust you, Aunt Fiona." She still held the gun in the other. She waved the gun at me. "But I can't have you ruining our mission just because you have feelings for the killer. Sit on the toilet and face the wall."

Feelings for the killer. Did she know about Archie?

She waved the gun at me again.

Never one to argue with a girl with a gun, I did as she asked.

She tied the rope around my wrists and then fastened it to a plumbing pipe. "Classic Highwayman's Hitch." She beamed with pride.

Poppy ran in circles nearby, yapping. I didn't know if the beast was amused or distressed by her mistress's transformation from pleasant schoolgirl to threatening spy.

"I'll be back when Mr. Fredricks is safely aboard the ship on the way back to England to pay for his crimes." She stopped at the door. "We do make an excellent team, you know."

"Do you always tie up your teammates?" I tugged at the rope. I had to give her credit. The girl did know how to tie a decent knot.

I cranked my head around to see what she was up to now.

"Only when they've lost their ability to remain detached from the situation." She grabbed a small cloth from the drying rack.

"I suppose you're an expert on knots, too." Another one of her hidden talents?

"No, I'm knot." She snickered.

"Very funny." When I tugged at the ropes, they cut into my wrists. My struggle was in vain. "At least tell me the truth." I twisted my neck to look at the girl. "Who are you really? And why are you doing this?"

She came at me with the cloth. I tried to wrest my head away, but tressed up like a Christmas goose, I couldn't get my balance. "I promise, I'll be as still as a mouse."

"You'll have a tale to tell." She smirked. "My name is Kitty Lane." She tightened the rope.

Ouch.

"Let's just say the coppers and I didn't see eye to eye when I was growing up on the streets." She smiled. "Blinker Hall caught me pinching his wallet and gave me another chance." She shrugged. "He sent me to France for training and made me part of Operation Petticoat, an elite squad of girls working for the War Office."

The frills, lace, and giggles... they'd all been an act? "What about Billy Buck?" How did he fit in?

"I met silly Billy aboard the *Adriatic*." She threw her head back in laughter. "Throw a stick in any direction and you'll hit an American soldier named Billy."

My head was spinning. Didn't Captain Hall send the girl to

America to keep her away from Billy? Was Captain Hall in on the Billy ploy? Or had the girl fooled him too?

The wretched girl stuffed the towel in my mouth and tied it around my head.

She waved. "Ta ta, Auntie."

"You evil girl!" My voice was muffled through the cloth. Who knows what she heard?

"Just keep calm." She smiled. "I'll be back soon." She stepped out of the lav and then peeked her head back in. "Oh, and I hope your headache is better soon."

Grrrrrrr. I wanted to throttle the girl.

Captain Hall had tricked me. I wasn't babysitting Eliza. She was babysitting me.

26

THE GREAT ESCAPE

As soon as I heard the door to the room shut, I tried yelling for help. It was no use. She'd tied the towel too tightly around my head. I shook my head. But without the use of my hands, I couldn't loosen the gag.

My arms were stretched behind me. I couldn't even lower myself off the commode without attempting painful contortions.

Bark. Bark. Bark.

Good heavens. The girl had left Poppy to guard me.

Since I was boxed into the corner between the commode and two walls, I leaned to my left and rubbed my head against the wall. If I couldn't loosen the gag, maybe I could scrape my wig off, gag and all. Bad idea. All I got was an awful crick in my neck.

Bark. Bark. Bark.

What was Poppy so excited about?

The lavatory door popped open, and Poppy trotted in. *Clifford's trick.*

The little pooch looked up at me with a question in those big dark eyes.

Yes, my little friend. Believe it. Your mistress did this to me.

I cranked my head around to watch the pup twirl in circles and then stop near the rope that held me fastened to the plumbing.

My eyes widened as the creature grasped the end of the rope in her maw and jerked her head back and forth like a lunatic. The Highwayman's Hitch gave way and the rope dropped in loops onto the floor.

Quickly, I pulled my arms loose from the plumbing. My poor shoulders. As I pulled, the ropes loosened around my wrists. Thank goodness. I wriggled my hands free and yanked the blooming towel out of my mouth. "Good dog!"

When I stretched my aching arms, the little beast saw it as an invitation. She jumped up into my arms. I kissed her furry head, and she licked my face. I was never so happy to have my chin soiled by unhygienic dog slobber in all my life.

As much as I despised Fredricks for his allegiance to the enemy, I did not approve of any man paying the price for another man's crime... even if that other man was my beloved.

Anyway, hopefully, Archie was long gone by now. If he left the country, maybe he'd be okay.

I just had to get to the nick, present the new evidence, and clear Fredricks's name. I cringed. In order to clear Fredricks, I'd have to implicate Archie. I'd have to tell the coppers about the banger, the golden thread, the seat cushion, Archie's citrus cologne, the frame-up, and Archie's confession... perhaps not his confession of love. I touched my warm cheek.

One problem. Those constables never listened to a woman.

The solution. Rear Admiral Arbuthnot. Everyone listened to him.

I slipped out of my frock and blonde bob and into the naval uniform, complete with trousers, jacket, cap, my favorite mustache, and a beard for good measure.

"Guard the place," I said to Poppy as I dashed out of the door.

Too impatient to wait for the lift, I galloped down the stairs. I'd just entered the lobby when I saw Eliza—er, Kitty—chatting to Clifford across the room. Blast.

I ducked into the women's lav, and came face to face with a familiar face, John Edgar Hoover's face, but on a woman. She was a stocky girl in a slinky red dress, crimson lipstick, and heavy eye kohl. I swear she was the spitting image of Mr. Hoover. Did he have a sister?

She stared at me, and I stared back. Uncanny.

Did Mr. Hoover use disguises in his undercover work?

"Excuse me," I said, doing an about-face and exiting the lavatory.

Get a grip, Fiona, old girl. You're in disguise, for heaven's sake. Just walk past with confidence and even Eliza Kitty won't recognize you.

When I peeked out into the lobby, both the evil Kitty and Clifford were gone. But where? Had they gone together? What did Eliza Kitty say to the old boy to put him off liberating his friend?

Taking long strides, I marched across the lobby. The doorman called me a taxicab.

"To the midtown nick," I told the cabbie.

"Huh?"

"Police station."

Already when we pulled up in front of the nick, I could tell something wasn't right. Several copper cars had their lights flashing. Were they transferring Fredricks to the ship for extradition?

I paid the driver and hopped out of the taxi. A cold wind ripped right through my uniform and stung my skin. Give me London's weepy skies any day over this frigid ice block.

Inside, officers were running this way and that. An exceptionally tall man barked out orders, along with epitaphs.

Weaving through the chaos, I made my way to the reception desk.

Blast. She beat me. Eliza Kitty was leaning against the wall, picking at her nail varnish. Had she already dispatched Fredricks?

Clearing my throat to conjure my deepest voice, I approached the officer at the desk. "I'd like to visit a prisoner." I coughed from the effort. "Mr. Fredrick Fredricks."

"Haven't you heard?" the officer asked, an excited spark in his eyes. "Mr. Fredricks has flown the coop."

"Escaped?" Good heavens. Leave it to Fredricks to make his great escape just in the nick of time.

"Escaped." Eliza Kitty smirked.

Bad kitty.

"Don't worry." She pushed off from the wall and stood facing me. "I'll find him."

"Not if I find him first." I gave a salute and made for the exit.

* * *

I knew Fredricks was long gone by now, so I headed back to the hotel. I needed a strong cup of tea for fortification before I called Captain Hall and demanded to know what was going on and why he'd sent Eliza, er, Kitty, to spy on me while I was spying on Fredricks. I was going to ask him point blank why he didn't trust me.

When I got back to the Knickerbocker, Clifford was waiting for me in the lobby. Of course, he didn't recognize Rear Admiral Arbuthnot. I slipped past him and hurried up to my room to change.

Poppy greeted me with a wag and a yip. She'd managed to

tear the corner off one of the bedcovers. I hoped the War Office expense account included damages.

At the dressing table, I carefully peeled off the mustache and beard. My poor face was as red and swollen as a tomato. I'd developed an allergy to spirit gum that should make me consider another line of work.

I went to the wardrobe, withdrew my small case, sat it on my bed, and then lovingly placed my favorite mustache back in the center compartment. I threw the beard into the tray underneath.

After I'd changed into a woolen skirt, heavy blouse, and my practical Oxfords, I tidied up the room. Between Poppy's antics and Eliza Kitty dumping the contents of my bag on the floor, the room was a mess.

Orderly on the outside, orderly on the inside, as my dear old grandmother always said. I gathered up my spy lipstick, lockpick set, opera glasses, and... where was the gun? Did the little minx take Mata Hari's gun?

I had a thing or two to say to Captain Hall about his "niece."

Once my belongings were back in their proper places, I surveyed the room with satisfaction. Apart from the shredded bed cover, everything was in order... except for the pocket watch.

I hurried to my night table. Archie's gold pocket watch. What was it doing here? Had he left it in the melee earlier? I didn't remember him putting his watch on my night table. Was he leaving a keepsake for me?

I picked up the watch and turned it over. It was heavy in my hands... and my heart. Oh, Archie. With a fingernail, I flipped it open. A small piece of paper fell out onto the night table.

Good heavens. He left a note. My pulse quickened. My heart was racing as I unfolded the paper. A faint scent of smoky rosewood drifted into my consciousness. I devoured the letter, trying to read it in its entirety all at once. Of course, that technique worked for taking a mental photograph, but not for under-standing what was written.

I forced myself to slow down and read.

Dearest Fiona,

By now you've heard that I pulled off another daring escape. Of course, my first thought was to visit you—that is to say, my first thought after planning how I would dispose of my adversary in all things, including for your heart.

I gasped. How did Fredricks acquire Archie's pocket watch? I shuddered to think. He would want revenge against Archie for framing him. What if he killed... No. I couldn't let my thoughts go there. If Fredricks harmed one hair on Archie's fine head, I would throttle the bounder with my bare hands.

I took a deep breath and continued reading.

I advise you to watch out for the girl. Miss Eliza is not what she seems. Indeed, she is another formidable adversary.

Thank God you, dearest Fiona, are more even-tempered and level-headed. You give me hope that we can stop this bloody war, even if the suffragettes can't keep the Americans from combat.

Conversation, if not compromise and conciliation, must be possible for any hope of peace.

Just as the Suez Canal facilitates commerce between the Red Sea and the Mediterranean, you and I will facilitate peace between your allies and mine, the Central Powers. We will find the shortcut together, my sweet Ficus carica.

Please don't follow me. It's too dangerous. I will contact you when it's safe.

Yours always,

Fredrick

Good grief. Why was Fredricks always so melodramatic? *Ficus carica.* Fig in Latin. Horsefeathers.

True. The bloody war was a tragedy for both sides. True. It must end. But why was Fredricks constantly going on about how *we* would end it?

I was just tied to a toilet by a schoolgirl and liberated by a Pekingese doing a rope trick. How could I possibly contribute to ending this blooming war? Was Fredricks completely daft?

Tap. Tap. Tap.

Before answering the door, I folded the note and tucked it into my skirt pocket. I slid Archie's pocket watch into my handbag.

"Clifford, dear." I opened the door wider. "Won't you come in?"

"I say, Fiona," he sputtered. "Where the devil have you been?" He paced the length of the room. "Eliza said you were ill. I was deuced worried about you."

Tongue lolling, Poppy did a little dance around his feet.

"Your mate Fredricks escaped from jail." I tilted my head. "What do you think of that?"

"Blimey." Clifford bent down to pat the pup.

When I told him what Eliza had done, he dropped onto her bed and sat there blinking up at me. "I say, Fiona. You have quite an imagination."

Huff. "I didn't imagine it." I held out my wrists and showed him the rope burns. "Exhibit A."

"Why would the lovely Eliza do something like that?" he asked, toying with his pipe.

I scowled at him, and he put the foul thing back into his jacket.

"Appearances are deceiving, especially when it comes to the lovely Eliza." I fingered the note in my skirt pocket.

Poppy jumped up onto Eliza Kitty's bed and licked Clifford's hand.

"Give me some of those dog treats." I opened my palm.

"I say, if you're hungry, we can go down to the canteen."

"Not for me, silly."

"Oh." Clifford dug in his trouser pocket and produced a handful of kibble.

I knelt next to the bed and fed the kibble piece by piece to my furry friend.

The door to the room opened, and Eliza Kitty stepped inside.

I brushed off my hands and stood up. "You have a lot of nerve, Missy."

"Apologies, Aunt Fiona." She smiled sweetly. "I was just doing my duty and helping you do yours." *Cheeky girl.*

"I don't need your help." Arms akimbo, I glared at her. "Especially when it comes to my duty."

"Brilliant." She produced a telegram from her skirt pocket. "Duty calls." She held it out to me.

"What is it?" Clifford asked.

"It's from your mates in Room 40." Eliza Kitty sat down next to Clifford, and Poppy leapt into her lap. "They've decoded a telegram indicating his next move is some sort of sabotage in Egypt."

"Egypt." I pinched the note in my pocket. "What do you know about the Suez Canal?"

* * *

Two weeks later, gray skies welcomed me back to dreary old London. I'd never been so glad to be back home to a long-awaited decent cuppa, a nice hot bath, and my own cozy bed.

After a month away, stepping into Room 40 was a thrill.

The men gathered round me, congratulating me on a job well done... which was deuced confusing considering Fredricks had escaped, and the true killer was still missing—not that I wanted him found.

"I always knew you were the right woman for the job." Mr. Knox slapped me on the back like I was one of the lads. "Good on you, Fiona Figg."

"Person," I corrected. "Person for the job." I filled the electric kettle and then rinsed out a teacup.

Mr. Knox cleared his throat. "Righto. Person it is."

"Cheerio, Miss Figg." Mr. Grey extended his mousy paw. "Well done."

Perplexed, I wiped my hands on a dishtowel and then shook his hand.

What did they know that I didn't?

After swishing hot water around to warm the teapot, I sprinkled in a healthy dose of black tea and poured boiling water over it. The smoky smell of strong English tea invigorated me.

A boy wearing three-quarter length woolen trousers and a cap poked his head into the kitchenette. "The Guv wants to see you, Miss Figg." He smiled at me.

"Captain Hall?"

The boy nodded.

As usual, Captain Blinker Hall was seated behind his mahogany desk. Dwarfed by the giant wooden fixture, he put me in mind of Lewis Carroll's *Through the Looking-Glass*. He stood up and came around to the other side.

"Congratulations, Miss Figg." He extended his hand.

Now, I stood blinking at him.

"Our agent in the field reports you did a splendid job in New York." He shook my hand vigorously. "I'm recommending you for a commendation."

"Agent in the field?" My heart was racing. Could he mean Archie?

A giggle from behind the door made me whip around.

"Don't look at me." Eliza Kitty raised her eyebrows.

"You two ladies make quite a team." Captain Hall gestured toward the girl. "You cracked the phenol plot."

"That was all Fiona's doing," Kitty said. "I was just along for the ride."

I couldn't help but smile... even though I was still annoyed at the girl. Not to mention my irritation with Captain Hall for tricking me.

"And Lieutenant Somersby finished the job." Captain Hall sounded like he was boasting. "I'm also putting him in for a special commendation."

So, Archie was acting under orders? He was sent by British Intelligence to assassinate Schweitzer. I closed my eyes, both relieved and appalled. *Is Archie an assassin? Does the country I love go around killing people in cold blood?*

"I knew Kitty would keep you on your toes, Miss Figg." Captain Hall chuckled. "She reports you didn't resort to those ridiculous disguises, and you stayed the course. Good on you, Miss Figg."

Eliza Kitty may have lied for me, but I still didn't trust her. I glanced over at her, sitting there in that frilly dress and bonnet, looking every bit an innocent schoolgirl. Ha! I knew better.

"You're obtaining invaluable information for the war effort by trailing Fredricks." Captain Hall dropped back into his chair. "That's why I'm sending you both to Cairo. You'll stay with my friend Hogarth and his wife." He opened his desk drawer, pulled out a box, and opened it. "Care for a cigar to celebrate?" he asked, jokingly.

Eliza Kitty jumped up, selected a cigar, and rolled it between her fingers.

Good grief. "Eliza, dear, you shouldn't—"

She gave me a knowing smile. "Fancy a cigar, Aunt Fiona?"

"No, thank you." I turned up my nose.

Captain Hall chuckled as he lit Kitty's cigar and then his own. Soon the room was suffocating in cigar smoke.

I stifled a cough.

"Trail Fredricks, get close to him, and report back." Captain Hall blinked and puffed. "Don't bring him in or stop him unless it is a matter of life and death." He puffed and blinked some more. "He's more useful to us on the loose."

"Keep your friends close," Kitty said between puffs. "And your enemies closer."

I gave her a knowing look, with my stinging eyes, as if to say, *see, I was right to want him free.*

"You gals best go and get ready for your trip," Captain Hall said through clenched teeth and his cigar.

"Perhaps you can send us separately." I waved my hand in front of my face. "Divide and conquer, and all that."

"I trust Kitty and so should you." His voice brooked no objections.

Trust Kitty? The bad kitty? Never. I nodded.

Captain Hall smiled. "Get whatever you need, new wardrobe. The War Office will pay all expenses."

Oh, that could be diverting. Not that it would make up for what the bad kitty had done to me or being forced to work with her in Cairo.

Still, I couldn't wait to do some shopping at Angel's Fancy

Dress. I rubbed my hands together. I already had some disguises in mind.

"No silly disguises." Captain Hall stared me down. "Got that, Miss Figg?"

I nodded. Why couldn't he see how useful those disguises were? They were a necessary tool in my espionage toolbox.

"From now on, you two are a team." Captain Hall smiled and waved his cigar. "And Captain Douglas will chaperone."

Was he having a laugh? If so, it wasn't funny. Clifford was bad enough, but now I had to put up with Eliza, er, Kitty, too?

"I don't need a babysitter—"

He cut me off. "Where one of you goes, so does the other." His tone was dead serious.

"And I don't need a chaperone." Kitty puffed on her cigar.

Captain Hall ignored our protests. "A pair of damned good lady spies."

Lady spies? How about *spies*, full stop.

Tightening my lips, I glared over at Eliza Kitty. I was stuck with the little minx.

She winked at me. Cheeky girl.

At least Captain Hall finally had recognized my value. Too bad I had to smile and share the spotlight with the bad kitty. If he only knew what she'd done to me. Blooming hades. For all I knew, he'd ordered her to tie me up. Apparently, the bad kitty was his go-to girl.

Kitty smiled and lifted Poppy's paw. "Wave goodbye." She waved the furry little beast's paw at me. "Bon voyage, Aunt Fiona."

"Where I go, she goes." I crossed the office to pet Poppy's furry topknot. "Right, pup?"

"Of course," Kitty smiled up at me. "Poppy is part of the team too."

"The best part, if you ask me." I forced a fake smile.

If I had to work with the wretched girl, I would find a way to get even with her for tying me to a toilet. From now on, I would beat her at her own game. And I would find Fredricks before she did.

Poppy barked.

"Whose side are you on, little beasty?"

"We're all on the same side." Kitty smiled.

Poppy jumped off the girl's lap. When Kitty stood up, her blonde curls bobbed. The pink frills on her skirt took flight as she twirled around. Poppy followed suit. Two whirling dervishes.

Heaven help me. I shook my head in disbelief. *Good grief.* These were my partners?

If Kitty's Eliza persona was an act, it was a devilishly good one. I would need to up my game if I was going to beat her to Fredricks.

Yes. I rubbed my hands together again and smiled. I knew just the costume to ensure my victory.

First stop, Angel's Fancy Dress.

Next stop, Cairo.

A NOTE FROM THE AUTHOR
FUN FACTS

Chaos at Carnegie Hall was inspired by several real-life characters.

Believe it or not, Fredrick Fredricks was the alias of a real World War I spy whose real name was Fredrick Duquesne. He was known for his brazen persona and daring escapes from prison.

Emily Hobhouse was a British anti-war activist who campaigned against the British concentration camps in South Africa.

In 1917, J. Edgar Hoover had just graduated from law school and was a fan of the late Postmaster General, Anthony Comstock, who is famous for the Comstock laws prohibiting obscenity in the mail. Information on birth control and contraception was considered obscene, and Margaret Sanger was imprisoned as a result. Hoover was also a closeted gay man, who reportedly sometimes liked to wear women's clothes.

Margaret Sanger was a nurse and women's rights activist known for founding Planned Parenthood and for promoting access to birth control, especially for poor women. She is also infamous for endorsing eugenics later in her life.

Several other real-life suffragettes appear in the novel, including Alice Paul, Carrie Chapman Catt, and Dorothy Paine Whitney. And the Women's Suffragette Party of New York frequently had meetings at Carnegie Hall. Many of the suffragettes were also pacifists and didn't think America should join the war.

Dorothy Parker, known in her social circles as Mrs. Parker, was a journalist known for her quick wit and for founding the Algonquin Circle, a group of New York intellectuals and socialites who met for luncheon at the Algonquin Hotel. Although inspired by the real-life character, my version is very much fictionalized.

Anna Case was an opera star. She did sing at Carnegie Hall in fall 1917. And she was a favorite of Thomas Edison. He employed her for his tone tests. She did *not* die in a stage accident. That is pure fiction.

Thomas Edison was the famous inventor, known for inventing the lightbulb, and phonograph recordings, and the electric chair. In the so-called "war of the currents," Edison tried to discredit George Westinghouse's alternating current (AC) by using it to electrocute animals in public displays. One of the most horrific was the electrocution of an elephant on Coney Island, which Edison also filmed. The film is still available today. Edison was a proponent of direct current (DC). Westinghouse won the war. Today, we use AC in our homes.

Dr. Hugo Schweitzer was a chemist and industrial spy who worked for Bayer Aspirin. He called the Great War the "chemists' war," and he was involved in the great phenol plot to divert phenol from American ammunitions into the American branch of the German aspirin company. He did purchase phenol from Thomas Edison. The phenol plot was discovered when Schweitzer's financier, Heinrich Albert, accidently left his briefcase on a train and it was filled with incriminating papers. Dr. Schweitzer was not assassinated at Carnegie Hall. Again, that is pure fiction.

ACKNOWLEDGMENTS

Thanks to Verena Rose for adopting Fiona when she was an orphan and seeing her through the first three books. I'm indebted to Verena and Shawn Simmons at Level Best Books.

Thanks to Tara Loder, my editor at Boldwold Books, for believing in Fiona and insuring there will be many more installments to come. It's been a delight working with Tara and the team at Boldwood.

Thanks to my rough draft editor and "cheerleader," Lisa Walsh, who accompanies me on an otherwise lonely writing journey.

Thanks to my writers' group, Lorraine Lopez, Susan Edwards, and Benigno Trigo, for giving me helpful feedback on the first chapter.

As always, thanks to Beni for listening, and thanks to the rest of my family for their encouragement and interest in Fiona.

Special thanks to my furry friends, Mischief, Mayhem, and Flan, for distracting me with cuteness and hairballs.

Now turn the page for a sneak peek at...

Fiona's Next Adventure

THE STRANGER

This bloody war had taught me nothing was black and white...
except perhaps a strong cup of tea with a splash of milk, when
you could get it.

As the carriage clacked along the tracks through the desert
from Alexandria to Cairo, I distracted myself from thoughts of tea
with Annie Pirie's *The Pyramids of Giza*. My mouth parched and
my bottom bouncing on the hard wooden bench I shared with
Captain Clifford Douglas, I glanced over at our carriage companions, Miss Kitty Lane—whom I'd known until a week ago as Eliza
Baker—and a stranger who leaned against the wooden armrest
reading a slim volume.

The Egyptian railway carriages were white wooden trollies.
Nothing like the black iron horses of the British railway. Deuced
hot, too. The soot flooding in through the window was the same.
British or Egyptian. It didn't matter. We all choked on the same
smoke.

My book in one hand, I held a lavender-scented handkerchief
to my nose with the other. If only I'd worn my goggles. I squinted
at the pictures, concentrating on keeping my breakfast down.

More astounding than photographs of massive stone monuments jutting up out of the sand were pictures of one diminutive woman in a plaid shirt and flowery straw bonnet working in the dirt alongside male archeologists. Not because a woman couldn't do anything a man could do—at least anything important—but rather, that out of jealousy men usually didn't allow it.

Annie Pirie claimed it was under one of these grand pyramids that she'd met her future husband while they were both laid up with food poisoning.

Having nursed soldiers suffering from that very same affliction back at Charing Cross Hospital, I didn't find anything romantic about the squalls of salmonella.

Still, there was nothing like the vulnerability of the body to move the soul.

Why not fall in love over a bedpan?

After all, I'd met Archie Somersby when he was laid up with a shot-up arm. He'd asked me to help him write a letter to his mother.

My cheeks burned. *Oh Archie.* Would I ever see him again? Did I want to see him again? Now that I knew he was a government-sponsored assassin?

I dropped *Pyramids of Giza* on the seat next to me and withdrew a fan from my bag. Even with the windows open, it was beastly hot, and the desert seemed to go on forever. Winter in Egypt was a far cry from the chilly dampness of London or the snow in New York.

Once we'd left Alexandria with its oasis of palm trees, there was nothing but sand and more sand. Only the sky changed from brilliant blue to hazy brown, and along with it the thickness of the air. Heavy with humidity, now it was also laden with fine particles of sand.

I wiped my eyes with my handkerchief. My head bobbed

along with the rhythm of the carriage, nearly lulling me to sleep. Withdrawing a fan from my handbag, I fluttered it in front of my face in hopes of staying awake.

Hanky in one hand and the fan in the other, I stared over at my traveling companion, Eliza. *Or should I say Kitty?*

Just days ago, I learned the young woman sitting across from me, whom I knew from my last mission as Eliza Baker was really Kitty Lane, petty criminal and reform-school girl who'd studied criminology in France. Or at least that was *her* story.

Truth be told, I didn't know her cover name for our current mission, which was to protect the Suez Canal from whatever fiendish plot Fredrick Fredricks—infamous German spy and social gadfly—might be planning.

I wasn't keen on teaming up with a woman who had recently tied me to a toilet, but orders were orders.

Oblivious to the carriage's shaking and clattering, Kitty sat across from me, her nose buried in the latest issue of *Vogue* fashion magazine. With her legs stretched across the bench seat, wearing dark glasses, a flowing pink chiffon skirt dotted with tiny roses, a white blouse with pearl buttons, and an adorable sailor's hat, she looked the part of a fashion model herself.

I, on the other hand, was wearing a cotton blouse, linen skirt with multiple pockets for carrying items essential to espionage— magnifying glass, spy lipstick, lockpick set, tracing paper, charcoal pencil. As usual, I had on my practical oxfords in case I needed to make a quick getaway. My only concession to vanity were deep purple flowers on my straw hat. The hat was anchored with pins to what was left of my auburn locks, which I'd sacrificed to my first mission. I pressed the hat to my head, and I prayed it didn't blow off, frightening my companions. Without a wig or a hat, I looked like a bleached porcupine.

Even Kitty's Pekingese pup, Poppy, didn't recognize me when

my quills were exposed; she barked like she'd never seen me before. I gazed down at the little creature, and she smiled up at me.

Poppy had a pink ribbon in her topknot that matched her owner's outfit perfectly. The furry nuisance was sprawled across Clifford's lap, her outstretched paw touching my knee. Since the animal had rescued me from imprisonment in a loo on my last mission, I indulged her encroachment on my person.

Clifford was another matter. Indulging him often tried my patience. Captain Clifford Douglas had been sent along by the War Office to chaperone us despite the fact I'd already completed four missions. And Kitty, well, for all I knew she was an assassin in petticoats.

While engrossed in his hunting magazine and fantasies of killing, at least Clifford was quiet for a change.

"I say!" Clifford looked up from his magazine.

Blast. I knew it was too good to be true.

"Gezira Sporting Club has fox hunts with English hounds." Clifford beamed. "Do you ladies fancy a hunt?"

My eyes met Kitty's and we both laughed.

"Don't laugh, old girls, Cairo has jolly fine sporting clubs." Clifford's blue eyes flashed with indignation. "The Jockey Club is famous for its world-class horse races. How about lawn tennis at—"

"We're not in Arabia for sports." I interrupted him before he listed every sporting club on the African continent.

Clifford grumbled into his magazine. "You know, I once met Egyptologist Lord Carnarvon at the horse races—"

I interrupted him before he could launch into one of his stories. "Hunting. Fashion," I said, gesturing from Clifford to Kitty. "You'd think we were on holiday instead of..." I glanced over at the stranger in our compartment. "Instead of on business."

"You're a fine one to talk, Aunt Fiona." Kitty smirked at me. "You and your Baedeker's Guide to Cairo." Although I'd only know her for a few weeks, the girl had taken to calling me "Aunt" on our last mission, and she couldn't seem to shake the habit. At twenty-five, I was only seven years her senior and hardly an old maid.

"Given your pile of guidebooks..." Kitty pointed at my one slim book, which was really more of a pamphlet. My Baedeker's and Murray's were packed away. "You're preparing to play tourist." She pursed her rosebud lips.

"I'm learning my way around, not ogling the newest fashions," I said—perhaps a bit too defensively judging by the stormy change in Kitty's countenance.

I wasn't just learning about Cairo and its environs; I was committing to memory every page of every guidebook. I never knew when my photographic memory might come in handy. Still, I wished the War Office would issue me one of those clever disc spy cameras to wear under my shirt with the lens peeking out of a buttonhole.

"Poppy, old thing," Clifford said, gazing down at the dog in his lap. "We're going to have such a grand time. I'll show you all my favorite haunts in Cairo."

If only Poppy knew Clifford was reading a special issue of *The Field* devoted to fox hunting in Egypt. Like me, I was sure she would not approve of blood sports, especially those in which her distant cousins served as prey.

As if reading my mind, with her tongue lolling, Poppy gazed up at me with those big dark irresistible orbs. I patted the little beastie's topknot, and she licked my hand.

"No!" Kitty slapped her magazine shut. "They might eat her."

"Good grief," I scoffed. "Who would want to eat Poppy?"

"Everyone." Kitty slid off her seat onto her knees and scooped up the pup. "She's delicious." The girl buried her face in Poppy's fur.

"I'm sure Egyptians don't eat dogs." Truth be told, I wasn't sure. I turned to Clifford. "Do they?"

"Muslims consider dogs impure and unclean." Clifford withdrew his pipe from his breast-pocket.

I scowled at him.

He ignored me and lit the foul thing.

"Poppy isn't impure." The girl cuddled the squirming ball of fur. "Even if she isn't always clean."

"Kitty." I gestured toward the seat. "Speaking of unclean, please get up off the floor, dear."

"You're sweet as Christmas pudding." Kitty pulled the pup onto her lap as she took her seat. "But don't worry, Pops, no one is going to eat you." She nuzzled her face into the dog's muzzle.

Speaking of unhygienic.

"But the Christians or Coptics might." Grinning, Clifford jerked away from an imaginary smack on the shoulder.

"That's not funny!" Kitty held the dog in a tight embrace.

"Don't worry, old dear." Clifford patted his side as if he had a weapon concealed under his jacket. "I'll protect her... and you, too."

As if Kitty Lane needed anyone's protection. I'd vowed not to let the girlish giggles and frilly frocks fool me again.

"What do you think of this ensemble for Lady Enid's fancy dress ball?" Kitty displayed the *Vogue* cover with an illustration of a woman wearing a gaudy orange hoop skirt and tricornered hat that made her look like an oversized pumpkin.

"Lady who?" I gaped at the girl. "What fancy dress ball?" This was the first I'd heard of a ball. We'd only just disembarked the ship from England. We hadn't even arrived in Cairo. How in heaven's name did the girl already have an invitation to a ball?

"Lady Enid Clayton, the wife of Sir Gilbert Clayton." Clifford puffed his pipe and then let out a great cloud of foul smoke. "Director of Military Intelligence in the Arab Bureau."

"Friend of our hostess, Violet Hogarth." Kitty placed Poppy on the seat, in between herself and the stranger. "And Gertrude the Great."

"Who?"

"Aunt Fiona, you really must keep up," Kitty teased. "You should trade those musty old books for the society pages."

"Petrie, The Hogarth's, Gertrude Bell, T.E. Lawrence, and that lot." Clifford held his pipe in front of his mouth. "Archeologists excavating the ancient tombs, don't you know."

"More importantly, they have exquisite balls beneath the southern stars." Kitty clapped her hands together. "Doesn't it sound dreamy?" When she cooed at Poppy, the creature smiled up at her.

If it hadn't been for the stranger sharing our compartment, I would have chastised my mates. While I was busy preparing for our mission by studying guidebooks, they were faffing about with pretty dresses, gruesome blood sports, and fussing over a spoiled little dog.

"I guess you can tell our priorities by our reading material." I held up my book. "Mine is written by a scholar and a lady explorer." I nodded for emphasis. "She—"

"If you want to get to know a people," the stranger interrupted, "study their poetry."

I sat blinking at him.

Who was this striking man? He wore a red fez hat, white trousers and jacket, and a wide black belt and tall black boots. Not to be outdone by his bushy eyebrows and full beard, his grand mustache curled up on the ends a good two inches on either side of his upper lip. In fact, his facial hair was *so* impressive, I wondered if it were fake.

"Read Hafez Ibrahim, poet of the Nile." The stranger opened both his hands in offering. "Or The Prince of Poetry, Ahmed Shawqi." He clasped his hands together in prayer. "Nations are but ethics. If their morals are gone, thus are they." He slapped both his knees. "Gone. I tell you, gone."

"Do I know you, sir?" Clifford asked.

There was something uncanny about the man. I too had the uneasy sense of déjà vu.

"You don't even know yourself." The stranger scoffed. "If you English can't make yourselves welcome with arrogant promises of freedom, you resort to armored tanks and Vickers machine guns." His mustache quivered.

I had a good many fine mustaches in my collection, but none quite as impressive as his. I touched the edge of my seat. Just thinking about my assortment of crumb catchers in the little case below made me as giddy as if I were sniffing spirit gum. I swore, even now, I could smell its intoxicating pungent odor.

"Well, I say." Clifford huffed. "No need to be rude." He tugged on the bottom of his jacket. Good old, reliable Clifford. Quick to defend King and country.

"Those hunting hounds were brought here to fulfill your countrymen's desire to turn every place into their homeland." When the stranger waved his arms, the loose sleeve of his jacket danced a jig. "They died from the heat." His dark eyes flashed. "Let that be a lesson to you."

"You know, it's rude to eavesdrop." I tilted my head and appraised this mysterious fellow with his obvious dislike for me and my countrymen.

"We're in a rattling coffin." The stranger winked at me.

Cheeky devil. My fan fluttered so fast in front of my face my wrist could barely keep up.

"Rather hard not to overhear your conversation." He lowered his voice. "Especially since you English love the sound of your own voices so much you project them at high volume—"

"Look here, whoever you are." Clifford stood up. "This is no way to talk in front of the ladies."

Good heavens. I hoped Clifford didn't do something stupid like challenge this fellow to a duel or punch him on the nose.

The carriage swayed and Clifford fell back onto the seat, nearly landing in my lap.

The stranger was right about one thing. With just two bench seats facing each other, and one small window, the compartment was small and claustrophobic.

"Now, now." I patted his arm. "The ladies can defend themselves, thank you."

I couldn't take my eyes off the stranger. There was something strangely compelling about him. Perhaps it was the faint scent of rosewood. Either that, or the resounding strength of his convictions.

"Do you read Arabic?" I pointed at the stranger's book, assuming it was the poetry of which he spoke.

"It's the only way to appreciate the character of the poetry and the people." He shook his head. "Of course, the English think everyone in the world should speak their language."

"I speak French and German," Kitty piped up. "And Spanish, and—"

"I suppose you learned a bushel of languages at that boarding school in Lyon." I cut her off. "Along with who knows what else," I said under my breath.

I too was fluent in French, thanks to Mrs. Boucher's French class at North London Collegiate School for girls. My German, on the other hand, was appalling. I had to admit, Kitty could come in handy when spying on Fredrick Fredricks and his German comrades.

"Mere European languages." The stranger held up his book. "Here, you must learn Arabic if you want to do anything but see yourselves reflected in a mirror of your own hubris." He stood up. "At least you have French, young lady." The stranger bowed slightly to Kitty. "Since Egypt was occupied by the French before the English, you'll get by passably well." He opened the door to the compartment. "And now if you'll excuse me, I too have work in Cairo."

As he crossed the threshold, a folded paper fell out of his book.

I reached down and picked it up. The paper was heavy and thick.

"You dropped something," I said to the closed door.

The stranger had vanished.

"What is it?" Kitty asked.

"I say." Clifford snatched it from my hands and snapped it open. "Why it's a map!"

"Good heavens." I gazed down at it. "Not just any map."

A map of the Suez Canal. Marked with a big black **X**.

I touched the spot on the map.

Lake Timsah.

Smack bang at the mid-point of the canal.

Could it be just a coincidence that Fredrick Fredricks had hinted at a plot involving the Suez Canal? Or the War Office had sent us to stop it?

"We have to go after him!" I waved the map in the air and sprung up from my seat.

Always obliging, Clifford jumped up from his seat.

When Kitty took to her feet, Poppy barked and wagged her tail, as if cheering us on.

Three trains converging on the same track, we collided trying to get out the door.

What a wreck.

No doubt the stranger was long gone by now.

MORE FROM KELLY OLIVER

We hope you enjoyed reading *Chaos at Carnegie Hall*. If you did, please leave a review.

If you'd like to gift a copy, this book is also available as an ebook, digital audio download and audiobook CD.

Sign up to Kelly Oliver's mailing list for news, competitions and updates on future books.

https://bit.ly/KellyOlivernews

ABOUT THE AUTHOR

Kelly Oliver is the award-winning, bestselling author of three mysteries series: The Jessica James Mysteries, the Pet Detective Mysteries, and the historical cozies The Fiona Figg Mysteries set in WWI. She is also the Distinguished Professor of Philosophy at Vanderbilt University and lives in Nashville Tennessee.

Visit Kelly's website: http://www.kellyoliverbooks.com/

Follow Kelly on social media:

twitter.com/KellyOliverBook

facebook.com/kellyoliverauthor

instagram.com/kellyoliverbooks

tiktok.com/@kellyoliverbooks

bookbub.com/authors/kelly-oliver

Boldwood

Boldwood Books is an award-winning fiction publishing company seeking out the best stories from around the world.

Find out more at www.boldwoodbooks.com

Join our reader community for brilliant books, competitions and offers!

Follow us
@BoldwoodBooks
@BookandTonic

Sign up to our weekly deals newsletter

https://bit.ly/BoldwoodBNewsletter

Made in the USA
Middletown, DE
14 March 2023

26775409R00166